Nightmare in Dreamland

Anna Sterling, provincial, introverted and self-contained, arrives in Los Angeles to carry out her dying father's last command to find her younger sister Julie who seems to have disappeared without a trace.

Caught up in a world of garish and sinister make-believe that both repels and attracts her, she discovers alarming truths about her tyrannical father, an acclaimed English author who had once been wooed by Hollywood, and her mother, as well as being forced to face some of her own inadequacies as a person.

As the search for her sister becomes increasingly labyrinthine, Anna realizes she is becoming enmeshed in a wider conspiracy of secrecy involving a bizarre cast of Hollywood characters, including the ailing, ageing agent Hilde Klein, her menacing son Bernard, the street-smart Mexican bit player 'Mabel', the James Cagney clone Mick Angelo, and the charming but feckless English actor George Allenby. Too late to draw back, she becomes aware that in searching for Julie she is putting her own life at risk.

MARGARET HINXMAN

Nightmare in Dreamland

THE CRIME CLUB
An Imprint of HarperCollins *Publishers*

First published in Great Britain in 1991
by The Crime Club, an imprint of,
HarperCollins Publishers, 77–85 Fulham Palace Road,
Hammersmith, London W6 8JB

Margaret Hinxman asserts the moral right to be identified
as the author of this work.

© Margaret Hinxman 1991

British Library Cataloguing in Publication Data

Hinxman, Margaret
   Nightmare in dreamland.
   I. Title
   823.914[F]

   ISBN 0 00 232346 X

Photoset in Linotron Baskerville by
Rowland Phototypesetting Ltd
Bury St Edmunds, Suffolk
Printed and bound in Great Britain by
HarperCollins Book Manufacturing, Glasgow

CHAPTER 1

On the day she arrived in Los Angeles crowds were gathered on the sidewalk and snarling up the traffic outside the forecourt of Mann's Chinese Theatre where Eddie Murphy was being immortalized on the Walk of Fame. The crush of bodies was so dense that it was impossible to identify the focus of attention. But she knew it was Eddie Murphy because the cab-driver had told her so, adding, without evincing or expecting much interest, that the comedian was one of the hottest properties in movies.

Apparently there was some sort of publication which listed everything of major or even marginal importance that was happening in town each day. And today Eddie Murphy was happening.

As the driver drummed his fingers impatiently on the steering-wheel, she peered at the gaudy mock-oriental façade of the theatre. It used to be Grauman's, she remembered from long ago, after the flamboyant showman who created it. But under new ownership even the name seemed devalued, like everything else on Hollywood Boulevard. Once it had been the emblem of glamorous extravagance in this small enclave of southern California that was synonymous with extravagant glamour for millions of people all over the world. A dream, not quite impossible but far enough out of reach to exercise a tantalizing magic. Now the dream was available to everyone, neatly packaged and tightly scheduled between Disneyland, Las Vegas and the Grand Canyon, flights, hotels and air-conditioned coaches included. And maybe those same pilgrims wondered what the dream had all been about as they posed for snapshots beside life-size balsa wood models of the famous, inspected the long forgotten names set in pink gilt-edged stars along the black pavement of Hollywood Boulevard and craned their necks for a glimpse of Eddie Murphy in the flesh.

'I didn't know they still did that sort of thing,' she said.

5

The cab-driver glared at a policeman in a stationary patrol car who was irritably waving the traffic past the theatre.

'Sure they do, lady,' he grunted. 'This is Hollywood.' As if she hadn't noticed.

He jerked a thumb towards the hills above Hollywood Boulevard where the letters of the legend were just discernible through the inevitable haze of smog. Although the gesture was dismissive there was a touch of pugnacious pride in it. He looked neither young nor old. There was an agelessness about him, like one of those weathered character actors in old gangster films that never date. He seemed a throwback to that other Hollywood.

'I used to work in movies,' he volunteered as if to confirm her impression. 'Came out here from nowheresville. Nebraska. Back in the 'sixties. I did some extra stuff, bit parts. But it was all going over to Television. So I wind up behind the wheel of a cab. It's a living. Just. These days you're better off being a black or a spic,' he grumbled *apropos* of nothing.

Racist, she thought. Back home she'd have sparked, but this was an alien land and she'd yet to discover whether the natives were friendly. Even on the drive from the airport she'd remembered just how alien it was although she'd have been hard put to explain exactly why. Maybe it was the blaring billboards, the streets that just began and then stopped, the buildings that had an unfinished look about them as if uncertain whether they were being put up or pulled down. Maybe it was the air of impermanence that was so unlike the contained order of Winchester in England where she lived, small of scale, with everything related to everything else through centuries of continuity and brutal change righteously resisted.

'First trip?'

'Sort of.' What had made her say that? It wasn't true.

'Say again?'

She shook her head. 'I mean, no. I was here once when I was a young girl.' But it hadn't been like this. Then it had been the Beverly Hills Hotel and welcoming baskets of fruit and flowers in the suite and Malcolm enjoying being fêted by the studio while knowing all the time it was just a silly charade with no substance.

But she hadn't known that and he'd never bothered to explain it to her. She was just excess baggage he'd brought on the trip, along with her timid, fretting mother. And she hadn't understood when the honeymoon was suddenly over and they were packing their bags to return home. She remembered that huge, intimidating lion of a man pacing the rooms and roaring insults at the 'philistines who run this accursed industry', the same philistines whose hospitality he'd relished and mocked and abused. His rages had frightened her then and continued to frighten her until she realized it was all just a game to him, no more serious than the unlikely possibility that he could adapt his immensely clever and impenetrably difficult prize-winning novel into a filmable screenplay which had brought him to Hollywood in the first place. All those years of being frightened by her own father and not understanding that the only reality for him was the current work in progress! At least until Julie injected another kind of reality into his life. She'd tried not to think about that during the last months of his dying, but now she had to. Julie was her reason for being here.

I hate this place already. Unfair, she knew, but thought it just the same. Julie would have loved it, though. Julie wouldn't have let anything cloud the dream. She'd have seen precisely what she'd wanted to see. Julie had always been like that. Unless something had happened to change her. But how would she know? It had been so long.

'Vacation?' The cab-driver's growly voice wrenched her back into the present from the painful recesses of memory.

'Hardly,' she said. 'You could call it a mission.' Damn fool thing to say.

'Life's a mission.'

She caught his eye in the rear view mirror and surprised herself by mustering a smile from the depths of her jet-lag. A philosopher, too. A racist, philosophical cab-driver. Welcome to LA!

The cab screeched to a halt outside the spruce, high-rising

Holiday Inn off North Highland Avenue. He dumped her luggage on the sidewalk and waited patiently while she counted out the money for his fare with fumbling fingers, realizing too late that the two-dollar tip was probably grossly inadequate. He looked at the bills in his hand and then at her with the merest trace of amusement and no resentment.

'Too bad you're staying in this neighbourhood. It's OK if you're a tourist. But there's a lot nicer places. Westwood. Beverly Hills.' How could he know that she had chosen it just because it wasn't Westwood or Beverly Hills or anywhere else that would remind her of Malcolm in his uncaring prime? 'You wanna watch your purse, too. Have a nice day!'

Before she could decide whether his salutation had been ironic or ritually courteous in the American way, he had driven off.

'Mrs Anna Sterling?'

The girl at reception flashed a dazzling smile revealing perfectly proportioned and polished white teeth. She was immaculately pretty in the fashion of the moment, almost too perfect to seem real. In that old Hollywood, Anna mused, she'd have been hoping to be spotted by a studio talent scout. Now she was probably more interested in climbing the Holiday Inn corporate ladder.

The smile switched itself off as the girl repeated a touch tartly: 'Mrs Anna Sterling?'

'Yes. Well, Miss—uh Ms—actually.' I must stop wandering like this, she thought. It's this place. It addles the brain. 'Rubbish!' The addling had begun long before her plane had touched down at the airport: a meticulous process of chipping away at that little nugget of self-esteem she possessed.

'I beg your pardon?'

'Nothing.'

The smile behind the reception counter switched itself back on again as the girl handed her her key and a couple of messages: one, friendly, from George Allenby, and the other, less friendly, from Mrs Hilde Klein.

'I'll need to hire a car.' Everyone said you had to have

8

wheels in California, although the prospect appalled her.

'There's a Hertz right here by the hotel garage. Have a nice day,' the pretty thing dismissed her briskly.

Once in her room Anna sank thankfully on to the king-size bed and closed her eyes. She knew she should start making her calls immediately. She was here for a purpose and it wouldn't go away just by thinking about it. But she couldn't yet bring herself to make the first move. She told herself it was just exhaustion after the flight. But she knew that was only part of it. The other crucial part was an unwillingness, beyond mere reluctance, to begin her search for Julie. Did she really want to find her? Did she really want to follow a trail that could only be dangerous, because Julie had always courted danger as assiduously as Anna had avoided it.

Damn you, Malcolm Sterling, damn you! Why couldn't you just die? Why did you have to leave this legacy? And why me? You didn't even care about me. 'You're so like your mother. She had a pretty little talent for concocting stories, too.' She could hear his voice as clearly as if he were in the room: not insulting (Malcolm's insults would never be wasted on unworthy recipients), just patronizing. A pretty little talent compared to his brutish, massive genius! Probably he hadn't even realized how crushed she'd been by that tone, that dismissive assessment of her pleasure in writing her slight, graceful stories. But at least she'd kept going. Her mother had given up her own writing under that withering contempt years before.

She'd often wondered why Malcolm had ever married that faded, anonymous creature, for that's how she had seemed to Anna during her formative years.

But perhaps she hadn't always been like that: living with and for and in the shadow of Malcolm must have exacted a terrible price. A stronger woman would have rebelled and left him. But Theresa had borne it with what now appeared to Anna a timorous dignity, a very small part of herself that she'd managed to preserve untarnished, undiminished by being the wife of Malcolm Sterling. Until the late birth of Julie and then, as if she'd completed the job God had

9

unfairly conferred on her, she'd simply given up. There was no other expression for it. The death certificate had specified complications following pneumonia. But Anna knew better. As her mother had meekly given up the writing, she'd equally submissively given up the life. When she thought about it now she was overcome by a sense of outrage on her mother's behalf. Yet hadn't she, too, adopted virtually the same role, the same unquestioning subservience to Malcolm's demands?

There was a time when she'd been proud to be the daughter of the great author; hovering anxiously in the background at the literary luncheons; soothing the feathers of friends, press and publishers he so recklessly ruffled; supervising the household, the nanny for Julie; keeping the messy periphery of his life removed from the important task, his work. Even her fear of him had given her a kind of perverse satisfaction. And knowing that he compared her disparagingly with her young sister Julie, who, when she was old enough to assert an attitude, treated him with calculated insolence, didn't diminish her awe of him.

'You're so—so old-fashioned, so nineteenth-century. So Henry James,' his literary agent, James Quill, had once said to her. He hadn't sounded unkind, just amazed, as if he'd stumbled on a well-preserved human relic frozen in the past.

'And me? What about me?' Julie had taunted him. She was only fifteen at the time but he'd looked at her as men always looked at Julie, weighing up the ripe potential of her approaching womanhood.

'You—you're Scarlett O'Hara.'

'Aren't you sorry you're not Rhett Butler?' she'd teased him. Even then she'd been able to make a man feel foolish and flattered at the same time.

'What the hell are you playing at, girl?'

They hadn't noticed Malcolm standing in the doorway. For a fraction of a second the expression in his eyes was more like that of a betrayed lover than a heavy father—or so it seemed to Anna.

'Games, *Daddy*, games. Just like you.'

Oh, Julie had known how to handle him all along, as if

she'd been born with the insights Anna had been forced to acquire so painfully, if indeed she'd ever truly acquired them.

But in the end, in the very end, he'd needed her as he'd needed no one else. That it was a selfish need was unimportant. It was as if all her life he'd cast a spell on her which sapped her will and independence. And now as he lay dying from that ravaging cancer he was calling in his favours.

'You must find Julie, make it right,' he'd whispered. He was a shrunken skeleton of his old self; only the blazing eyes in that death's head retained the energy that had fuelled his creative powers.

He'd gripped her wrist, the dry, bony fingers exerting a surprising pressure. She'd looked at the wasted figure in the huge bed and wondered at the irony that this pathetic, dependent invalid was the man who had dominated and contorted every aspect of her existence.

'You haven't been fair to me, Father,' she'd said quietly. Such a reticent reproach for so many hurts. So old-fashioned. So Henry James.

His eyes had stared back at her without comprehension. Even approaching death he couldn't understand what he'd done to her. The ego was as strong and intact as ever.

'You must find Julie, make it right,' he'd repeated.

They were the last words she'd heard him speak. The next morning he'd died and she'd felt nothing but a kind of numb contentment that in the end he'd had to turn to her. And after the eulogies, the funeral, the ordering of his affairs and the memorial service she'd been left with the legacy.

'Now you can begin your own life and not before time,' Hugh had said. 'A whole world has passed you by while you've been ministering to that—'

'Tyrant?' She'd smiled. Decent, dependable Hugh who had waited so patiently and couldn't bring himself to speak ill of the dead. 'Not yet. Not until I've found Julie.'

'You don't even know where to begin to look. It's been two years. And how do you know she wants to be found?

11

If she did she'd surely have made contact. Wherever she is, she must have heard about Malcolm's death. How often have you heard from her in that time? Once? Twice?'

'I know all that. But I have to do it, Hugh—or, at least, try. I don't want any old debts to Malcolm hanging over me.' Only then could she come to terms with their fraught relationship and learn to live in peace with it. But she hadn't said that to Hugh. 'You should appreciate that. Clean sweep.'

Clean sweep, clean sweep . . .

She must have dozed off, fully clothed, when the telephone woke her up. For a moment she thought she was back in the cottage on the outskirts of Winchester, smugly sheltered in mellow, green English countryside yet within strolling distance of the Cathedral and College whose proximity Malcolm for some reason had found both reassuring and necessary when he was working. Then her eyes took in the bland, comfortable hotel furnishings, the characterless room; her ears became accustomed to the distant yet still harsh thunder of traffic heading for the Hollywood freeway twenty storeys below.

Blearily, she propped herself up on her elbow and lifted the receiver.

'I thought you'd never answer. Or maybe you were jet-lagged dead. They told me in the hotel you'd arrived. Hugh said you'd be in need of serious care and protection, that's why I . . .'

'Hugh!' She rubbed her eyes and slowly came to life. 'I'm sorry. You must be Mr Allenby. You're very prompt.' Even in her dazed state she hadn't taken to the flippant tone or the 'serious care and protection' routine. Hugh would never have said that.

'George. Call me George. Or Georgie. Or "you dirty bastard!" This is Hollywood. Surnames are for screen credits. I woke you up! Right? Didn't anyone ever tell you that the worst thing you can do after a transatlantic flight is to take a nap? You have to forget you're tired and go with LA time. That way you'll get a good night's sleep.' His voice was light yet fruity, the accent not quite English and

12

not quite American, the words fluent but thoughtless, like that terrible dubbed dialogue in foreign language films.

She was wide awake now and her head ached. 'I'm sure that's very true, *Mr* Allenby,' she said pointedly, deliberately choosing to sound like some affronted Victorian maiden and then regretting the childishness of the gesture.

But before she could apologize for the frosty tone he picked up on it. 'Whoa, there! Hold on. I'm only trying to be helpful. I promised Hughie. We Wykehamists have to stick together.'

Hughie! Georgie! She supposed the diminution of perfectly good Christian names had something to do with shared schooldays.

'I was hoping we could get together this evening.'

'I—I really don't know that I feel up to it, George.' She conceded a half-measure of familiarity. 'I haven't even unpacked and . . .' She couldn't think of any other plausible excuse for not facing George Allenby today beyond the weary prospect of listening to that voice rattling on for hours. She knew she should be grateful. After all, he'd taken the trouble to contact her. He didn't even know her, except through Hugh.

'Look, Anna—or may I call you Miss Sterling?—no, scratch that.' His voice sounded more serious, less lightweight. 'Look, Anna, I don't know how determined you are to find your sister. You can put it off until tomorrow or the next day or the next day. But that might be too late. I'll pick you up in thirty minutes. If that's not OK, just say so. And we'll forget it.'

His sudden switch in tone seemed oddly disturbing as if he were deliberately attempting to provoke her.

She laughed nervously. 'You're trying to scare me.'

'Yes, I am. Because, sight unseen, you sound like a woman who would benefit from a good scare every so often. Never do today what you can put off forever—I'd guess that's your philosophy?'

'You're taking a lot for granted,' she bridled, partially because he'd read her so accurately. 'And what's so urgent anyway? *Have* you found out anything about Julie or—?'

13

'I got Hugh's letter about your coming over a few days ago,' he interrupted her abruptly. 'He sent me a photograph of your sister. Just on the off-chance, I guess. I can't be sure but I think I saw her at a club off Sunset Boulevard.'

'You actually *saw* her! When?' She was conscious of not sounding as relieved as the news seemed to warrant.

'Well, don't raise your hopes too high. But you don't forget a face like that easily. Only her name wasn't Julie Sterling. Or Julie anything. She called herself Scarlett O'Hara. Some gag, huh?'

He expected some sort of response—surprise, derision, outright disbelief, anything but her unnerving silence.

'Am I making any sense?'

'Yes,' she said finally. 'Julie's kind of sense. I'll be waiting for you in the lobby in half an hour.'

CHAPTER 2

'Where are you taking me?'

In the sudden, brief dusk between day and night Hollywood Boulevard made her feel uneasy. A throbbing army of colours and races, mostly loud and young and watchful, cluttered the sidewalk. Cruising cars clogged the road. Streetwalkers with savvy doll faces, in mini-skirts and thigh-high boots, patrolled the Walk of Fame. Gaudy neon signs advertised the clubs, pizza parlours and other more dubious pleasures. The whole scene seemed to have been orchestrated to a brutish rock beat.

A bag lady squatted in the doorway of a boarded-up shop singing a frail song in a high, clear voice, apparently impervious to the noise and wash of humanity around her.

I feel like her, thought Anna. Displaced.

'Into the combat zone.' He caught the look on her face and laughed reassuringly.

He was slighter, more English than he'd sounded on the telephone, his clothes casual in the manner of the place but probably expensive. He looked, she thought, like his brother

14

Hugh would have looked if he'd spent over fifteen years acquiring a tan and rattling around on the fringe of show business as a not very successful actor in California instead of teaching history at Winchester.

'I'd still like to know where you're taking me and what this has to do with Julie.'

He manœuvred his nippy hatchback past a bright yellow elongated convertible that was double parked, shot off at a right angle and then, after several more detours, stopped outside a sign that flashed the logo 'Double Take' over interchangeable faces picked out in neon. Off the main noisy bumper-to-bumper strip it appeared almost restrained.

He rested his elbow on the wheel and turned towards her. The same blue, inquiring eyes, the same leanly sculptured features, the same receding hairline that gave him a bookish air, like Hugh. Yet, oddly, it was the fact that they were Wykehamists rather than brothers that seemed to relate them.

'This—' he gestured towards the sign—'is where I'm pretty sure I met, well, saw, your sister.'

'*Here!*' She looked at the garish entrance to what appeared to be a club or saloon of sorts and shivered. 'It's horrible. You must have been mistaken.'

But even as she said it she knew she didn't believe what she was saying. If she were honest, it was exactly what she'd expect of Julie.

He lifted his hands as if capitulating to some implacable enemy. 'OK. If that's what you think, I'll drive you right back to the hotel and you can sit on your butt and order room service and watch Television. You can sort things out neatly and tidily in your mind and then venture out into the safety of daylight to look for someone you don't seem to care whether you find or not . . .'

'That's not true.'

'And furthermore,' he went on, paying no heed to her protestation, 'do you have to judge everything by appearances? To you a bunch of kids on a sidewalk is a threat, a building site is a disaster zone and a bar with a comic name is a den of iniquity. So, you're right, Los Angeles is

15

aggressive, bizarre, weird, crazy; but, Christ, it's *alive!*'

She felt the adrenalin that seemed to have drained out of her on the flight surging through her veins.

'The implication being that I'm not alive. Well, look, *buster*—' The expression popped out unexpectedly from her subconscious, overheard perhaps at the airport or from a movie or remembered from her visit here before, so long ago.

'Buster!' His lips twitched with amusement and then she, too, found herself giggling, like a child released from the strait-jacket of manners. He nudged her shoulder gently. 'C'mon. I want you to meet a guy who may be able to help you.'

She nodded. 'Thanks. You know, you were right,' she said haltingly.

'About what? You—and Julie?'

She nodded again. 'I *am* scared. Julie has always scared me. Not physically, I mean. How could she? She was so much younger. Thirteen years younger.'

'You said "was".'

'Did I?' She looked puzzled and alarmed as if she'd been caught off-balance. Why had that use of the past tense slipped out so readily? She shrugged off the question and the antagonism she'd felt towards him from that first exchange on the telephone returned. 'Why do I feel with you that I'm being studied under a microscope like a newly discovered microbe?'

'Something Hugh said.'

'What?' she said suspiciously. She didn't like the idea of Hugh discussing her, particularly with this judgmental brother.

'Rather nice, really. He said not to be taken in by the surface. You were an enigma he hadn't yet solved. Maybe I'd have better luck. He loves you, you know.'

'I know,' she said quietly. She was staring straight ahead at the tail lights of the cars swishing past them. The sound they made was like waves breaking on the shore and oddly soothing after the loud bustle of Hollywood Boulevard.

He lifted his hand and let it hover for a moment above

16

her shoulder, then, changing his mind, he clamped it firmly round the steering-wheel. 'So, what scares you about Julie?' He changed the subject.

'What she might do, what—situation, I suppose—she might get herself into.'

'Then it's worth finding out that your fears are groundless—or not. Either way it's better than not knowing.'

'Good God!' A young, smooth Hispanic face was peering at her through the windscreen.

'He's just curious. A couple of people sitting in a parked car for no particular reason in this neighbourhood. If he were a mugger or worse the windscreen would be shattered and we'd be bleeding on the pavement. He may even be a cop.'

He wound down the side window. 'What gives, man?'

The boy—for in Anna's estimation he was no more than sixteen or seventeen—looked wary, then, having sized them up, grinned. 'You dealing, buying?'

'Neither.'

He shrugged and moved on. But not far, just a few steps to the nearest doorway. He lounged there for a minute or two watching them. She noticed George reach towards the glove compartment, his eyes not leaving the boy. Then they heard the skirl of a police patrol car growing louder. The boy froze momentarily, then mooched off into the night with the easy, rolling gait of an Angeleno swagman.

'He's probably a little out of his territory. There's usually more than one.'

She felt as if she'd been holding her breath throughout the whole episode and she let it out slowly through her mouth with relief. 'What's in that glove compartment?'

He opened it and she saw, resting on a nest of papers and used Kleenex, a gun.

She stared at it and then at him. 'You mean you actually have to carry that thing around all the time? How can you *live* in this place?'

'Sure, I carry it around in case it's needed. I haven't had to use it yet. And in answer to your other question: I live here because I work here—sometimes, that is—and I like it. I like the climate, the informality, the people—the ones I associate with, anyway—and the challenge. Here you have to be tough and flexible. Nothing's certain, nothing's forever. That's what destroyed me about back home. The prospect of being safe and secure in toyland for the rest of my life. Satisfied?'

She shrugged. 'It's your life. Personally I don't consider safety and security dirty words. And I'd hardly describe the home counties as toyland. You've been away too long.'

'Maybe. Anyhow let's go inside and you can experience another culture shock.'

'Is it safe?' She choked on the word. 'Sorry! I mean, your car.'

'Like I told you, Miss Prim, nothing's safe in LA. That's half the fun of it.'

He didn't attempt to open her door or help her out of the car.

The narrow exterior of the 'Double Take' led into what appeared at first a murky interior, dimly lit like some cult movie of the 'forties in the *film noir* genre. But as her eyes became accustomed to her surroundings she began to realize that the effect had been carefully designed to resemble just such a film set. The spacious area had been portioned into booths, increasing the sense of intimacy, of shadows and corners. The walls were festooned with giant glossy photographs of movie stars in famous roles from what was popularly known as the golden age of Hollywood. She had the feeling of huge eyes, gaunt cheekbones, improbably lush lips bearing down on her from everywhere. There was a small bar and tiny tables crammed a central area that took the overspill from the crowded booths. At the far end on a poky stage someone, who could have been male or female, was impersonating Marlene Dietrich singing 'Falling In Love Again' from *The Blue Angel*, although the celebrated huskiness resembled more the croak of someone in the early stages of a bad cold. But the effect was strikingly authentic.

A smoky haze seemed to overlay the room like a cloud hovering just below the ceiling. That, too, appeared to be a

18

special effect for there didn't seem to be much serious smoking, at least not the tobacco kind.

'How goes things, you dirty rat?'

She jumped.

'Slow down, sister. I'm the good guy.'

The voice matched the short, feisty figure who was breathing down her neck. The man looked so exactly like James Cagney in his heyday that you might have imagined the ghost of the actor had returned to haunt the town that had created and nurtured his screen image. He was holding himself in precisely the same tense, punchy way, shoulders hunched, arms flexed, fists restless, as if he were perpetually on the brink of picking a fight.

It was all, she knew, an illusion. Like this factory town for manufacturing dreams. An illusion that no longer fooled anyone, not even the public.

He clapped George playfully on the shoulder and, playfully, George faked a fall. 'Long time, G.A.'

'I've been spending six weeks being frightfully *Briddish* interrogating a Russian defector in Montreal. At least, Sean Connery—or is it Michael Caine?—does most of the interrogating. I just get to nod and stroke my nose wisely when the chief says something incredibly bright. But the money's good. Fortunately for me they had to keep rewriting the script as even our thick-between-the-ears producer realized that *glasnost* had broken out and the Russians were no longer the baddies.'

'Who's it for?'

'Arnie Beckman.'

'Arnie Beckman! His last movie really cratered.'

'Well, he must have climbed out of the crater smelling of roses—or, better yet, money. Mick, I want you to meet Anna Sterling. I talked to you about her on the phone.'

She felt George prod her elbow and she rewarded him with an icy stare. 'Thanks for remembering me,' she muttered.

'How could I forget you,' he muttered back. We sound like a warring old, married couple, she thought. 'This is the proprietor of the club—Mick Angelo, known to the paying customers as Jimmy Cagney.'

19

Cagney's *doppelgänger* grasped her hand in both of his and held on to it longer than necessary for courtesy's sake.

'No one's ever called me a proprietor before. That's what I love about Georgie. He's so civilized. Not like us peasants'.

He screwed up his eyes and stared hard at her, his head cocked to one side as if framing her in a camera lens. 'You know, you'd be a great Joan Fontaine.'

She remembered *Rebecca*, blushed and felt oddly flattered. She'd never been overly conscious of her looks and no one, not even her father or Hugh, had commented on them except to mention on special occasions that she looked 'nice'. And then only grudgingly.

'What do you mean—*be* Joan Fontaine?'

'Look around you.'

She scanned the photographs on the walls.

'No. Look around you.'

It was then she noticed an eerie familiarity about the waiters and waitresses who were weaving through the tables adroitly with trays of drinks. Each of them bore an uncanny facial resemblance to some famous movie star. On closer inspection the resemblance was fleeting, a disguise that owed more to the art of make-up and hairdressing. But the disguise was good enough to create the impression that the punters were being served by a bevy of Joan Crawfords, Ingrid Bergmans, Lana Turners, Humphrey Bogarts, Rita Hayworths and Clark Gables.

Mick beckoned over a Bette Davis. 'How's tricks?' he said. And winked.

She winked back. 'Fasten your seat-belts, it's going to be a bumpy night.'

He grinned broadly. '*All About Eve*. They know them all. All the best lines from the best movies. "I am big, it's the pictures that got small." "Play it Sam, I'll hum it for you." For an extra buck, they'll throw in a song.'

'And on the stage?' She gestured towards 'Marlene'.

'They're amateurs. Fancy themselves as movie impersonators. They get up there each night and make a fool of themselves. Sometimes they don't.'

So that was it. She remembered why she was here and

the old sense of unease flooded back. 'Then—that's how you met my sister. You did, didn't you?'

He looked at her keenly, no longer smiling.

'Sure, I met her. She worked the tables here. Only a few days. Maybe a week. Six months or more ago. Dead ringer for Vivien Leigh as Scarlett. Never did say her real name, though. I only made the connection when I spoke to Georgie here. I'll tell you one thing. That broad was in trouble.' He touched his nostril with a knowing finger. 'Oh, Christ!'

His attention was drawn to the stage. Marlene Dietrich had retreated under a barrage of insults to be replaced by Mae West, a buxom blonde bulging out of a liberally sequined hour-glass 'nineties gown with a train she wasn't quite sure of and a feather boa that threatened to strangle her. She teetered on stage, swivelled her hips, patted a hair-do set in concrete and invited a large, red-faced man squeezed into a small chair at a small table to come up and see her sometime.

'Kentucky fried chicken,' murmured Mick.

'Who?'

'The guy. Tourist.'

'Go west, Mae—like Okinawa,' yelled someone in the audience.

For a moment, the fake Mae looked nonplussed, a tiny brain behind anxious eyes seemed to be searching for an escape route. Then, like the real trouper she fancied herself to be, she bounced back into a brick wall of cat-calls.

'It's better to be looked over than over-looked,' she purred with pride as if she'd suddenly been touched by Mae's very own *chutzpah*.

A groan rippled round the tables gathering force and momentum like a soccer anthem.

Mick looked as agitated as his pugnacious features would permit.

'I've gotta get Mae off. She never learns. Look, you guys, order yourselves a couple drinks and we'll talk later.' He conducted them to a reserved booth near to the bar and relatively far removed from what appeared to be the beginnings of a *fracas* that was developing on stage. But he seemed

21

reluctant to leave them, as if there were something he needed to say first. 'You know, I met your father, too. Malcolm Sterling. When I was at UCLA. He'd just published *Beauty's Summer Dead*. Great book. Shakespeare—the title. Don't look so surprised.' Her expression must have given away her sense of amazement that this funny little phoney James Cagney had actually been to university and, even more astonishing, knew her father's work. '"I'm an intellectual mountain goat leaping from crag to crag",' he quoted.

'*Young Man With A Horn*,' she quoted back at him.

'Right on. Lauren Bacall, Kirk Douglas,' he said approvingly. 'OK, folks! Mae has another urgent engagement.' He shooed the hapless Mae West off the stage. 'What'll it be?'

'Judy!'

'Marilyn!'

'Rita!'

'What can I get you folks?' The lisp preceded the look. The waiter was undeniably Humphrey Bogart.

George raised an eyebrow at Anna. But she found she was getting used to being addressed by long-dead film stars.

'I'm terribly hungry. I haven't eaten since the plane. What do you suggest?'

Bogart scratched his chin thoughtfully. 'We don't do anything fancy. Burger and fries, pastrami on rye, ham and eggs, a reuben . . .'

'What's a reuben?'

'Any leftovers from the kitchen between ten slices of bread. I'd settle for the ham and eggs,' George proposed. 'Coffee for the lady?' She nodded. 'Bourbon for me.'

'Got it, folks. "Here's looking at you, kid!"' With that Humphrey Bogart took himself off as unobtrusively as he'd appeared.

She realized that George was scrutinizing her with renewed interest. 'How the hell did you know that? The intellectual mountain goat stuff. That's one of Mick's trick quotes. Strictly for buffs. I didn't figure you for a movie buff.'

'I'm secretary of a film society back home. We had a Doris Day season recently.'

22

'But . . .'

'Doris Day was in the film, too.'

She placed her hands firmly folded on the table. 'What else can I tell you? I sit on charity committees, I do meals on wheels, I lobby the council on conservation issues. And in my spare time I write slim volumes of short stories. They get reviewed respectfully and only sell enough to warrant publication because occasionally there is a small demand for them when they are read on "Woman's Hour". But as I have no ambition for larger fame it doesn't bother me. What else? Oh yes, I'm the daughter of a great and demanding writer which took up a lot of time, at least until he died. Actually, it seems to be taking up quite a bit of time now that he's dead. That's why I'm in this—this—crazy place looking for my sister. Because I promised him I would. Basically I'm a small town girl with small town aspirations and small town talents. A conclusion you've no doubt drawn anyway. Does that satisfy your curiosity.'

The note of sarcasm wasn't lost on him. He held up his hands, palms outward, in mock alarm. 'Pax!'

She relaxed, slumping into her corner of the booth. She felt physically weary yet oddly buoyant of spirit. 'Sorry! It's just—I hardly know what's hit me.'

'What did you expect? You're looking for someone who presumably doesn't want to be found. Did you think you could just file a name and photograph with Missing Persons and get an instant identification and address? This is as good a place to start as any. At least she was here and not so long ago.'

She looked around her at the familiar but phoney faces. 'It's just—just so daft. All these people pretending to be other people. I mean, why do they do it? And who comes to see them?'

'Quite a few Hollywood people come for a gag because they're friends of Mick. Mostly it's tourists. Why do they do it? Maybe because they don't like who they are. You liked being compared to Joan Fontaine. I could tell. You blushed.'

23

She felt herself blushing again. 'It's something to do with having a too thin skin and it's hot in here.'

'Don't apologize. It's attractive. Not many women blush these days—even if you could tell under the make-up.' He could see he was embarrassing her and changed the subject. 'Some of the people who wait on tables or go up on stage get lucky. Producers making TV biopics are in the market for extras or bit players who look like celebrities and sometimes they find them here. You know, in the old days there used to be a bordello where all the girls looked exactly like the movie queens of the time. So if you fantasized about laying Myrna Loy you picked the hooker who looked like Myrna Loy.'

'Is that what this is?'

'A bordello?' He laughed. 'Not officially. What the help do in their spare time is their business.'

'Hi, Georgie!' A very tall, very slender, very beautiful, olive-skinned Mexican girl in designer jeans, shocking pink jogging sweat shirt and trainers leaned over the table. The overall effect was stunning.

'Mabel!' He hailed her. 'Her name's really Consuelo, but she likes Mabel better.' He noticed Anna peering hard at the gorgeous creature. 'No. She's not trying to be anyone else. She's just Mabel. An original. Mabel meet Anna. Mabel's in the sitcom *Southern Comfort*.'

'Was!' Mabel slid into the seat beside him. 'My darned fool agent had words with the producer. They wrote me out last week.' She took a pack of cigarettes out of the pocket in her sweat shirt, selected one fastidiously and lit it. 'I hear you're asking about a girl who called herself Scarlett?'

The question caught Anna unawares.

'Did you know her? The only contact I have here is Hilde Klein, my father's agent.'

Mabel took her time before answering, drawing languorously on the cigarette, as if practising her timing for the next TV sitcom role.

'Vaguely,' she said finally. She had a subtle but definite Spanish accent that suggested mystery even if none existed.

24

'But if you ask me you're wasting your time. She was one screwed-up lady. Kinda sad, too.'

'Julie? Sad? We *are* talking about the same girl?'

'Julie! Was that her name?' She studied the photograph Anna had produced from her bag, then flicked it on to the table. 'That's her. You're not much alike, are you?' She sounded too casual, too carefully non-committal.

'No—no, I suppose we're not.' Anna was uncomfortably conscious of Mabel's bold, dark eyes weighing up this strange Englishwoman in these strange surroundings.

'Maybe you don't know your sister as well as you think you do. No offence. But it happens in families. I haven't spoken to my sister in Tijuana in ten years. Which is just as well, because if I had I'd probably have killed her. Maybe you feel the same way.'

Mabel-Consuelo's artful smile gave no hint whether she was kidding or serious.

CHAPTER 3

Hilde Klein hoisted herself awkwardly on to her good side in the lounger by the pool and poured herself another dry martini from the silver shaker at her elbow. The stroke she had suffered six months before had been less severe than had at first seemed probable, but it had left her partially paralysed down the right side, with an all but useless arm, limited mobility and a permanent facial disfigurement. In repose one half of her face was as alert and vibrant as it had always been. The other half was sunken and wasted, the eyelid drooping, the mouth dragged down into a perpetual scowl of discontent. This half she kept as hidden as possible with large, brimmed straw hats, upturned collars, gracefully arranged gauzy scarves.

She had always been a vain woman, using her looks and coquetry to disguise a steely skill in getting top dollar for her clients from the 'sharks', as she termed them, who ran Hollywood and fancied themselves tougher than she. She

25

could cope with the physical disabilities, the need to use a walking aid, the ministrations of a nurse and physiotherapist and the stylist who dressed the wigs to cover her sparse grey hair. She even rather enjoyed the amount of sympathy and the sense of power her condition engendered. Health was better: but money and status, especially in Los Angeles, made the lack of it comfortably tolerable.

Since she had arrived in California as a refugee from Germany over fifty years before she had always contrived to be the centre of attention: at first among the small group of fellow refugees who had supported her and whom she had quickly discarded when they were no longer useful to her; then, progressively, in the larger, harsher world of agents and studios and entrepreneurs. From virtually nothing she had built up her business and gained the reputation of being one of the sharpest agents in Hollywood. She had briefly craved the limelight of stardom herself. But she soon realized that the real power resided behind the scenes in the front offices where the deals were made, the bargains were struck, careers were launched and as calculatingly destroyed. And that, she'd decided, was where she wanted to be. That she was quick and witty, with a deceptive, waif-like Piaf pertness, was no disadvantage.

As a semi-invalid she found to her satisfaction that she was still the focus of attention, even though her agency was no more, swallowed up—for a vast sum shrewdly negotiated by Hilde—by one of the huge show business conglomerates. She had been glad to unload it, the industry now being managed, she railed, by idiots, crooks and riffraff. But she was still Hilde Klein, the legendary Hilde Klein. Old friends and enemies, colleagues and clients, still came to pay court, even if they tended to avert their eyes when they came into close contact. She knew she'd never been loved. But, by God, she'd mattered. And she still mattered.

It was only when she looked at her face in the mirror, which she tried to do as little as possible, that she raged against the stroke that had hit her so suddenly. She knew she had to live with that lop-sided face for the rest of her life. And it was all Louis's fault. Louis's and that girl's!

26

She drained the martini glass and stared sullenly at the dark, lapping water in the pool. Below her in the distance the lights of Hollywood twinkled irreverently, seemingly mocking her secure, safe and constricted comfort high in the hills.

She'd neglected to switch on the patio floodlight and was startled by the sound of footsteps on the tiled surround. The shock was only momentary. Even the way he walked condemned him as weak, devious, covetous. She longed for Louis's firm, aggressive tread. Only she knew she'd never hear that again.

'I don't want to see that woman, Sonny,' she threw into the blackness behind her, knowing he was there, listening, waiting. But he was all she had, her only flesh and blood.

'Sitting in the dark, drinking, Mother mine? Naughty! Is that your fifth or sixth martini?' He spoke in a silky, insinuating drawl which many unwary women had found attractive.

'Who's counting?' She shaded her eyes as he flicked on the light switch. 'Did you hear what I said, Sonny?'

Sonny controlled a desire to wince. He wouldn't give her that much satisfaction. His name was Bernard and for a man in his forties to be addressed in the same way as he had been when a child would have seemed demeaning if he hadn't his own good reasons for ignoring it. He was well aware of his mother's contempt for him, but he could bide his time. And occasionally she took his advice, even when his motives for offering it were mischievous—like now.

'Why did you make me?' she persisted fiercely.

'Because it wouldn't look good if you didn't see her.' He could always appeal to her pride in keeping up appearances.

She still put up a resistance, although less forcefully. 'Wouldn't look good to whom?'

'Well, it wouldn't look good to the woman—Anna Sterling. After all, you were Malcolm Sterling's American agent.' He paused. 'Among other things. And you were the daughter's sponsor when she came over.'

He'd moved into the light and for the first time she faced him. A faint smile flickered around the mobile corner of her

27

mouth. '*The* daughter. How very discreet of you, Sonny.' She held out her glass for a refill. 'I suppose you're right,' she conceded. 'After all, what harm can it do? It's just—being reminded of that little bitch.

'How was I to know what she'd be like?' she flared. 'And Louis was so—so insistent. It was nothing to do with me. You know that's true, don't you, Sonny?' The question sounded very like a plea for mercy, a rare admission of vulnerability from this tough, proud woman.

But he wouldn't let her off the hook. 'I don't know what's true, Mother mine. I barely knew her. When she arrived I was away on that wild goose chase to Europe you sent me on to get me out of the way when you concluded the deal to sell the agency. Remember?'

'You'll never let me forget, will you, Sonny? You couldn't have managed the agency. You'd have run it into the ground in two years. You haven't the head for it—or the flair—or the stamina. You're like your father. Poor Max! He never understood the first thing about making it in this town. Only you're worse. You can be a cruel bastard. Max was kind, too kind for his own good.'

For a moment she indulged a fond thought for her first husband. Poor Max Klein! So eager to please, so anxious to be considered part of that elite group of European refugees, Bertolt Brecht, Thomas and Heinrich Mann and the others, hoping their genius might rub off on his own meagre talent. But Hollywood had never had any time for third-raters, particularly those as modest and unassuming as Max. At first she'd thought she could inject into him some of her own pushy drive and aggression. But it had been a losing battle. 'I'm not like you, Hilde,' he'd said in his hopelessly mangled English. He'd never learned to master the tongue of his adopted home. She sometimes wondered why she'd married him. Not out of pity. She was incapable of pity. Weakness was a sin. Out of need, perhaps. It hardly mattered. She'd barely noticed when he'd died after the war; they'd drifted so far apart. The only memory he'd left her was their son. Bernard. Sonny.

When she thought about Max, which she seldom did, she

28

suppressed any sense of guilt with the belief that it was just as well he hadn't lived. If he had, he—and, by association, she—would have been drawn into all that UnAmerican Activities trauma and that would probably have been the end of her career. As it was, she'd been able to distance herself from his radical friends and left-wing causes. Even at the last, poor Max had done the right thing by her. Not like Louis. Louis had been *her* weakness. Maybe it was a sort of retribution.

'Don't you think you're a little old to be jealous?'

'Of what?' For a moment, lost in the past, she couldn't follow her son's line of thought.

He'd placed his hands on the arms of the lounger and was leaning forward so that his face was inches from her own ravaged face. She flinched slightly, not enough to concede defeat but enough for him to register it. He was handsome, Sonny, younger-looking than his years, California fit, no trace of grey in his jet black hair, hardly a line marring his even features: the product of easy, moneyed living. Only she noticed the slackish jaw, the heavy-lidded eyes that always seemed to be weighing up a situation to his own advantage. She'd made a mess of Sonny, she thought. She and Los Angeles.

'Of Julie, of course,' he reminded her. 'Louis was so taken with her, wasn't he? Do you remember how he kept on at you when there was all that talk of re-making *Gone With The Wind* about what a marvellous Scarlett she'd be? Not that there was anything you could do about it. You'd given up the agency, you had no clout and she wasn't even an actress. But he behaved like a crazy kid in love who can't think straight. You'd never think he was—'

'*Stop it*, Bernard!' she commanded. Her delivery was slower since the stroke, the pitch more gravelly, but when she demanded attention her utterance could still pack a powerful punch, like Bette Davis accepting an Academy Award she felt was her due.

He backed away from her and, almost without realizing what he was doing, stroked his cheek as if it were smarting from a hard slap. But his tone remained exasperatingly cool,

29

in control. 'Thank you, Mother. It always works. If I get you angry enough, you stop calling me Sonny.'

Very deliberately he poured her another large martini. 'Here, dear, console yourself. I have to be going.'

He sounded somehow final, as if this departure might be his last, thus feeding her unspoken fear that, sooner or later, unlikeable as he was, he and everyone else would desert her. She'd be left: an old, infirm relic of the past, cocooned in heavily protected splendour, alone except for a housemaid, a fussy cook-housekeeper, a boring nurse and a Vietnamese gardener who spoke no discernible English except when he was berating the man who came to vacuum the leaves off the immaculate and expensively watered lawn.

She looked at Bernard anxiously. 'You'll be here.' She tried to sound peremptory as if she were merely confirming a matter of fact, but it came out like a plea for help. 'You promised. When she comes. That Sterling woman.'

He smiled. He'd redressed the balance. 'Of course, Mother. I wouldn't miss it for the world. Now . . .' He grasped her frail shoulders and pecked her cheek, the wasted, sunken one, rejecting the good side she offered him: an habitual gesture calculated to discomfort his mother.

'You could stay for dinner. Myrna can rustle up something. It won't take a minute. Or a drink.'

'Sorry, dear. I'm late already.'

'Who is it this time?' Realizing his mind was made up, she had no need to be friendly, or even circumspect.

'Her name's Kelly.'

'That's not a girl's name,' she sniffed. 'Are you going to marry this one, too?'

'Why should I? Three down. Why try for four?'

'It's not like my day,' she grumbled. 'In my day they *married*. Even in Hollywood they married—eventually. The studios made sure of that. If you want to play around, keep it quiet and keep it out of the papers, they said. No hanky-panky or we'll have you up on the morals clause.'

'Those are movie stars you're talking about, Mother. It's all different these days,' he said with an elaborate show of patience. When her mind retreated back into the past, as it

30

did more and more frequently these days, she lectured him and anyone else who happened to be around as if they were children.

'All right. Go! Go! Go! You and your dumb *shiksas*!'

She waved him away before he could throw Louis up in her face. She didn't really feel as angry as she sounded. She knew he wouldn't let her down. He'd be here if only to enjoy the encounter, to see which of them—she or the Sterling woman—would draw blood. Well, let him enjoy. She'd show him.

'Mrs Klein. It's time.'

Hilde sighed again. Everyone told her they should be so lucky to have good, reliable, loyal, live-in help like Myrna, these days. But Myrna was a trial: she had been for her thirty years of service in Hilde's employ. Hilde supposed she should be grateful but gratitude was not one of her virtues. And she shuddered to think of the consequences if Myrna should ever decide to call in her favours.

'OK, Myrna, wheel me in. And, Myrna, fix me another batch of martinis.' She crooked her forefinger and beckoned the bulky woman forward. 'But don't let on to that dragon of a nurse.'

As Anna Sterling drove the compact Toyota she'd rented with extreme caution through the heavy Hollywood traffic up towards Beverly Hills she reflected on her telephone conversation with Hilde Klein that morning and the strange turn events had taken the previous evening. The girl on the hire car desk had provided her with a detailed map of Los Angeles but she still didn't feel easy behind the wheel in this motorized city. Already she'd been stopped and scrutinized by a policeman behind forbidding dark glass in a patrol car. She'd been dawdling suspiciously through the increasingly more affluent avenues and drives lined with the homes of the seriously wealthy guarded by security gates, sophisticated burglar alarms and intercom systems. The cop had been courteous but firm: idle curiosity was discouraged in this area. And if you didn't know your way to your destination you'd better find out fast. 'Have a nice day!'

he'd said, but, having set her straight on the right direction, he'd watched her narrowly until she was out of sight. After all, you never could tell these days.

On the phone Hilde Klein had sounded chilly, hardly welcoming, although she had conceded that she remembered Anna as a gawky thirteen-year-old when she'd visited all those years ago with her father and mother. But she really, *really*, couldn't cast any light on the whereabouts of her sister and she'd *hate* to waste her time. For Malcolm's sake she'd been happy to sponsor the girl in the States, help her get her green card to work there, but she hadn't actually *seen* her for months. She'd just vanished.

It was all so pat, so positive. I'm damned if I'll let you get off that easily, thought Anna. If the woman was holding something back there was one sure way of making her more amenable. 'I see,' she said sweetly. 'That's awkward. I contacted the British Consulate in Los Angeles before I left England and apparently they could find no trace of her. So . . . well . . . it's awkward . . . as I said. I've no other option. I suppose I'll have to go to the police. If I give them all the details about her . . .'

'No!' A hint of agitation cracked the icy chill in Hilde Klein's voice. 'No, I'm sure that won't be necessary.' The voice recovered it's hard-edged composure. 'Would eleven-thirty this morning be convenient?'

Anna allowed herself a faint smile of triumph as she put down the phone. It was amazing how responsive even the most implacable people became at the threat of calling in the police. She was learning. She'd never been devious before, never needed to be. But she was learning.

What bothered her was her lack of concern. She should be distressed about Julie's apparent disappearance, instead of just calmly plotting her next move. But all she felt was a hollow nothingness. She'd never warmed to her sister and now she didn't much care. She was only fulfilling her promise to Malcolm. Maybe that girl, Mabel, had been right. Maybe she didn't know Julie as well as she thought she did. 'You're a cold fish,' Malcolm had once accused her. And she'd angrily cited her work on behalf of the deprived, the elderly, the disabled. But in her heart she'd known he was right: compassion for the many had always been a convenient substitute for real concern about those closest to her.

Well, hadn't he made her the woman she was, taught her to erect defences around her emotions against possible hurt? It wasn't much of an excuse, but it was all she had.

She only knew she wanted to leave Los Angeles, get it over with as quickly as possible, return to the quiet, ordered life she'd left behind. To Hugh who made no demands. To the friends who kept their distance. To the routine of charity work and committees and fund-raising teas. To the story world in which she could lose her own unadventurous identity on the old-fashioned manual typewriter she insisted upon using. It was too late to change the kind of person she was, she told herself, suppressing the knowledge that it was never too late.

Perhaps it *was* a matter for the police. That way she could leave this glittery, alien city and its weird inhabitants with a clear conscience. She'd have tried. What else could she do?

That's what George Allenby had said last night. Quite suddenly, disturbingly. 'I know a cop in the LA Police Department. I can get him on to looking for Julie. See what he turns up. It could take a while and you'd be wasting your time hanging around here. It would be just as easy to contact you at home. You'll have done all you can.'

It was after Mabel had left that she'd caught that look between him and Mick. 'Suddenly you're anxious to get rid of me,' she'd laughed nervously.

'It's not that, Anna,' he'd said soothingly. 'It's just I'm beginning to realize that you're unlikely to make much mileage this way. Right, Mick?' Having settled Mae West's hash, James Cagney had reverted to his real self and was refreshing himself with a diet Coke in the booth with Anna and George.

'Sure, honey. Like I said, she was only here a few days and some guy came to see her.'

'What guy?' she persisted.

33

He shrugged. 'Some guy. And she took off. She said she was going up the coast to Vancouver. She just took off. Canada's a big country. She could be anywhere.'

'But if she went to Canada surely there would be some record of her entry.'

'Could be. Maybe you should try up there.'

'And you said she was in trouble.'

Mick played with a book of matches as if seeking inspiration from the exercise.

'I meant—she was troubled. Yeah—that's what I meant. Troubled. Maybe she wasn't feeling so good. This town, it does things to people. They're up, they're down. You never can tell.'

Anna looked from one man to the other, now alert despite her fatigue. Neither gave anything away. 'Why do I get the feeling you're trying to fob me off?' She wanted to add 'with a pack of lies', but something, which she wouldn't admit to herself might be a sense of self-preservation, prevented her.

'Who's fobbing who off, honey? I'm just telling you like it was.'

She turned to George who was unconcernedly sipping his bourbon. 'Then why were you so keen to bring me here?' she challenged him. 'A matter of life and death, you implied. You could have told me this, mentioned your friend in the police department, on the phone.'

His smile was patronizingly indulgent: the sort of smile she'd seen time and again back home on the faces of pilgrims to the temple of Malcolm Sterling forced to put up with his dim daughter until the great man was ready to receive them. You're not so different, she thought: Los Angeles on the outside, but Winchester at the core. 'Calm down, Anna. I just wanted you to meet Mick. I thought he might have more information about her than he did. But at least you know that when last seen she was fine and—' he hunched his shoulders and raised his hands as a comment on the vagaries of the female sex—'for reasons of her own she didn't want to hang around LA.'

'That's not the way Mabel told it,' she said coolly.

'No one pays attention to Mabel. She's a good kid but any Mexican with her build and looks who prefers to call herself Mabel has to be crazy. Anna, she's an actress. She dramatizes everything.'

'And you're an actor. Not a very successful one, I understand,' she couldn't resist adding. It was a cruel remark and the mean glint in his eyes as she said it made her realize that she'd scored some kind of bullseye.

That an elaborate performance had been put on for her by George and Mick she had no doubt. But why? What had Mabel said to effect such a change in George, so helpful at first and now so dismissive?

She shouldn't waste her time, he'd said. Hilde Klein hadn't wanted her to waste her time either. Neither had Mick Angelo. So many people worrying about her wasting time! Hardly a coincidence. Did they really think she was that thick?

Despite herself, she felt a sudden surge of rage at being treated like a ninny, an innocent abroad. If not for Julie, for herself, she wouldn't give in now.

She plunged down hard on the accelerator of the Toyota and headed up through the deserted, palm-lined thoroughfares of Beverly Hills to the house off Benedict Canyon.

CHAPTER 4

It wasn't, after all, a house in the English sense of the word. She'd remembered it as grand and intimidating, like those National Trust stately homes which seem to stare down aloofly at the groups of visitors upon whom they depend for their upkeep.

In fact it was just a fair-sized, whitewashed, mock-Spanish villa set in a sprawling plot. Sprinklers played on the vividly green lawns which swept down on either side of the drive to an electronically controlled main gate, beside which a eucalyptus tree stood solitary sentry duty. Clumps of fleshy brilliantly coloured azaleas preened themselves in the sunshine which had escaped the mid-morning smog below.

It was unnaturally quiet. That was the first thing that struck her. When she'd been there before with her father and mother it had been buzzing with noise, chatter, music, voices raised in anger or drink or maybe drugs—cocaine was chic in those days. On those Sundays there had been a passing show of celebrities, would-be celebrities and has-been celebrities. And for a while Malcolm had been the centre of attention, until he'd stormed out of Hollywood vowing that no cretinous movie producer would ever get his hands on one of his books again. Later, he'd grudgingly conceded that BBC TV had done a very decent job on *Beauty's Summer Dead*, insisting, she always felt a little too much, that small is better. Secretly he'd probably regretted that he couldn't lick the Hollywood system—although he'd made damned sure that it didn't lick him.

The interior of the bungalow was cool and spacious. Nothing seemed to have changed. The same pristine white tufted rugs on tiled floors. The same soft furnishings in blends of soft grey and lilac. The same arrangements of garish outsize blooms in costly Venetian glass vases precisely placed on the low tables that were scattered around the room. The same gallery of photographs, all featuring Hilde Klein with some notable or other, papering the walls and weighing down the unopened flat top of a white baby grand piano. Anna wondered if it had ever been played and by whom. A room for display, no well-thumbed books or trifling ornaments or sentimental bric-à-brac. She looked idly through the floor-length windows which opened on to the terrace which in turn led to the kidney-shaped pool. It had always been the focus of activity on those Sundays. People diving into it, splashing around in it, lounging around beside it. And talking, always talking. Now it was so silent.

She felt a sudden chill which she couldn't explain.

'I remember you. You were a skinny little thing, always hiding in corners.'

Anna stiffened. She hadn't heard Hilde Klein enter the room or maybe she'd been lost in the past, conjuring up a

36

long-gone scene. When she turned to face the woman she managed to cover up her surprise with practised discretion. Years of voluntary work with the disabled and sick had conditioned her to never reacting to a person's physical appearance.

Hilde Klein seemed disappointed at the lack of response. Attention, after all, should be paid if only for the pleasure it gave her in disparaging it. 'You've grown up,' she said stupidly.

'It's been twenty years. Thereabouts.'

'Of course. Thereabouts!' In repeating the word she belittled it and, by association, Anna.

'I don't suppose you remember my son, Bernard.' She waved her good hand imperiously over her shoulder where Sonny was leaning against the wall by the doorway. He felt worn and irritable after a heavy night and a raging row with his latest lover Kelly. But the sight of Anna, standing there, neat, serene and self-contained, cheered him somewhat. After the flamboyantly aggressive Kelly she could be a soothing antidote, he speculated. He nodded, affably enough.

'Vaguely,' Anna replied. But there was nothing vague about it. He'd seemed like a dark young god and he hadn't even noticed her. 'It's good of you to see me, Mrs Klein. I hadn't realized . . .'

'Oh, this!' Hilde tapped her walking aid and sounded satisfied. Attention had been paid. 'A stroke. Six months ago—after my husband's death.' There was a note of challenge in her voice as if she were daring Anna to question what she'd just said.

'I'm sorry.' She regretted it immediately. What had she got to be sorry about? Yet, looking at this ruin of a woman who had once been the famous Hilde Klein, she did feel sorry.

'He was killed in the San Francisco earthquake. He'd been driving up to see a client. Everyone thought at first it was the big one they'd been expecting. But apparently it wasn't. That figured. Louis couldn't even get himself killed in the big one.' She spoke matter-of-factly, without bitterness. 'You probably remember him—vaguely—too. Louis Lederman. He was an art dealer. I never used his name. I was too well known as Hilde Klein,' she continued proudly. 'That's him. It was taken not long before he died.'

She pointed a wavering finger at a photograph which was set apart from the rest, the only one which didn't include his wife in the frame. The man who stared out at the unseen camera was floridly handsome but going slightly to seed. He had obviously been quite a bit younger than Hilde.

Anna inspected the photograph, at first out of politeness, then with a sense of disturbing recognition. In her mind's eye she stripped the face of the excesses of the years. She saw it clearly, but not in isolation. There was another face, stricken and concerned, caught in some unsavoury act. It was her mother's face. Louis Lederman and Theresa Sterling.

'Goodness, dear, you surprised us—me,' her mother had said when Anna had come upon them in the pool house on one of those Sunday mornings. 'Mr Lederman was just . . .' Her voice had trailed away and his had taken over, smooth and soothing. 'Mr Lederman was just being nice to Mrs Sterling.' He'd chuckled as he'd said it, as if it were of no importance.

She'd closed the pool room door quietly, as if not wishing to disturb them, and taken herself off to a quiet corner of the terrace where she could see her father entertaining the cluster of admirers around him with wicked stories of the English literary scene. She'd told herself that she wouldn't think about her mother and Mr Lederman and it was easy because Theresa had behaved as if nothing untowards had happened at all. It seemed as if that was the moment when she'd learned to keep herself and her thoughts to herself. And she'd learned the trick so well that she'd almost forgotten the pool house and Mr Lederman, until the photograph brought it back with startling clarity. Having kept the world at bay for so many years, she realized the world was now forcing itself back into her life.

She felt suddenly drained of energy and she clung to the cluttered piano for support.

'Are you all right?' Sonny's hand was on her shoulder, his grip strong but surprisingly gentle. 'Myrna can get you something. Tea, coffee, a drink. Myrna!'

A plump, dumpy woman appeared instantly as if she'd been expecting the call. She looked first at Hilde Klein, then, satisfying herself that her employer was not in need, she puckered her lips and raised her eyebrows at Sonny. 'You called,' she said with a touch of acid in her voice which clearly indicated her opinion of Hilde Klein's son.

'I think Miss Sterling would appreciate a brandy.'

Anna waved the suggestion aside. 'No—really.' She felt more composed now and looked up at him gratefully. 'Really, it's much too early and besides I'm perfectly all right. Perhaps some coffee.'

'Coffee, Myrna,' commanded Hilde.

'Right. Coffee,' Myrna responded, making it plain that she only took orders from the lady of the house.

'I can't think . . .' Anna began as she allowed Sonny to settle her into one of the deep, suede-covered settees that lined the room. She noticed that the suede was wearing thin on the arms and felt the clammy presence of her mother and father who might have sat in this same settee. Is this why Malcolm had been so insistent that she come to LA? Not just to find Julie but to find out about so much that she'd deliberately shut out of her life.

'Oh yes you can, my dear.' Hilde Klein had manoeuvred herself into the specially constructed upright chair that accommodated without contorting her feeble frame. 'You were put out at seeing that photograph of Louis.'

'Hilde, do you have to?' Her son sounded as angry as his laid-back nature would allow.

'Hilde, is it? Not Mother any more? My, my, it's amazing what a pretty face does for you, Sonny. Well, hardly a pretty face. Nothing like her sister's. Let's say a damsel in distress. You know, I didn't want to see you, but now you're here I'm rather enjoying myself.'

Anna had never been so conscious of malevolence as a positive force before. It was so tangible that she felt if she

39

reached out her hand into the space between her and Hilde Klein she would actually feel its venomous sting.

She turned to Sonny for some sort of support. He seemed, after all, less antagonistic than his mother. But he was studiously examining a rogue hang-nail on an otherwise impeccably manicured forefinger. And she noticed how soft, almost cherubic, he looked underneath the California tan. A mother's boy? In his forties? Or more likely a son who had a very good reason, whatever that might be, for maintaining an uneasy peace with his mother.

Part of her wanted to leave as quickly as possible and with as much dignity as she could muster, which, in the circumstances, would not be a lot. That would be her natural response, to remove herself from unpleasant situations so that she could conveniently forget that they had ever happened. That was how she had conducted her life before her father's death had plunged her into this unwanted quest.

But now she was aware of a new, unsettling curiosity stirring within her, a desire to confront the disagreeable rather than retreat from it. Maybe, after all, the air of recklessness about this appalling city, as she still regarded it, was having its effect on her.

'What have you got against me, Mrs Lederman?' The steel in her own voice and her use of the discarded surname, as she dealt out each word with calculated precision, surprised her. It surprised Hilde Klein even more. She observed Anna through those lop-sided eyes with a cunning respect, as if suddenly recognizing, if not an equal, a worthy antagonist.

'I only came to ask for your—your advice—in finding Julie. Is that so strange?' Anna continued. 'Yours is the last address I have for her. And the British Consulate haven't been able to turn up any information.'

'And you threatened me with the police if I didn't help.'

'How can I threaten you if you've nothing to hide?'

A low gargling sound spewed out of Hilde Klein's twisted mouth. For a moment Anna thought she might be having a fit, then she realized that the gargle was a chuckle.

'Is that what you think? Your sister's body is buried in

40

the back yard. My, my, aren't we fanciful! Is that what you think?'

There was a dull thud as a heavy marbled ashtray thumped on to the rug by the piano. Unless the ashtray had a life of its own, it had slipped from Sonny's fingers, either from nerves or as a warning. 'Nothing broken,' he said, retrieving it. He flung himself into the settee beside Anna and she could sense the tension in his restless body.

'If you're so bored, go and jog round the garden. That's what you do, isn't it? Jog.' She waved her son away as if he were some aggravating insect.

'I thought you wanted me—I mean, I thought . . .' He stood up, undecided.

'Well, I've changed my mind. I like this Anna. We're going to have a nice chat. A few home truths.'

'I don't think . . .'

'I wish you wouldn't think, Sonny. You're not good at it. Remember?' The question carried more weight than it seemed to warrant. Without a word to her or to Anna, he stalked out through the patio doors to the pool as Myrna came in with the coffee.

'Black or cream?' she asked Anna.

'Black.'

As the coffee was poured into the elegant Rosenthal cup, Hilde continued to observe Anna.

'Myrna is a little short on manners,' she said as if the woman were invisible, a clinical subject for examination. 'You may have noticed that.'

'Not really,' said Anna, uncomfortable for herself and embarrassed for Myrna, who seemed, however, supremely unembarrassed.

'Myrna's never felt the need of manners. It comes from being brought up on a farm. Her family were sharecroppers in the south, dirt poor. She came to Hollywood to make her name like all those other silly girls from all over the States. Well, she did. On a police file. Prostitution, robbery . . . small stuff. I suppose you could say I rescued her.'

She turned her head awkwardly towards Myrna as if

41

noticing her presence for the first time. 'You could say that, couldn't you, Myrna?'

The woman smiled, seemingly enjoying a secret she shared with her employer. 'You could say that, Mrs Klein.'

'When she came out on probation I vouched for her and she's been with me ever since. Ever since when, Myrna?'

'Ever since Bernard was a little boy, Mrs Klein.' She kept on smiling without animosity, long used to being the anecdote her employer trotted out to entertain her guests.

'We've been through a lot together, haven't we, Myrna?'

'Oh yes, Mrs Klein, we've gone through a lot together. Is the coffee to your liking?' she asked Anna with exaggerated courtesy. She had, noted Anna, the same kind of cunning eyes as her mistress, which seemed out of place in her pleasant, plum duff face. The image of the faithful retainer receded. Just for an instant she seemed more like a faithful accomplice. Hilde's accomplice. More than long service and a salary bound them together, thought Anna.

But the instant passed.

'That'll be all, Myrna,' said Hilde, as if wearying of the subject of the hired help.

'You don't approve of my talking about Myrna like that,' she went on as Myrna left the room.

Anna was about to say that it wasn't for her to approve or disapprove; instead she observed: 'I think you and she have a lot in common.'

'Bad manners or bad memories?'

'Maybe both,' she replied boldly, surprised at her own daring but guessing that Hilde would be the sort of woman who might admire her for her candour. Just as Malcolm might have admired, loved her even, if she'd had the guts to stand up to people, to him, instead of turning the proverbial other cheek. But it was too late for that now.

Damn the past! Damn her wilfully blind ignorance or innocence—she couldn't tell which. And damn this bantering match in which Hilde Klein was forcing her to participate.

'I'm really not interested in your relationship with your housekeeper, Mrs Klein . . .'

42

'You can call me Hilde.'

Anna felt like screaming at her to stop evading the issue. Instead she said brusquely, 'About Julie. What can you tell me about her?'

Again, that awful gargling chuckle. 'What an impatient woman you are. I don't get many visitors these days. People I used to know well are embarrassed by the look of me. It reminds them of their own vulnerability to disease, misfortune. It's against the rules in Beverly Hills to be less than one hundred per cent in every department. You should humour a sick old woman.' The attempt to sound both coquettish and pathetic was so grotesque that Anna would have been tempted to laugh if she hadn't been sure that Hilde Klein would not have enjoyed the joke at the expense of her bruised vanity.

'A few hours ago you didn't want to see me at all.'

Hilde flicked an imaginary fly from her line of vision. 'I changed my mind. Do you know anybody here?' she changed the subject abruptly.

'Only an actor, not well known. George Allenby. He's the brother of a friend of mine back home in Winchester.'

'Is he your lover, the friend?' There was a gleeful look in the cold eyes.

'Yes—I don't think—what business . . .?' The words came out in a jumble of tried and discarded responses. She wished she were better at parrying this sort of intimate probing. The sense of outrage the question provoked was mixed with a *frisson* of pleasure that anyone should be remotely interested in her undernourished love-life. Somehow the companionable but hardly passionate sex she shared with Hugh didn't seem particularly relevant to Hilde Klein's greedy inquiry.

'You're quite right. It's none of my business. You just look as if you could do with a good lover. My son would put it a little less elegantly. But I don't hold with such vulgarisms. Only the over-educated or the under-educated can carry them off naturally. Half-educated people like me have to observe the formalities. The school of life: that was

43

my alma mater. There's a cliché for you. I used to sit at the feet of Brecht and Werfel and all those other expatriates, listening and not understanding a word. But I learned from them about style and I learned how to handle people and I was born, as they say these days, street-wise. It was all the training I needed in my career.'

The time for reminiscence threatened to be endless, but as suddenly as she'd started reciting the credentials of her early struggle, she stopped. 'George would be a good lover,' she mused. 'If he could make up his mind.'

'You know George Allenby?'

'I know everybody.' She shrugged. 'Does he still hang out with those *nonentities*—' she spat out the word as if it were contaminated with failure which in her estimation it was— 'the ones who deck themselves up as stars?'

'At the bar he took me to last night. Somewhere in Hollywood.'

She shrugged again. 'I never venture down there now. All that—seedy, mean, nothing but panhandlers, perverts and tourists. It wasn't like that in the old days. A premiere at Grauman's Chinese! That was something. You see those pictures on the piano? Now *they* were Hollywood. Go on, go on, take a look.'

She shooed Anna over to the piano. Anna took up the first photograph to hand and looked at the grinning David O. Selznick with his arm affectionately around the shoulder of a diminutive, flirtatious Hilde Klein.

'"To Hilde—the only agent who is tougher than my brother Myron,"' recited the old stricken woman who obviously knew the placement and inscription of every photograph. 'That was taken long after *Gone With The Wind* and Myron was dead. Poor David! He was cursed with knowing that he could never top having produced the most famous movie ever made but he kept on trying. Myron was the agent who introduced Vivien Leigh to his brother on the night when they burned Atlanta on the backlot of the Selznick studio. "David, meet your Scarlett." You must have heard that old chestnut. She was quite fascinated, more than that, obsessed by that photograph. She'd dance

44

around with it in her hands as if it were a sort of talisman, tossing her head and batting her eyelashes like Scarlett.'

'You mean Julie?'

Hilde nodded.

'Well, she'd always had a thing about being so like Scarlett. Vivien Leigh as Scarlett. It was a childish obsession. She should have grown out of it.' Anna put the photograph back in its place with a gesture of exasperation. 'My father encouraged it.'

'Ah yes, Malcolm! He would. He liked little girls and their fantasies.'

'I never saw my father like that,' Anna said irritably.

Hilde Klein looked at her shrewdly. 'Maybe you never really saw your father at all. Or Julie, come to that.'

'What do you mean?'

'You *do* know that your sister was seriously unhinged.'

'Unhinged? Hardly. Flighty maybe.'

'My dear Anna, where have you lived all your life? Have you any idea why she should suddenly have decided she wanted to come to America?'

Anna hesitated. She felt in a curious way beleaguered as if her motives, not Julie's, were being questioned. 'It was nothing. Just a fit of depression. She was run down. Nothing,' she insisted. 'She'd been studying hard for her A-levels. Well, maybe not that hard. But you know what teenagers are like. Everything is larger than life.'

'But you weren't like that, I suspect.'

'No, I wasn't like that. I wasn't like Julie. She'd always wanted to travel. To America. Malcolm was against it. But the doctor thought it might be a good idea—to get away. We'd no idea at the time that she wanted to stay away so long, work here. Eventually . . .' How was it, eventually? What had brought her to Los Angeles and Hilde Klein? Think, Anna, think! 'Eventually Malcolm agreed. And I suppose as you'd been his agent here, he thought you might—well, keep an eye on her.'

'You suppose! Is that how it was with you? Rather suppose than inconvenience yourself by discovering the truth.'

Anna turned angrily on Hilde Klein. 'What truth? What

45

damned truth are you talking about?' She noticed Hilde's good hand, clawed round the arm of her chair, was shaking. 'What truth?' she repeated.

The shaking increased, the rings on Hilde's fingers battering the side of the chair like pebbles rattling around in a high wind. 'She came to see her father, you fool. Didn't you have any idea? Louis, my husband, Louis Lederman was her father.'

CHAPTER 5

For several minutes the room was silent but for the rings tapping out their morse code on the wooden arm support of Hilde's chair. But gradually that, too, stopped as the hand ceased shaking.

Anna fixed her eyes on the woman, not seeing her as a whole person, although each individual detail would be permanently etched on her brain. The frenzied expression in the eyes. The twisted mouth. The dead, useless arm and the agitated, active one. The shrunken body disguised by a prettily draped lilac silk smock, below which the stocky legs, brittle as branches on a diseased tree drained of sap, disappeared into sturdy white lace-up nurse's shoes encasing the unsteady feet. She would remember the suede-covered settees and the grinning photographs and the coffee congealing in her cup and the sun pouring brightly through the patio windows. And she would remember the question echoing over and over again in her mind in those frozen minutes: 'How could I not have known?' The vision of Louis Lederman and her mother in the pool house returned: her mother's embarrassment and Louis's unfeeling response. 'How could I not have known?' And the answer, the only possible answer—'because I never wanted to know'— would continue to reproach her.

For twenty years she had lived with her father and the child born to her mother, cared for them in a careless way and insulated herself from any real knowledge or understanding of them. Was it out of genuine love and concern for her mother that Malcolm had proclaimed Julie his own child—or merely a need to protect his bruised vanity? And when had Julie learned the truth about her parentage?

Finally she drew a deep breath. 'Maybe—maybe I'm the one who is unhinged.' It came out like a casual joke. She should have said something of importance, something to rebut Hilde and reassure herself. But all she could think of was a trivial joke.

She didn't know how Hilde would respond but when she did it was totally unexpected. 'I'm afraid I was lying. You must forgive me. But you goaded me, you see.' Her voice was surprisingly firm and positive as if daring Anna to disbelieve her.

She sounded dismissive as though she had been guilty of nothing more shattering than a joke as feeble as Anna's.

Anna stared at her, trying to convince herself that she should make allowances for a sick, ageing and probably embittered woman tormented by the knowledge that the world of which she had been such a central force was passing her by. In similar circumstances what games would one play to keep the spirit alive!

But then she detected a trace of fear in those challenging eyes. Hilde Klein hadn't been playing games with her, she was trying to retrieve an advantage she'd unwittingly relinquished.

'I don't believe you,' said Anna.

'Then that's all right,' Hilde replied, misunderstanding her. The flicker of fear disappeared.

'I don't believe you were lying,' Anna continued. 'Only suddenly you wish you hadn't told me that your husband was Julie's father. And I can't help wondering why. How many more "whys" are there that you won't answer?' She'd been trying to contain her anger at Hilde's deceit, her arrogant assumption that Anna was a dim-witted innocent who could be fobbed off with any old story to fit the situation. But now that anger was free and growing. She realized that her voice was becoming louder, more aggressive. 'What right have you to treat me like an idiot? What right have

47

you to judge my family relationships? No, I *didn't* know that Malcolm wasn't Julie's father. Are you satisfied? You lob that little nugget of information at me like a hand-grenade—and then you try to say, "It's not a hand grenade at all, it's a marshmallow. Forget it! It's just my bit of fun." What did you say? Humour an old woman!'

The release of the tension she'd felt as soon as she'd entered the house gave her a strength and a cruelty of which she couldn't credit she was capable. 'I'd as soon humour a tarantula.'

She advanced slowly upon Hilde Klein, who sat there in that stiff, upright chair, helpless against the force of fury she had unleashed. She raised her head to confront Anna now standing over her. Her mouth was moving dumbly but the eyes refused to concede defeat. It was as if she were facing a firing squad but was too proud to ask for a blindfold.

'What happened to Julie, Mrs Klein? That's all I came to ask. What happened to Julie? Where is she?' Suddenly she realized that her voice had risen to a shriek and as quickly as the anger had exploded it disintegrated into shame. She was conscious of how appalling she must seem: a strong, healthy woman verbally and psychologically battering a cowed, frail invalid. How many times in her charity work had she come across cases like this? How many times had she counselled from the safe confines of reason without benefit of personal experience? Now, here I am behaving like a poverty-line single parent taking out her misery on an elderly dependent relative.

She took a backward step from the chair and raised her arm towards Hilde Klein, then, as the woman shrank away from it, she let it fall limply to her side. 'I'm sorry. I don't know what came over me. It was unforgivable to harass you like that.'

And again Hilde Klein surprised her. 'You shouldn't be so concerned about how you affect other people. It's healthy to let it all out, sometimes.'

Anna smiled, a faint, grudging smile. Whatever Hilde Klein wasn't, she *was* resilient. 'I hardly ever do. Let it all

out. Keeping it in is much less wearing. All the same . . .'
She cocked her head to one side, begging the question.

Hilde Klein nodded her head slowly, a gesture of triumph
now that she was firmly back in control. Ruthlessness, she
implied, didn't bother her. She could deal with ruthlessness,
she always had. It was fecklessness and the untidy messes
it made that offended her. But that would be dealt with,
too: it was just more difficult.

'She came here, as you know, nearly two years ago.
Malcolm had written to me and I was happy to let her stay
for a while.' As she mentioned his name her voice took on
a gentler tone. 'Malcolm always knew I'd do anything for
him, even though he left Hollywood in—let's say, embarrassing circumstances. We had plenty of room. Louis was
having business problems and I thought a young thing
about the place would be nice.'

'Louis who wasn't her father,' Anna prompted her sarcastically.

The old mouth tightened into a thin, bitter line. 'Louis
who wasn't her father,' she insisted defiantly. 'She obviously
hadn't been well and, as I said, she seemed unhinged. That
wasn't a lie. Los Angeles appeared to agree with her. She
said she'd like to work here. I honestly believe she thought
she might get into movies. Silly girl. They're all silly girls.
Louis offered her a job in his gallery in Westwood, not a
serious job. A receptionist, pretty girls out front are always
a useful acquisition. She did quite well. Between us we
managed to get her a green card to work. Then—then I
think she got involved with someone. Some boy or other.
She said she wanted a place of her own. I suspect she wanted
to move in with him. She said she'd be careful and keep in
touch. She did for a while. And then—she just vanished. I
tried to find out what had happened to her. But it's easy
enough for people to disappear in this country. Also, soon
after, Louis was killed in the earthquake and then I had
this damned stroke. I was in no fit state to worry about a
stupid girl who'd gone missing.'

'Even though you were responsible for her.'

'She was responsible for herself. And what about *your*

49

responsibility, Malcolm's? How come it took you so long to take an interest in your sister?'

Anna sighed. 'If I could answer that, maybe I wouldn't have needed to be here. She wrote at first, just postcards, the usual thing. Then—nothing. At first I was concerned. But Malcolm said whatever it was she'd have to work it out on her own. It would all be all right. I felt he was holding something back. But that was between her and Malcolm. By then he was seriously ill. I tried to reach her. I phoned here several times but I kept getting the maid—Myrna, I suppose—who told me Julie had left long ago with no forwarding address. And then there was so much else to worry about.'

She paused, reluctant to admit what she knew to be true. 'Julie—Julie and I were never very close. Not close at all, really. I suppose I resented her because of her bond with Malcolm. I did everything for him but it was Julie he truly cared about. I was just—useful to have around, you might say. Unpaid help.'

'Such self-pity!' The ridicule in the remark was inescapable. Self-pity was not one of Hilde Klein's indulgences.

'I know. It's not a pretty trait. I used not to be aware of it, but I am now.' She spoke as if to herself not to the woman who had goaded the confidence out of her. 'Couldn't you have told me all this earlier, without beating about the bush? Are you so short of entertainment that I had to supply the need?'

'You're not so very entertaining.'

'Who were her friends? Maybe they know something,' Anna persisted.

'Young people she picked up on the beach. They all look alike to me.' The woman closed her eyes wearily.

Anna had the feeling that the interview was over and nothing she could do would resuscitate it, nothing she could do would make Hilde Klein reveal the secrets she must still have hidden. Nothing—for now.

As if on cue Myrna bustled into the room. She looked accusingly at Anna while bending over to whisper in Hilde's ear.

'The person . . . contacted . . . here . . .' Anna caught a few disconnected words.

'All right, all right, Myrna,' Hilde said irritably. 'You can see Miss Sterling to the door. Tell the person to wait in the kitchen.' She turned to Anna. 'Extra help for a little party I'm giving. Maybe you should come. If you're good.'

Anna found herself standing outside the front door still pondering the strangeness of Hilde Klein's last remark.

She turned her face to the sun enjoying the warmth of its rays and the fresh, smog-free air. For all its spaciousness and light and bright decor, the house she'd left had seemed airless and dark as if the secrets inside the head of the old woman had pervaded the atmosphere, creating dingy corners and malodorous crevices where none existed.

Her Toyota was parked incongruously beside a glittery white Porsche Cabriolet, like a humble mongrel snuggling up beside a thoroughbred. Bernard Klein was lounging on the hood, one long leg stretched out in front of him, the other wedged against the near-side tyre. The indolent stance was misleading, though. He was alert and watchful and obviously waiting for her. She thought again what a handsome man he still was and a wave of nostalgia reminded her of how she, a gangly thirteen-year-old, had worshipped him all those years ago.

'Couldn't they do better than this for you?' he said, patting the hired Toyota.

'It's about what I can handle. Anything more—' she jerked her head at the Porsche—'would be inconvenient. I'm not used to Los Angeles traffic.'

'I heard raised voices.'

She paused, her hand on the handle of the car door. 'Mine, I'm afraid. I lost my temper.'

'Mother has that effect on people. What did you lose your temper about?'

She was about to say 'nothing', then she looked across at Bernard and read the question in his eyes. Maybe his question would answer hers. At least for her own peace of mind.

She slammed the door shut again. 'Can we walk a little?'

51

He looked surprised. 'Sure.'

The sprinklers had been turned off but the coarse grass was damp beneath their feet. Los Angeles grass. Not the soft, feathery English grass that required centuries of rainwater to nurture in those Capability Brown gardens the Americans so admired.

He linked his arm into hers as if it were the most natural thing in the world. Old friends renewing their acquaintance. Perhaps he'd persuaded himself that he remembered her better than he did.

She decided on the direct approach. She'd had enough of verbal fencing, the rules according to Hilde Klein. 'Was Louis Lederman Julie's father?'

He took a long time before answering, measuring his stride in unison with hers, although his legs were longer. 'Why do you ask?' he said finally.

She pulled her arm away from his irritably. 'Look, for God's sake, a straight answer to a straight question. I'm sick of skirting around the facts. Lies, half-lies. What is it with you people? What is it with *all* you people?' She threw out her arms embracing the whole of Los Angeles. 'Yes or no?'

He puckered his mouth, not meeting her eyes, then as if having reached an expedient decision: 'Yes. How did that come up?'

She laughed in his face. 'I'd have thought it was a pretty natural thing to come up. After all, I'm her sister.'

'It's a wise child . . .' he said mockingly.

'*Stop* it!'

He raised his hands in mock fear. 'I'm stopped.'

'Hilde let it out. Then almost immediately she withdrew it, said she'd lied, that I'd chivvied her into telling a lie. But I was damned sure she wasn't lying. Now you've confirmed it. Why would she do that?'

Bernard shrugged boyishly. He really is a 'Sonny', she thought. 'I guess she had second thoughts about throwing that at you all of a sudden. Sure, he was her father. When you were over here, your mother and he—well, it's obvious, isn't it? No big deal.'

52

'What do you mean? No big deal! Maybe not to him or Hilde. But it bloody well must have been to my mother and to Malcolm. In the circumstances I think they both behaved admirably,' she said knowing how prim that must sound to Bernard.

He shook his head pityingly. 'Oh, how deluded you are, little girl. Your father wasn't all that admirable. He may have been about that. But not about other things?'

'What things?'

'He's dead, isn't he? So forget it. Enough is enough. Sometimes enough is too much.' He looked at her with what appeared to be genuine sympathy.

'When did Julie find out?'

It was addressed to herself rather than Bernard. (She racked her memory trying to visualize the moment when she might have realized that Julie was nursing some traumatic knowledge she wouldn't or couldn't confide to Anna.) He answered it all the same.

'Not long before she came over, apparently. It seemed Malcolm told her. Odd thing to do after all those years of keeping it secret. Don't ask me why.' He shrugged again. 'I hardly knew her. I don't live in Hilde's pocket—however it may seem. I only know Louis was tickled pink at being the father of such a dish. He paraded her around as if she were the greatest thing since—since Scarlett O'Hara.'

'And you're telling me a girl as distinctive as that could just suddenly vanish? No trace?'

He yawned. 'I'm not telling you anything. This is boring. You know how boring this is? And you know something else? You wanna lighten up. Have some fun. This is a fun town. I know lots of places.'

'I'll bet you do.' She flicked aside the invitation. 'I heard she worked in a club for a week or so. I think it's called the Double Take.'

He yawned again, more pointedly. Maybe he really is just plain tired, she thought. 'I know it. Off Sunset. It's possible. After she took off I guess she needed to make some dough. Girls do all sorts of things to make a buck in this town.' His meaning was obvious, but she preferred not to add that fear to all the others.

'The man who owned it, Mick Angelo, I think . . .'

He nodded, but without much interest. 'Yeah, I know him too. Crazy guy.'

'He said she was troubled, something on her mind.'

He sighed. 'So, who isn't troubled? Me, I'm troubled. You're troubled.'

He was being deliberatelye evasive, she knew. Bernard might not be over-bright but he was canny enough not to tell her anything he didn't want her to hear unless she shocked it out of him. And that, she realized with a sense of helplessness, was her only hope. Where else could she turn?

She drew a deep breath. 'I think Julie's dead. I'm just beating about the bush not going to the police.'

He rounded on her, no longer bored or indolent. 'If you go to the police you'll *never* find her.' He stopped abruptly, then continued in a more conciliatory tone. 'Can't you get it through your head that Julie didn't give a shit about you or Malcolm or her life in England? That's what she was doing when she came to America. She was escaping. She *wanted* to get lost. So why should you give a shit about her? It's needle in a haystack time, honey. This is a big country.'

'I know,' she said quietly. 'Everyone keeps telling me. But I'll find her. One way or another I'll find her. Maybe neither of us gives a shit—as you so delicately put it—about the other. But I'm fed up with being given the runaround by you and your mother and those—those other people. So you can deliver *that* message to Hilde Klein and anyone else who might be interested.'

He looked at her, half admiring. 'I'll say one thing for you. You've got guts.'

'It's a novel experience. It requires novel responses. For me, that is.'

'Come again?'

'You wouldn't understand.'

'Bernard!'

They'd been so absorbed that they hadn't noticed

54

Myrna's stocky figure approaching the parked Toyota. Then, spotting Bernard and Anna, on the lawn, she called again. 'Bernard, Mrs Klein wants you to do an errand for her.'

Bernard, ignoring the overt humiliation in the command, smirked. 'She who must be obeyed.'

'Why?'

He shrugged. 'Sometime maybe I'll tell you.' He seemed to be nerving himself to say something against his own better judgement. 'You want some advice?'

'Not particularly.'

'I'll give it anyway. For free. Don't push it. For your own good.'

He touched her cheek with the back of his hand. She felt his manicured nails cool against her skin. 'I'll be in touch.'

He turned brusquely away from her and strode towards where Myrna was standing waiting. She was looking at Anna, with an expression on her face of pure spite.

CHAPTER 6

Before the door was firmly closed, she heard his voice raised in anger floating across the sun-drenched lawn. 'You fool, Hilde. You couldn't leave it alone, could you? You . . .' The rest was swallowed up along with all the other secrets in that benighted house.

Anna walked slowly towards the car, then changed her mind. She wasn't by nature an eavesdropper, but whatever argument was going on in there concerned her directly. Her and, by association, Julie. And the events of the past two days had taught her that the only way she was ever going to find out anything to help her in her search was to be as devious as those who were intent on withholding it. Whatever she'd said to scare Bernard, she was sure that Julie was alive. If she were dead she'd have been notified by the British Consul or the police. That she was in some kind of trouble was more likely. Anna wouldn't yet allow herself

55

to speculate whether the trouble might also be actively dangerous. But her habit of caution was dying fast.

She took off her shoes and edged her way round to the side of the sprawling villa. A low, wrought-iron gate separated the front from the back. Someone had left it ajar. She eased through and, pressing herself against the wall, inched round the side of the patio, avoiding the embrace of the fleshy shrubs that hugged the stucco walls. The windows on to the patio were open and she could see the flimsy curtains playing in the slight, cooling breeze that had suddenly whipped up. A short flight of wide-spaced steps assembled in a semi-circle led down to the pool.

Crouching low she could, she judged, edge towards the window without being seen by anyone inside. In other circumstances she would have been appalled at the situation in which she found herself. Doubled up on her haunches in hiding to overhear a conversation that wasn't meant for her ears. The correct, unadventurous, uncurious, law-abiding Anna Sterling behaving like a prowler or a sneak thief! If those Winchester worthies back home could see her now! But she was beyond being appalled at anything very much in this bizarre, alien community, least of all the effect it was having on her.

She tucked her shoes firmly between her knees in case she was required to beat a hasty retreat and then strained her ears to catch the gist of what was being said inside the patio room.

At first all she could hear was an indistinct murmur like running water. Then the words began to separate, some lost completely, others quite clear.

'. . . wormed it out . . . about Louis . . .' Hilde's muffled voice sounded plaintive.

There was a silence. Then: '. . . so, she knows . . .' Another silence. '. . . can't do any harm . . . a wrinkle . . . can do without . . .' Clearly, Bernard's anger had evaporated as quickly as it had erupted. Anna assumed they were talking about Hilde's revelation, so hastily withdrawn, that Louis was Julie's father. She could see the pool house, now smothered by voracious climbers, beyond the pool and the image of her mother's anguished face assailed her like a sharp knife thrust. She ordered it out of her mind. This was surely not the time and hardly the place to probe the wounds and the repercussions of that sorry little infidelity she knew she'd have to come to terms with sometime.

'I don't like it . . . never liked it . . . an easier way.' Bernard again.

'. . . told you, Sonny . . . insurance . . . just in case . . . a while longer . . .' Hilde seemed more in command. '. . . fixed it . . . I told you . . . use the user . . .'

'Bullshit!' The voice was neither Hilde's nor Bernard's. It was flat, cold and young and it could have been male or female. Clearly there was another person in the room.

For a moment Anna was overcome by a dizzying certainty that the voice was Julie's, until it repeated the expletive, but with a more agitated emphasis. 'Bullshit!' And she realized that it wasn't Julie.

'. . . damned window . . . it's got cold.'

Anna heard someone move towards the window and pressed closer back against the wall. She could just see Bernard's hand reach out to rescue the fluttering curtains and heard quite plainly the goading drawl Hilde habitually used in addressing her son.

'You have to be nice to her . . . know . . . nice . . . best thing you do.' Then the window was slammed shut, leaving Anna wondering who Bernard was required to be nice to and whether it might be her. If her ridiculous exercise had proved nothing else, at least it had revealed that the Kleins had something to hide which probably involved Julie.

She moved back round the side of the villa, her knees still bent in a squat position. As she reached the side gate she straightened up, her shoes in her hand. She was easing backwards through the half-open gate when she felt a light tap on her shoulder. It might as well have been a blow from a crowbar. The oxygen seemed to drain out of her lungs as if sucked out by a whirlwind. The tap was repeated but now it was more like a prod, a threat.

She tried to will herself to turn round but the effort seemed beyond her. She felt dizzy: whether from squatting awkwardly against the wall, trying to catch her breath or just plain fright at being caught out hardly mattered.

'Anything I can do for you, miss? Maybe you left something behind.'

Maybe my sanity, thought Anna. Talk your way out of this one. She was breathing more easily now and the churning in the pit of her stomach was calming down. She didn't know who she expected to find sneaking up behind her or what they intended to do, but the Myrnas of this world she could cope with.

With as much nonchalance as she could muster she finished slipping on her shoes, then turned round and faced the woman squarely. She had the benefit of height, she was almost a head taller than Myrna. But then she saw the expression in Myrna's eyes, tough, pugnacious, prepared to doubt and deride whatever Anna said. She remembered her look of spite as she'd summoned Bernard from the garden. And suddenly this Myrna acquired another disturbing dimension which set her apart from all the other manageable Myrnas. Anna shivered.

'No, thank you,' she said with a show of confidence she didn't feel. She made an attempt to duck round the woman and walk away with a modicum of dignity. But Myrna blocked her path.

'Are you sure, miss?'

The provocation in her voice eroded what little self-assurance Anna had been able to summon up. 'There was something else I remembered . . .' she found herself burbling nonsensically as if called to account by some authoritarian headmistress.

The eyes, like shrivelled currants in a whey-coloured bun, were triumphant, enjoying her discomfiture.

Under their challenging stare, Anna's unease disintegrated. She felt a surge of indignation, welcome and sustaining. 'What business is it of yours?' she exploded.

The eyes didn't waver. 'Everything about Mrs Klein is my business. She's not a well woman. She don't take kindly to surprises. When she's unsettled, I'm unsettled.'

Anna moved a step closer to Myrna. 'Was my sister

unsettling, Myrna? You must remember her.' The woman started to back away, the first time she'd shown any lack of nerve. Anna pressed her advantage. 'What did you think of her, Myrna? What was she like? What *happened* to her, Myrna?' I could go on and on, she thought. I could make her tell me what she knows. I could twist her arm, I could hit her. Wildly, she raised her hand and saw the woman flinch.

'I'm just the help. I don't go around spying on people.' Despite her momentary panic, Myrna's voice was calm and implacable and it had the effect of shaming Anna for a second time as she realized that for a mad moment she had been capable of striking her.

'Myrna! Anna! I thought you'd left.'

In her anger, Anna hadn't heard Bernard crunching up the path to the gate. She dropped her hand to her side, not able to look at him, to confront his measured assessment of a situation in which she, of all people, was the aggressor.

'Given the circumstances, there's a savage in all of us, even you,' Malcolm had told her once when she'd been particularly pious about football hooligans and louts who mugged pensioners. She hadn't believed him, hadn't wanted to concede a fundamental weakness in the human race that only needed to be triggered to surface. Now she wasn't so sure. What other suppressed aggressions had she been harbouring, all unknowing? There was so much she had become unsure about in the last two days. Was it only two days? It seemed so long ago since she'd left that sheltered, ordered life buttressed by its impregnable certainties.

'I was just about to go,' she said. She looked at Myrna, but the currant bun eyes gave nothing away except a fleeting glint of victory. Hers.

As she nosed the car down the drive, waited for the remote-controlled security gates to open and turned into the road, Anna tried to banish the jumble of thoughts that were churning around in her mind and concentrate on the driving. She couldn't take another ticking off from a vigilant traffic cop.

A car, parked some distance away on an incline, started

59

up. But it was a while before she realized that it was cruising steadily behind her, not closely but keeping her in sight. It sat there in the rear-view mirror, looking not at all menacing. But it still crossed her mind that she might be being followed. She shook her head crossly. I'm being paranoid. From hunger, she decided. She had taken only juice and coffee for breakfast and the ham and eggs she'd had at the Double Take last night were just a greasy memory.

She noticed a Denny's on the way back down to her hotel from Beverly Hills and turned into the parking area at the rear of the coffee shop. From the corner of her eye she noticed the car that had been tailing her following her into the park. Now that she could see it more clearly she remembered it. It was the same model as the one she was driving, but electric blue, not red. She stalked across towards it and flung open the door. The driver smiled up at her, half apologetically, like Hugh late for an appointment.

'They really shouldn't let you loose on the streets of Los Angeles. I've known twelve-year-old kids who are better drivers,' said George Allenby. Winningly, she had to admit.

'You've been following me,' she accused him, ignoring his aspersion on her driving skills of which, on her own home ground, she was rather proud.

If she expected him to mock up some explanation she was disappointed. 'That's right,' he admitted genially. 'It seemed like a good idea. I missed you at the hotel and the girl at the Hertz counter told me where you were headed when you picked up the car and anyway you mentioned Hilde Klein last night.'

She looked at him dubiously. He really couldn't be as guileless as all that. 'That doesn't explain why you should follow me.'

'Let's say, I'd nothing better to do. Also I felt badly about last night. I guess we—I wasn't as helpful as you'd hoped.' He turned away from her, fiddling with the key in the ignition for no particular reason. 'Did you find out anything? Anything about your sister, I mean?'

She weighed her words carefully before answering. She was beginning to learn that trust was an expensive com-

60

modity: if you conferred it too lightly you might have to pay dearly. 'Sort of,' she hedged.

He smiled, as if satisfied that she'd said the right thing. 'Let's eat.' He thrust his hand under her elbow and propelled her towards the entrance of the coffee shop. His proprietorial manner irritated her. As she pulled away from him, he looked at her peevishly. 'I gather that's why you stopped off here.'

A chunky, middle-aged waitress who seemed several sizes too large for her Denny uniform took their order, provided iced water and perked coffee with the speed of a willowy teenager. 'You British?' she asked Anna as she scrawled on her pad, only mildly surprised that anyone would want a side order of pancakes and incinerated bacon with chicken salad.

Anna nodded.

Her suspicion confirmed, the waitress said pleasantly: 'We get a lot of you guys out here.' All, presumably, with eccentric tastes in food.

'You've made a hit,' said George, sipping his iced water and lighting a cigarette. 'You don't mind?'

She shook her head. 'Live and let live—or die, as the case may be. I smoke occasionally. But today my sin is bacon and pancakes with maple syrup which I adore and don't get very often at home. The chicken salad is conscience food.'

As he flicked the ash into the ash tray, she noticed that smile playing around the corners of his mouth. It reminded her of Hugh and that she ought to telephone him sometime. In his own quiet, introverted way he was probably concerned about her. 'What's so funny?'

'You. You're a funny lady, Anna Sterling. Not a barrel-of-laughs funny, an unfathomable funny. Where do you hide it all? You must be worried or you wouldn't have come all this way in the first place. You must be frustrated because you don't even know where to begin to look for Julie. And I guess you must be frightened, too. Alone in a hostile land? Isn't that how you read it? A lot of other women would be falling apart or taking the next plane back home or something . . . But you, you don't show a thing. You sit there telling me how much you love bacon and pancakes. You make jokes, not very good ones, it's true, but the effort is admirable. You bridle about little things like me saying you're a dodgy driver and yet you keep a stiff British upper lip about the one thing you should really be raising the roof about. The whereabouts of your sister. Like I said, you're unfathomable.'

'Maybe that's my oriental blood. Inscrutable.' He raised his eyebrows as if actually debating whether there was a touch of the oriental in her ancestry. She forked a mound of syrup-drenched pancake into her mouth with a show of dreamy delight. 'Sold to the gentleman on my right. For a moment you actually wondered if there might be some rogue Chinese grandparent or Japanese geisha in my background. That's good. It means I can fool you as capably as you can fool me. Besides, you should have seen me at Hilde Klein's. I wasn't so damned stiff upper lip then. Now, *there's* inscrutable for you. But of course you know that.'

She watched his reaction while concentrating on the pancakes and bacon. He was toying without enthusiasm with a club sandwich. 'What's that supposed to mean?' he said.

'When I mentioned Hilde Klein last night you suddenly decided it really wasn't worth my while hanging around trying to look for Julie. And Mick backed you up.' He was about to protest but she cut him short. 'Look, I wasn't that jet-lagged. A bit puggled, maybe, but not completely *non compos mentis.*'

He shoved the plate of half-eaten sandwich away from him. 'Hilde Klein can be dangerous,' he said flatly. 'She likes to manipulate people. It's not wise to get mixed up with her. Even now, she's still a power in the land. Money can unlock a lot of doors, but it can lock them too.'

'You mean she likes to put people in her debt?'

He shrugged. 'That's part of it.'

'What has she got on Bernard?'

'Sonny!' He screwed up his mouth in a gesture of derision.

'He's almost middle-aged and she winds him round her little finger. No son who didn't *have* to mind his manners would behave like he does. Incidentally, what does he do, for a living, I mean?'

He looked at her curiously. 'Why this sudden interest in Sonny? Don't tell me you've fallen for him, too?' He seemed to weigh up the question, then shook his head. 'No, that wouldn't fit with old inscrutable Anna. What does he do? Mostly he fails at what he does. His mother, who is loaded after selling the talent agency although you might not think so from the way she lives, puts up the dough and he blows it on one or other no-hope scheme. He part-owned a club which went bust, he put money into movies which flopped, he choked on a chain of Mexican eateries downtown. Now he's stuck with a health club that's seriously unsuccessful. It's a piece up the coast near Santa Barbara. Another guy runs it and he comes across with the sales spiel. A few minor celebrities looked in to give it a touch of class at first but now they're fading away. No one likes to back a loser in this town.'

'Except a possessive mother,' she volunteered, feeling enormously fortified by the unseemly intake of carbo-hydrates.

'Except a powerful mother,' he corrected her. 'I guess he's harmless enough. By that I mean he probably hasn't been booked on a drugs charge or caught with a smoking revolver in his hand.'

'What about caught with his hand in the till?'

Again he regarded her with respectful curiosity. 'You really are sparking on all cylinders this morning.'

'She has to have some hold on him,' she said reasonably, separating the chicken pieces from the mountain of salad.

'Rumour has it that she covered for him when it was discovered he was ripping off clients at the agency. He worked there for a while but his employment was abruptly terminated. The clients were not unnaturally anxious to recover their money or sue or both. Hilde took control of the situation. Don't ask me how. But she carried a lot of clout especially in those days, with the studios, the artists and, more than likely, the police. It was all hushed up, or as hushed as anything can be in Hollywood. But you can be sure Hilde retained enough evidence to screw Sonny if he ever stepped out of line.'

'How do you know all this?'

He beckoned for more coffee and lit another cigarette. 'There was a time when Hilde took quite an interest in me. Let's just leave it at that.' He took her hand in his, playing with the gold signet ring on her little finger, a school-leaving present from Malcolm with a characteristically down-putting inscription: 'To Anna who could do better.'

'I've always been a bit of a drifter, Anna. Hugh must have told you that,' he went on. 'All I knew when I came out here was that I wasn't a bad actor. But I never had the drive, the will-power, to really make good. But Hilde saw to it that I did make a living. I still do.'

'When did she stop taking an interest in you?'

'When I got married.'

She jerked back, registering surprise.

He grinned. 'You didn't think I was the marrying kind. Or maybe you thought I was gay. It didn't last long. She was an actress and the thespian twain should never marry. Since then I've—I've made ends meet and had a good time. People here like me and I like them. I've a nice little apartment off Wilshire. The coast is thataway and the mountains thisaway, San Francisco is a few hours' drive and Las Vegas an hour's flight. It's a great life. You're not even listening.'

It's true. She wasn't. Or just barely. 'Sonny knows. Sonny knows what's happened to Julie. And I think he likes me. Is he in the book—the telephone directory?'

'Look, Anna. Don't mess with Sonny. For God's sake, as Hugh's brother, I'm telling you. Presumably you'd pay attention to Hugh.'

She got up and ostentatiously picked up their joint check. 'As Hugh's brother,' she said deliberately, 'you can go take a running jump and get on with your life.'

He made to grab the check from her hand but she

snatched it back. 'Let's just say this is in payment for information received,' she said as she counted out the dollar bills at the cash desk.

CHAPTER 7

The car park was practically empty when they left Denny's. The regulars ate lunch early and the casuals were otherwise occupied. There was a somnambulant calm in the air which was almost certainly deceptive. By day Los Angeles was a community of worker bees buzzing away in their separate hives until dusk cast its exotic neon glow over the city.

For all her show of bravado Anna felt suddenly at a loss. And lonely. It was all very well to hint boldly at coaxing Bernard Klein to drop his guard and tell her what he knew about Julie. Actually doing it was something else.

'So, what now, Miss Fix-it?' said George as he walked her to her car. He was echoing her own thought but she didn't intend to give him the satisfaction of admitting it.

'We'll see,' she replied, hoping she sounded both enigmatic and decisive. 'What the hell are you doing?' She felt his hand gripping her arm as he swung her around to face the red Toyota. She tried to break free but his grip tightened. 'Will you please tell me why—' she started to say angrily.

He shoved her forward. 'Look!'

She followed his eyes which were directed at the panelling on the side of the car. 'Good God!'

The red façade was scarred with a message scrawled in large, uneven letters, presumably with an aerosol paint spray. 'Get Lost.'

She stared at it, at first with disbelief, then mounting horror. The pancakes and bacon and chicken salad churned around inside her and she felt sick to her stomach. 'Oh my God!' she repeated and realized that her legs were buckling under her. 'I think I'm going to be sick.'

He folded her in his arms, hurried her to a bench by the wall and pushed her head down between her knees. She heaved deeply but nothing came up. 'Stay still for a minute, you'll feel better.' Gradually her breathing became calmer and the nausea receded although not the fright that had induced it.

'OK now?' he asked. He sounded solicitous but also vaguely surprised at her extreme reaction. She supposed this sort of thing happened all the time in Los Angeles.

She nodded and leant against the wall, her eyes closed.

'Who'd do such a thing?' she whispered.

'Kids? Someone who doesn't like Brits,' he volunteered flippantly.

As she regained control of herself and her digestive tract, a wave of indignation replaced the unreasoning fear that had swept over her. 'Why would kids pick on this car?'

'It's red.'

'Can't you take anything seriously?' she rounded on him. 'Doesn't it occur to you that it isn't just random, but deliberately planned. As a warning. Get lost! Anna Sterling, get lost! Stop poking around!'

'Now you're just being fanciful.'

She shrugged away from him. 'Someone must have seen who it was. One of the waitresses perhaps in there—or the cashier.'

'How? There are no windows looking out on the parking lot,' he pointed out.

'You can think up more arguments for doing nothing about anything than a Tory MP with a comfortable majority,' she said grimly.

'What's politics got to do with it?' he called after her helplessly as she walked purposefully back into the coffee shop, narrowly avoiding collision with an overflowing litter bin.

The cashier was built like a football player except for the excess layer of fat round his girth which suggested he'd been overdosing on Denny's french fries and burgers. He was polite but perplexed, when she explained what had happened. His round, red face composed itself into an expression of concern. 'That's real terrible, ma'am, but there's no way you can see anything from in here. Some guys park there and don't even

66

eat here.' He spoke to a couple of the waitresses and the fast food chefs who were equally unhelpful.

The middle-aged waitress who'd served them said it was a shame and that the cops ought to do something about this sort of thing. It gave the city a bad name. And why didn't Anna have a nice piece of pie and coffee to take her mind off it? After all, she implied, it was only a car.

'She's right,' said Anna as they left the coffee shop. 'I want to go to the police. Not just about this, but about everything. I should have gone to them as soon as I arrived, if you hadn't side-tracked me,' she accused George.

He shook his head while letting out a sigh of deep resignation, his silence defusing her temper.

'Not so inscrutable as you thought,' she muttered, trying not to sound too apologetic although she realized she'd been unfair to him.

'So, I'll take you down to the Hollywood station on Wilcox,' he explained very patiently. 'And what'll you tell the police? That some graffiti junkie *you* didn't see and *neither* did anyone else, this graffiti artist sprayed your car with a not very friendly message. They have one of the biggest drug, homicide, violence and vice problems in the United States. You think they'll bust a gut over your little mystery?'

'But it's their job,' she protested. 'And what about Hilde Klein and Bernard and Julie? Where's Julie? I still want to see someone in authority.'

'OK, OK!' He lifted his hands as if warding off further argument. 'I told you I had this buddy who's a cop in the police department here. Joe Hatchett. I'll call him. I said I would last night only you were so determined not to believe anything I said. He could at least run Julie through the computer. I doubt whether there's much he can do about that.' He nodded at the vandalized Toyota. 'Satisfied? Great balls of fire! You're smiling.'

'Hatchett? A policeman named Hatchett?'

He returned her smile. 'Yes, well, don't go getting any wrong ideas. He's no Rambo. He'll never make detective, first class. But at least he's the law which is what you seem so anxious to drag into this case.'

'You agree, then, it's a case.'

'Oh, sure. Some fool girl takes off without telling anyone where she's going and the earth has to stop spinning on its axis so that you can find her, slap her wrists and take her home where she belongs.'

She puckered her lips, considering what he'd just said. 'You make it sound pretty silly. But there's more to it than that, a lot more. I discovered today that Malcolm isn't her father, Louis Lederman is. I wasn't going to tell you. I don't know why. I suppose because I haven't yet fully taken it in myself.' She searched his face looking for some hint of surprise if nothing else. But he betrayed no emotion beyond a mild interest. Then again, why should he? He didn't know Julie or Malcolm or even Anna herself, except for these past two days during which she hadn't seemed truly herself at all.

'Is that supposed to be earth-shattering?' he said.

'It's a shaker for me,' she said quietly.

He yawned, not pointedly but as if he were genuinely bored by the subject. 'I can see it might be. Look, I'll be in touch. Meanwhile I'll give you my phone number and address,' he said, jotting down the information on a paper napkin he'd fished out of his pocket and stuffing it into her hand.

The numbers and letters swum crazily in front of her eyes. He's washing his hands of me, she thought.

'I'll get hold of Joe at his home and you can meet him,' he assured her. 'Informal. Better not at the office. You wouldn't like LA police stations.'

Did he think she was some kind of shrinking violet? She marvelled at his apparently endless capacity to say exactly the right thing to annoy her. But she let it pass.

She unlocked the door of the car, ruefully surveying the damage. 'What'll I tell the hire car company?'

'Why not the truth?' He laughed. 'Is that what's bugging you, Anna? That's what your insurance is for.'

His laugh was contagious. It was, she realized, a pretty foolish worry to add to all the others.

He was, of course, infuriatingly right. The agent at the

Hertz desk at the hotel dealt efficiently with the paperwork and provided a replacement car. A Toyota Corolla. Red.

There was a message for her at reception. A Ms Lopez had called and left a number. Anna puzzled over the name.

'Are you sure that's right? I don't know anyone called Lopez.'

The girl was already busy with another guest who was large, demanding and wore a Texas stetson.

'Miss!' Anna insisted.

Miss turned away from Stetson impatiently. 'That's what it says. Ms Mabel Lopez.' Of course! She had never caught Mabel-Consuelo's surname at the Double Take the previous night, Anna remembered. 'Oh yes. And someone was asking for you,' the girl added almost as an afterthought. 'I guess she didn't wait.'

Now she tells me, thought Anna irritably. 'Well, did she say what she wanted?'

The girl sighed. 'Look, ma'am, I just work here. Maybe she's around the lobby someplace.'

'No name?'

'No, ma'am, *no name!*' The latter enunciated through gritted teeth.

Stetson smiled courteously at Anna. 'Take all the time you want, little lady. I'm in no hurry.' The girl shot him a furious look which clearly said that while he might be in no hurry, she was. A trickle of guests was already standing in line behind Stetson, requiring information, maps, bookings for tours and instant attention for leaking plumbing. 'Harry,' she called into the office behind her, 'I could do with a little help here.' Harry responding to her testy tone, emerged sheepishly, straightening his jacket.

As she walked through the lobby to the elevator, Mabel's telephone number clutched in her hand, Anna heard her name called in a carrying voice that rose above the indistinct babble of other voices. It was definitely not that of the hostile receptionist.

She turned round but could recognize no one in the queue for the lift behind her.

She heard her name repeated and homed in on the

69

location of the voice. Lining the corridor which led through to the parking lot were a few booths: a news-stand, boutique, gift shop. The gift shop was empty but for one customer who was waving in Anna's direction. It was a girl in canary yellow shorts, sneakers and a purple top which flopped untidily over one shoulder. Her clothes looked cheap and uncared for, but it would hardly have mattered what she wore—a potato sack would have done as well. What you noticed was the raven hair curling freely into the nape of her neck and framing an exquisite oval face: boldly shaped black eyebrows, green, cat-like eyes, a perfectly formed mouth at once ingratiating and challenging.

As the overhead beam in the shop spotlighted the face, Anna gasped. 'Julie!' she breathed.

She took a step forward and then stopped abruptly. She felt a lurching shudder of disappointment. It was, after all, just a trick of the light. Like everything in this city whose fame was founded on a trick of the light. It wasn't Julie, just someone who looked like Julie.

'I know,' the girl replied. Her voice was smoky, sensual but it hadn't managed totally to eliminate traces of a flat prairie twang. Like most Los Angelenos, she had come from somewhere else. 'We always did look alike. Don't you remember me?' She held up a T-shirt she'd been fingering emblazoned with the legend 'I love Los Angeles' woven through a map pinpointing Hollywood's famous landmarks. The fact that Hollywood was just a small part of the vast, sprawling city was irrelevant. 'Neat, huh?' she said, then pulled a face just like Julie. 'Neat? *Ugh!*'

As she looked at the girl more closely the resemblance was less marked. She was older than Julie. The oval face was more gaunt. There were dark rings under her eyes and the nose was puffy. 'Bettylou Valentine,' she said helpfully. 'I met your sister at a disco. We did a Scarlett O'Hara turn in a competition. I came out to your house once.'

Yes, now Anna remembered. 'You were on some sort of student exchange.'

The girl chuckled, a low, gurgling, provocative sound. 'Is that what she told you? I was just bumming around Europe.'

70

Of course, she had been the gullible one. Malcolm hadn't been so easily taken in. She remembered that, too. The dreadful, clashing row between him and Julie which she hadn't wanted to hear.

'That girl's a bad influence,' he'd said. 'Student! She hasn't even heard of any of my books,' he'd added as if that omission condemned her lack of scholarship as final and irrevocable. He'd always assessed people by their response to his own celebrity. It was the yardstick for all his judgements. She'd sometimes wondered if all great authors were as vain as he, but, as with so many other things, she hadn't given it serious thought.

'What gives you the right to judge everyone?' Julie had challenged him. 'I like her. She's fun. She doesn't have hang-ups. She just likes to have a good time. Why shouldn't I have a good time?'

'Because you're . . .' With the painful knowledge of hindsight, Anna recalled how he'd drawn back from making the obvious claim: 'because you're my daughter.' 'Because you're mine,' he'd said. And it had seemed such an odd thing to say, almost obscene in its possessiveness. Julie was his.

Julie had felt it, too. 'I'm not yours. I'm mine,' she'd exploded. But what *had* she felt? Why hadn't Anna bothered to inquire? Why had she turned her back and busied herself with all the peripheral things that didn't concern her family?

She rubbed her forehead with her hand as if trying to wipe out the memories that kept haunting her.

She let her hand fall limply to her side. 'Have you any news of Julie? I came here looking for her. You see, her father, that is Malcolm,' she corrected herself, 'Malcolm died and we couldn't reach her and haven't heard from her except the odd postcard since she came to Los Angeles.'

Bettylou continued to examine the gaudy T-shirt. 'Sure I know that. I know about Julie. That's why I'm here.'

The woman behind the counter who had been beadily observing Bettylou's careless handling of the merchandise interrupted. 'Are you buying that shirt?' she sniffed.

Bettylou flung the offending article down on its pile of

71

neatly folded companions. 'I wouldn't be seen dead in it,' she said loftily.

'I think maybe we'd better go up to my room to talk,' said Anna hastily before the saleswoman could muster a riposte to match the offensive gesture.

As she entered Anna's room Bettylou gave it a speculative once-over, sizing up its deadening uniformity: the matching patterned bedspread and curtains, the built-in wardrobe and dressing-table, the bland pictures on the bland wall-paper, the low easy chairs by the floor-length window which weren't as comfortable as they looked. It was impeccably clean and soul-less.

'I hate these places. They all look alike.'

'It's serviceable and convenient,' said Ann, feeling un-accountably affronted.

'I like a mess. Just born untidy my old mother used to say. God rest her soul.' The way she said it, it didn't sound like a blessing.

'Born untidy.' That's what Anna used to say to Julie when she surveyed the state of her room. She moaned. Get thee behind me, memory!

'You OK?' said Bettylou as she plumped down into one of the chairs, her long, tanned legs sprawled out in front of her. She didn't wait for an answer. 'Got anything to drink?'

'I could ring for room service.'

Bettylou shook her head. 'I'm not planning to stay. I just thought you might have a bottle in the room. And I guess you wouldn't have any dope.' She laughed, 'No, I guess the uptight, upright Anna Sterling wouldn't have any angel dust lying around.'

'No, she wouldn't,' said Anna, barely containing her aggravation. 'You said you had news of Julie. When did you last see her? I'm—I'm out of my mind with worry.'

The girl looked at her through heavy-lidded eyes. 'You could have fooled me. Sure, I've seen her a lot since she came to LA. I was doing a little bit of this and a little bit of that, clubs, movies—'

'What movies?'

72

Bettylou smiled sweetly. 'Not the kind you'd like.'

'Did Julie—'

'Hold your horses. Julie didn't need to do that stuff. She was staying up in the hills. Glitzy life. New father.'

'You knew that.'

'She told me. She'd just learned that Louis Lederman was her dear, old pop before she left home. But I guess she never told *you*?' she guessed shrewdly.

'No.'

'Well, that figures. You weren't close, were you? She used to say that talking to you was like talking to a committee that never made decisions and never passed judgements. Those were her very words, not mine.'

Another blow to her self-esteem! Anna could hear echoes of Hilde Klein in Bettylou's manner, her pleasure in tickling a wound just sharply enough to be painful but not so deep as to draw blood.

'Where is she now?' she prompted the girl.

'She took off. A while ago, a few weeks. She'd met a guy and they'd fallen for each other. And he was going up north and she was going with him.'

'To Canada.'

Bettylou frowned, as if not sure how to answer. Then she seemed to decide to agree. 'Yeah! Sure. Canada.'

'And you've no idea where she is now?'

'No. But she said she'd let me know as soon as they were settled. She was happy, real happy. So, you see, you've nothing to worry about.'

'Why didn't she answer my letters? Why didn't she get in touch when Malcolm died?'

'Look, Anna. You don't mind me calling you Anna? She just wanted to get away from her family. She had her reasons.'

'What reasons?' Anna rounded her.

'That's for her to tell you. She'll come round. You'll see.'

'And who was this—this guy—she went off with?'

'She never said. Leastwise, not to me.'

'How did you know I was over here, where to reach me?'

'I heard it around. At the Double Take. That's right, at

73

the Double Take. And I just figured I could reassure you, let you know everything was OK.'

Anna looked down on the girl slumped in her chair, so like Julie. And yet . . . and yet what? What would Julie look like now? 'That was thoughtful of you,' she said with a trace of sarcasm.

'You do believe me?' There was a note of anxiety in Bettylou's voice which wasn't lost on Anna.

She didn't answer. 'It must have been a shock for her when Louis Lederman was killed in the earthquake.'

'Earthquake! You're kidding!' She'd caught Bettylou unawares and it took the girl a moment to recover. 'I mean, it sure was a shock.' Then it was as if a beam of light switched on in her brain: 'I guess that's why she fell for this guy. On the rebound. From the shock,' she bubbled eagerly. She glanced deliberately at the ugly man's watch on her wrist. 'Is that the time? Bullshit! I'm late. For an appointment. I gotta run. Nice meeting you. And remember. There's not a thing to worry about. Julie's fine.'

It was all so convenient. The explanation of Julie's disappearance. The reason why she shouldn't have made contact with her family. The assurance that Anna needn't trouble herself about her sister. And now, the hastily contrived need to depart.

'When can I call you?'

Bettylou flickered the fingers on both her hands indicating constant flight. 'Oh, I shake down all over the place. I'll call you sometime.'

She was out of the room before Anna could stop her and it was as if she had never been there. Only her dark little reminiscences and glibly produced excuses for Julie's behaviour remained, lurking in the corners of the room to emerge and taunt Anna.

'Bullshit!' She wasn't sure if she believed the girl, but she was very sure that she was the third unseen party she'd overheard in the patio room at Hilde Klein's villa.

CHAPTER 8

Mabel Lopez's apartment block beyond West Hollywood was one of the remaining remnants of the old Hollywood, where hopeful starlets hung around waiting for the phone to ring between checking on the 'trades' and hustling for bit parts that just might lead to the big time; where struggling writers struggled and old timers who never were famous settled for a future of knowing they never would be. It was a complex of peeling stucco buildings surrounding a meagre swimming pool and flanked by that crazy confusion of vegetation that grows rampant in Los Angeles: huge sensual lilies, honeysuckle, California poppies, Venus fly-traps, and the ubiquitous palm trees.

It housed a convivial community: the cast list contemporary in dress and outlook but not too dissimilar from the inhabitants of the 'thirties. Mabel's apartment was up a flight of stone steps on what Anna regarded as the first floor and the Americans the second. A balcony wound beneath the windows, the width of the apartment. The interior was darker than that of the glossy, modern apartment blocks that were gobbling up green spaces of the city and spreading through its suburbs. Having been built at a time when air-conditioning was not so common, it adopted the Spanish style of blocking out the blinding sun to preserve a cool current of air inside. At least that was the theory.

To Anna it looked more like home than anything she had seen in Los Angeles which, admittedly, wasn't extensive. She supposed there were pleasant residential areas for ordinary people as distinct from the filthy rich but tourists didn't often get to view them: after all, they weren't what Hollywood was all about and that's what tourists came to see. They had enough of seeing ordinary people back home.

She didn't need to ring the bell to the apartment. Mabel was looking out for her. She was wearing a bikini top and

75

a colourfully patterned skirt tied at the waist. Her dark hair was sleek and damp and she'd obviously been swimming in the pool.

When Anna had returned her surprising call, she had been insistent that Anna came round. She'd been surprised because Mabel had been so dismissive, almost insulting, the previous evening. She'd even asked her why the sudden interest.

'You look forlorn,' Mabel had joked, then, more seriously, 'Besides I guess I didn't tell you the whole truth about your sister. That is, all I knew about her. I wasn't sure I could trust you. And the company wasn't right.'

'The company?'

'Well, Georgie. He's kinda flaky. And he and Mick are thick as thieves. Anyway, it's not much fun staying in a hotel. You could put up with me for a day or two. I've plenty of room. My guy's in Texas on location for a movie. And my girlfriend comes and goes. She won't bother you if you don't bother her.'

'I—I don't know. It's very kind of you.' And, suddenly, the idea of not being alone in this formidable city seemed very attractive to Anna, even though she barely knew Mabel, was dubious about her flatmates and wasn't at all sure why she was being invited to share her apartment anyway.

'Just come along—and then you can see. I've been alone in Los Angeles, too,' she said, reflecting Anna's feeling. 'But that's another story.'

She was getting used to the Los Angeles traffic and, able to avoid the freeway which was always jam-packed, as Mabel had warned, she found the apartment house quite easily, set back off the road in its own quaint little bygone world.

'You made it!' Mabel hailed her. 'Hey—Sissie. This is the stray I told you about.'

A coffee-coloured black girl, quite as tall, slender and staggeringly beautiful as Mabel, loped out of the front door, smiled warily and gave Anna a half-hearted wave. 'Hi!' Then she loped back in again.

'Don't mind Sissie. She's between guys. It always makes her itchy. She's a good actress, though. Sissie Carradine. You've heard of her?'

'I think so. Wasn't she in that Civil War TV mini-series?' She was still feeling slightly put out at being designated a 'stray'.

'Nominated for an Emmy. Then—nothing. It's like that in this business, specially if you're black. It's easier for hispanics like me. We're supposed to be exotic like Dolores Del Rio but not so exotic as to be uncomfortable. You know, half the men in Hollywood were supposed to be in love with Dolores Del Rio. C'mon in!'

She beckoned Anna into a large living area separated into two sections by a couple of steps. The basic furniture—tables, chairs—was pared down to a bare minimum. Her first impression was of a riot of colour, like the first impression of an abstract art exhibition. Ethnic rugs were strewn across the floor, jazzy batiks decorated the walls and cushions in all shapes and sizes were littered around for sitting and sprawling on. Plants in crude peasant pots, unevenly patterned, shot unrestrained to the ceiling winding their tentacles around anything handy. A minute kitchen led off the upper eating area and Mabel indicated the location of a bathroom and a couple of bedrooms.

Oddly, despite the blaze of clashing colours, it felt cool and looked homely. Unlike Hilde Klein's villa, apart from her gallery of personal photographs, it was an expression of its owner, Mabel, and, possibly, Sissie.

'You like?'

Anna nodded. 'I like.' She didn't know why. It would have been anathema to her at home, restless, untidy, unco-ordinated, probably harbouring several weeks' deposit of dust and grime. But here it seemed like a haven of undiscriminating normality.

Mabel plumped down on a huge, squeegy cushion, winding her legs easily under her. Anna followed suit but more awkwardly. She was still wearing the neat linen dress that had seemed like suitable attire for Los Angeles when she was packing. Since arriving, though, she'd realized that it was quite out of place, proclaiming her status as an outsider.

Mabel watched her, amused. 'You wanna buy something more comfortable. But I guess you haven't had much time to shop around. So, what's the story?'

It was as if Anna had been waiting for just such an invitation. Suddenly it didn't seem to matter whether Mabel, like everyone else, was just putting on an act. Instinctively she felt she could trust this warm, unlikely accomplice. And she poured it all out. Hilde Klein. Bernard. Louis Lederman. George. The graffiti scrawled on her car. The surprise visit from Bettylou. Even her unseemly eavesdropping on the conversation between Hilde Klein and her son and the sinister intervention of Myrna.

'You've had quite a day,' breathed Mabel. 'It's lucky I called.'

'Lucky?'

'You need a friend.'

'George seemed anxious to be my friend.'

Mabel watched her carefully. 'But you didn't buy that?'

'I wasn't sure.'

'Wise girl.'

'He did offer to set up a meeting for me with his policeman friend.'

'Well, make sure you ask to see his badge first.'

Sissie emerged from one of the bedrooms. She was dressed for something special and carrying a small bag. 'I guess you'll be using my room, honey. Feel free, just don't mess with my things.'

'Tonight's the night,' mouthed Mabel at Anna.

'I heard that,' said Sissie amiably. She walked over to the fridge in the kitchen, took out a bottle of chilled Californian wine and opened it expertly. 'You look like you could use this.' She placed the bottle on the floor together with two tumblers. 'See you guys.' She sauntered off, leaving the front door wide open. The sun shot a beam of light into the darkish room.

'That's Sissie for you. Here today . . .' Mabel handed Anna a full tumbler of wine. It tasted tart and fruity and sent a pleasant glow down to the pit of Anna's stomach.

'Do you mind if I ask you a personal question?' said Anna cautiously, unused as she was to asking anyone personal questions.

'Shoot!' Mabel raised one delicately arched eyebrow.

'Why Mabel? Consuelo is so much prettier.'

Mabel laughed, showing perfect teeth, crowned, Anna judged, at some cost.

'It sounds so *Ingleesh!*' She mimicked a broad Mexican accent which she'd no doubt been born with but which had been largely eradicated en route from Tijuana to acceptance in Los Angeles.

'But you don't look English at all. You look gorgeously Latin.'

'That's the trick in this town, honey. They look at your name and then at you and they think: She isn't an Anglo, why does she call herself Mabel? You don't necessarily get the job but at least they give you a second look.'

Anna took another sip of wine. 'I hadn't thought of that. It's just so strange. It's all so strange. At home where I live the most you do is shorten your name from Elizabeth to Liz or Kathleen to Kate.'

'You poor kid!' Mabel shook her head wonderingly. 'Here you have to know the angles. If you don't, you're dead. Sometimes you're dead even if you do know the angles.'

'Is Julie dead?' Perhaps it was the wine that made her ask the question that she'd so rigorously refused to countenance.

'Maybe,' Mabel replied honestly. 'But I doubt it. If she is, you'd more than likely have known about it. From the police or somebody. It's possible, though, that she's in hiding. There are a lot of secrets in this town and a lot of people who don't want them out in the open.'

'The Kleins?'

'Maybe,' Mabel repeated. 'I'll tell you what I know. That's all.'

'You knew Julie better than you indicated last night, didn't you? I think I could tell. That talk about families and not understanding them,' she added bitterly. The bitterness directed not at Mabel but at herself for being so blind.

'I first met her when she'd left the gallery where she worked for Louis Lederman . . .'

'What about Bettylou?' Anna interrupted her.

'Sure I met her, too, with Julie. But she was just an airhead—a druggie who picked up guys to pay for her habit.'

Anna winced. 'Not Julie!'

'No, Julie had different problems. They may have been close once, but not any more. Julie had class, like you. But she was a real mixed-up lady.'

'You mean, learning that Louis Lederman was her real father,' Anna assumed.

'Not just that. Something deeper. Something that had happened in England that had really wiped her out. It was as if she couldn't put enough distance between herself and whatever it was she was trying to work out of her system.' She looked inquiringly at Anna.

Anna shook her head. 'I've no idea. She was bright, popular, Malcolm adored her. It was a happy home life.' Even as she said it Anna began to doubt it. What, after all, had she really known about how Julie felt? She'd accepted the surface for reality because it was more convenient that way.

Mabel smiled at her ruefully. 'Show me a happy home and I'll show you a lie.'

'Why did she leave the gallery?' said Anna abruptly, changing the subject. It was too late to ruminate about her sins of omission.

'I gather there'd been some sort of bust-up. I didn't know who with then but I can guess now from what you've told me. Hilde Klein didn't like the amount of attention Louis was paying to this new-found daughter of his. She held the purse strings so she made the rules.'

'Did you ever see her with Louis?'

'Sure. At the Double Take. At least I'm pretty sure it was him. They were very cosy. He was excited about something, something he wanted her to share. But you could never tell what *she* was feeling. Either she was up or so far down she was out of sight. Around here you'd guess she was on drugs, but I doubt it. I saw him hanging around the set a few times, too, before that, only I didn't make the connection until later. That's when I first met her.'

She poured them both another glass of wine. 'Look, I know I wasn't straight with you yesterday, but I figured Julie was as entitled as anybody else to her secrets. Then I thought about it and . . . well, here we are.'

Anna looked at her, puzzled. Mabel had a way of leading a conversation in one direction and then darting off on a detour that might make sense to her but not to Anna. 'What did you mean "around the set"? When you first met her? I thought you'd just seen her a few times at the club.'

Mabel smacked her own cheek with the palm of her hand. 'Jesus Christ! Didn't I say? It was on one of those TV movies about the good old days of Hollywood. I had quite a nice little bit as a south of the border señorita who tries to make it in pictures and is screwed by the big producer and all that stuff. There were some scenes of those Pickfair parties and premieres where they needed a lot of extras who looked like movie stars. Bettylou and Julie were among them. Bettylou knew the ropes but it was a first for Julie. Together they looked so alike and so cute that the director dreamed up a few shots for them to be dressed up like Scarlett O'Hara at one of these parties. It didn't make much sense because the period was pre *Gone With The Wind*. But he figured the viewers wouldn't know and anyway it was a nice touch. It was, too. Crazy. But nice. I'll show you the tape.'

Anna held up her hand, fearing that Mabel would go off on another of her tangents. 'And you got to know Julie then?'

'That's what I'm saying. There's always a lot of hanging around even on a TV movie if you're not the stars, in which case you're kept pretty busy all the time. Julie looked sort of forlorn among all those hardboiled extras. Bettylou had dumped her. And during the lunch-break we got talking. She told me she was from England and she'd just lost her job at an art gallery in Westwood and she needed the money. She was worried sick. Strictly speaking, she shouldn't have been working on the movie, because she didn't have a ticket.

But that wasn't what was really worrying her. I could tell that. Then this guy—I guess Louis Lederman—came to pick her up after shooting. I don't think she liked that. It sort of made her uncomfortable. I felt sorry for her.'

'And after the movie?'

'A few weeks, I guess. I went to the Double Take with a couple of out-of-towners. Tourists like all that pretend Hollywood. There was Julie, waiting tables. We said hello, but she didn't seem to want to prolong the conversation. I saw her once or twice after that. But then, like Mick said, she just split.'

'And you've no idea where she went?' It was hardly a question. Anna knew the answer already. She'd heard it before. It was as if Julie had disappeared in a puff of smoke like the victim of some weird conjuring act. Only there was no conjuror to make her miraculously materialize for the final curtain.

'None. But I couldn't help feeling she was scared. Something to do with a caper this guy—Louis—was involved in. But in her state anything would have made her jittery.' She was silent for a moment, watching Anna with an expression in her eyes of grudging pity: grudging because, perhaps, she was wondering whether Anna deserved the pity. 'I never knew her before, but it was like the spirit had gone out of her. She wasn't at all the fun person you describe.'

Anna forced herself to ignore the reproach. For now. 'Did you know Louis Lederman was dead? He was killed apparently in the San Francisco earthquake last year. According to his wife.'

Mabel shrugged. 'No—no, I didn't. If I'd read it his name wouldn't have meant anything to me. That sort of puts a different complexion on it, don't you think?'

'How do you mean?'

'He's hustling her. Then he's dead. And she vanishes. Or makes herself scarce. It's easy enough to lose yourself in California provided you keep clear of the law. You can fake some identification—or someone could do it for you.'

If that were the case, thought Anna, she might as well do

what Hilde Klein and George had been urging her to do. Go home.

'Of course you could hire a private dick,' said Mabel, reading her thoughts. 'But it would cost. Maybe you should wait to hear what Georgie's cop pal has to say. If he is a cop. How are you fixed for dough?'

'Enough. But not much more,' Anna calculated. 'My father left some money, but not a great deal. He was more of a critical success than a bestseller.'

'Malcolm Sterling. Right? I've heard of him from an old writer in this apartment block. He once worked with him.'

It came out casually as if it were of little importance, just in passing. Mabel could hardly have guessed how momentous that chance remark was to Anna. 'I'd like to meet him,' she said.

'Sure. He's usually around.'

'Funny. I once wrote a short story about a runaway girl. That's what I do. Write short stories. Mostly for women's magazines. My father thought they were trivial and, by his standards, I suppose they are. I wrote this story, full of pain and anguish, but it all turned out right in the end. Because it had to. They wouldn't have published it otherwise.' She wasn't sure why she should start ruminating about her own work in this manner, but it seemed somehow relevant. She'd been quite proud of the story, convincing herself that it was true and real. After all, hadn't she interviewed parents of runaway children and the children themselves in the course of her volunteer work? Hadn't she tucked away their reactions at the back of her mind for future reference? 'You think you know,' she went on bitterly, continuing out loud her silent meditation. 'But it's all second-hand. You're not in there feeling it, experiencing it. You're weighing up the evidence and the choices and giving practical advice. Only people aren't practical, are they? They do what they do for reasons nobody else can truly understand. It's taken me an awful long time to start learning that.'

Mabel was looking at her, puzzled. 'I don't follow you.'

Anna smiled, cutting off the flow of confidences that had

been pouring out of her. 'I hardly follow myself. I'm sorry. I was just thinking out loud.'

A tall, blond, muscular Adonis in bathing trunks paused in the open doorway to Mabel's apartment, blocking out the sunlight. He flashed a mouthful of dazzling teeth at Mabel.

'Hi, Gus!' she waved. 'How goes things?'

'Slow. But my agent says there might be something at Warners.' All the time he kept jogging on the spot, pumping his brawny shoulders from side to side. 'He's a zombie, but he's all I've got. Tells me the Robert Redford look is out, as if I didn't know. It's all Tom Cruise now. And I don't look like Tom Cruise. So I say to him: I'm taller, handsomer, sexier than Cruise. I'm the great white hope. Make me fashionable, I say. It's a waste of time. Still, you never know.' He dazzled them again with his teeth and jogged on along the balcony.

'Good luck at Warners,' Mabel yelled after him.

'How does he live?' said Anna. 'I mean, make money to live.'

'He parks cars at the Beverly Wilshire, pumps gas, carries old ladies' groceries at the supermarket. Anything! Mostly legal. In a few years he won't be so beautiful and he'll get the message and go back home to Ohio, marry the girl next door, settle down, raise kids and work for the rest of his life in his father's construction business. Or he'll stay put and end up in the sleaze and drugs market. Meanwhile—he hopes!'

'I can't believe this still goes on,' said Anna wonderingly. 'I know it used to, but now?'

'It doesn't go on so much. But all the time they make movies and TV and records in Hollywood there'll be kids who come here like migrating birds. They're brighter now. They actually go to classes. Try for theatre work—not that there's much in Los Angeles. But back of it all they want to be discovered—just like Lana Turner and Tony Curtis and all those others.'

'Is Gus a boyfriend?' They'd looked so friendly and comfortable together.

'Sort of.' Mabel paused, seeming to size up Anna before finding her wanting. 'I swing both ways.'

Having caught the look, Anna preferred to ignore it. 'You and Sissie?' she asked.

'Shocked?'

Anna smiled. 'Not that easily. It happens in my country, too.'

Even in properly conservative Winchester. Biddy and Mercy of Rose Cottage preserving their open secret for twenty years. She wondered what Mabel and Sissie would make of those two outwardly prim and passionately devoted English ladies, beyond their sexual kinship.

'Don't worry,' said Mabel. 'I figured I wasn't your type—nor you mine. You're strictly a meat and potatoes woman. I'm just a sucker for lame ducks.'

'All things considered,' sighed Anna. 'I feel more like a sitting duck.'

'How well do you know Georgie? George Allenby,' Mabel said suddenly.

'Hardly at all. I just met him when I came here. He's the brother of a friend of mine. Hugh.'

'A good friend?'

Anna considered. 'Most people think we'll get married. He teaches at Winchester College. He's not at all like George, except physically. George left home almost twenty years ago, I gather. Wanted to be an actor. He didn't do too well in England so he came out here. But Hugh and he have kept in touch, so naturally he told his brother that I'd be arriving in Los Angeles and why.'

Mabel stroked her chin as if searching for a rogue spot in that flawless skin, then got up and riffled through a line of video tapes stacked underneath the window.

'I've just remembered something. Let's watch a movie.'

CHAPTER 9

The TV movie, *Starlit on Sunset*, that Mabel had slotted
into the VCR was the kind that Anna would have watched
over a plate of comfort food late at night while thinking
of six other things at the same time. It was an indul-
gence that had amused Hugh and infuriated Malcolm who,
after his brief sojourn in Hollywood, persisted in regarding the place and anything to do with it as beneath his
contempt.

It hadn't yet been shown in Britain, if it ever would be.
The story was so numblingly familiar you could recite the
dialogue and predict the outcome almost from the start. But
it was lavishly and quite lovingly produced. A nostalgic
journey into the past, holding up its hands in horror at the
iniquities of the old studio system while at the same time
thoroughly relishing them. A typical example of Hollywood's love-hate relationship with itself.

There was a lot of fast-forwarding through the major bits
in which Mabel, heavily over made-up to fit the accepted
stereotype of a Mexican beauty, didn't appear.

With her finger poised on the remote control button she
wiped out whole sections of two quite renowned TV stars
playing a famous producer and his recklessly self-destructive
protégée, declaring, then denying and then dying for love of
each other. 'Boring!' she dismissed their energetic emoting.
'Now. Watch this!'

She ran the video back to the beginning of a glamorous
gathering in a huge, Gothic Hollywood mansion like the
one inhabited by Gloria Swanson and a dead monkey in
Sunset Boulevard. All the principals were present: drinking
fake champagne, dancing, whooping it up, making love,
engaged in monumental rows and either inviting or fending
off lecherous propositions while advancing what passed for
a plot. Their numbers were padded out with a couple of
dozen extras who at a quick glance could be mistaken for

86

some Hollywood luminary: Gable or Cooper or Lombard or Harlow or Selznick or Mayer.

Mabel was there, batting several layers of false black eyelashes and thrusting her bosom at a skinny little man who was supposed to be the powerful Irving Thalberg. She clucked her teeth at the exaggerated image of herself on the screen. 'Geez! What a load of garbage! And I actually thought I wasn't bad . . . Now!' She gripped Anna's arm, her long fingernails biting into the flesh.

Two young girls entered the frame and sashayed across the floor of the crowded ballroom in identical off-the-shoulder green-sprigged crinolines, their shiny black hair parted in the centre and drawn back off the forehead with matching bows. They did indeed look like twin Scarlett O'Haras, an impression fostered by make-up and a brazen bearing. Bettylou and Julie. While the former obviously enjoyed the exposure, Julie seemed awkward and uncomfortable.

The camera lingered on them as they minced towards the player impersonating Selznick, curtsied, giggled behind their hands and said in unison 'Mr Selznick, we want to be your Scarlett!' 'Selznick' looked perplexed, annoyed and then let out a loud guffaw as he realized the girls had been put up to it as a joke on his long-running search for the perfect 'Scarlett' by a friend, a shadowy figure who had been observing the little charade in the background.

The figure moved forward, waved at 'Selznick' and, linking arms with both 'Scarletts', escorted them out of the scene and, presumably, the picture, before returning to resume his own role of an English actor desperately trying to resuscitate his ailing career in Hollywood.

Mabel stabbed the 'pause' button. There was no mistaking him.

'George!' Anna sat there, stunned, staring at the still screen and the familiar face with its smile and its eyes that so reminded her of Hugh. 'He said he'd never seen Julie except once I think at the club.'

'Yeah—that's what I remembered. Not straight off. But later, I remembered he had a couple of days playing this

Ronald Colman type. He was between pictures at the time. Normally he wouldn't have taken such a small part. But he did it for the producer because the guy they'd got for it originally copped out at the last minute.'

'But—but why would he want to lie about a thing like that?'

'I guess he didn't *lie* exactly.'

'You mean he was just economical with the truth?'

Mabel frowned. 'I don't get you?'

'It's just a saying. Sort of lying by omission.'

'You English!' Mabel sighed.

Anna unwound herself from the cushion on the floor and stretched her back which was beginning to ache from the unnatural squat. She felt angry and confused and, above all, frustrated. 'What the hell am I going to do, Mabel?'

'Like I said, there's the police or a private dick or you could just ask Georgie why he kept quiet about knowing Julie. Mind you, he wouldn't have had to *know* her. They were just a couple of girls he had to walk across the floor.'

'It's not only that, Mabel. It's the whole business. Ever since I can remember, the world seemed to circulate around Julie. It still does. And yet . . .' She was staring out of the open front door. Below the balcony a foursome was lounging beside the pool, bronzed and oily with sun lotion, two boys and two girls. Anna could hear the muted thump of some unidentifiable rock number. They all looked so easy with themselves and each other. She wondered who in the world had time to sit by a pool in the middle of the afternoon on a working day. Then she recalled that this wasn't the world as most people knew it; this was Hollywood. Had Julie become part of all this, whatever *this* was?

'And yet?' Mabel prompted her.

Anna shivered and turned back into the room. 'I'm scared.'

'For Julie?' Mabel examined Anna's face intently, then shook her head. 'No, not just Julie. You're scared for you, aren't you?'

'This place! It contaminates you. It contaminated Julie.

I saw her on that film. It's the first time I'd seen her since she left England . . .'

'You can't tell anything by how people look on the screen. The camera's a weird thing. When you're not in the business you can't understand how weird the camera can be.'

'That's not what I mean,' Anna protested. 'I know enough to realize you can't take anything at face value on the screen, but it was much more than that. I could see deep down the strain she was under. You told me that yourself. I almost felt she was hating herself for doing what she was doing. Once she'd have loved it. Hilde Klein said she used to prance around posing as Scarlett, just like she used to do at home. So, what happened to change all that? What happened to change *Julie*?'

'Ask yourself another question. Why should you believe what Hilde Klein tells you about Julie?'

Anna stepped back on to the balcony. One of the couples was in the pool. They were ducking each other and screaming. The other couple had retreated behind their sunglasses, ignoring them. So young! No older than Julie, probably. She felt Mabel's hand on her shoulder.

'Cute? Huh? Don't be deceived by appearances,' she said as if reading Anna's thoughts. 'They know their way around better than any LA cab-driver. Tough as nails. Real smart-ass tinsel town babes,' she dismissed them. 'You didn't answer my question. Why believe what Hilde Klein tells you?'

'Because if I didn't I'd have to believe that what changed Julie happened before she left home. And then I'd have to blame myself for not being aware of it. Before he died, Malcolm, my father, said: "Find Julie. Make it right." I didn't know what he meant. But I should have known.'

'And you did what he asked. Dying request. All that bull.'

'You didn't know Malcolm.'

'Maybe I'm beginning to get an idea. Stop being such a tragedy queen. You're only feeling guilty because you were jealous. Whether he was her father or not, she was his favourite and you were the doormat. And when she left home, you were glad. Admit it! It's no big deal.'

89

'That's not true,' Anna rounded on her, angered at hearing the truth she'd feared to acknowledge from a virtual stranger.

'Look, I told you about this old guy who knew your father when he was over here. I'll take you to see him. Maybe you'll learn a thing or two about your father you didn't know. Meanwhile I'll give the company that crewed up that movie a buzz and see if they know anything about Julie. It's a long shot. But, it seems to me, long shots are all you've got.'

'I'd be grateful,' said Anna, grateful not just for the offer of help but for Mabel's sturdy refusal to allow her to wallow in the self-pity that kept threatening to engulf her. 'I'm not sure, now, that I want to meet . . .'

'Asher Kowalski. That's his name. And, yes, you *do* want to meet him or if you don't you should. It's time you got this father of yours into some kind of perspective. Saint or sinner. When you're dead it's all the same.' She crossed herself hastily as if caught out in a blasphemy, then smiled apologetically. 'Old habits! My family may have been dirt poor, but they were more Catholic than the Pope.'

Asher Kowalski's apartment was tucked away from the main block and the lively sociability of the pool, fronting the road on the corner. Mabel hadn't needed to make an appointment. 'He doesn't go out much. Except to the kosher deli for lunch sometimes. He sits and writes stuff that never gets produced and kids himself that he's still a big wheel. But apart from the odd TV spot his agent gets for him he hasn't written anything for years. In the 'fifties and 'sixties he was a somebody. Now he's nobody. That's how it is in this town. I don't know how he makes out. But I guess he had some dough put by from the good times. That—and his memories. Old guys like that live on their memories. And the hope that some film whizzkid will rediscover him.'

She painted such a sad picture of disintegrating old age that Anna was amazed when the apartment door was opened by a spry septuagenarian in a threadbare but once natty three-piece suit, totally unsuited to the California climate both of the times and the weather. His almost white hair was cropped close to his head giving it a curiously bullet-shaped appearance. His eyes were bright and dancing and eager to be surprised.

'My favourite lady!' The gap-toothed smile he beamed at Mabel hinted at the courtly charmer he must once have been and still, to an extent, was, for she chucked him under his flabby chin with obvious affection. 'To what do I owe the enormous pleasure?' He stepped aside, waving them into the shabby apartment. Unlike Hilde Klein, he hadn't lost his thick Middle European accent despite years in California. Perhaps he hadn't wanted to. In common with many expatriates, he clung to it as both a crutch and a comfort, an assertion of identity in a community of vagrants.

Mabel flicked her eyes over the cluttered living-room, piled high to the ceiling with books, filing cabinets, old newspapers and magazines and decorated with cobwebs. There was a musty smell of undisturbed age. The furniture was dark and heavy and far too large for the room. Every spare inch of surface supported mementoes, ornaments, bits of porcelain, mosaic snuffboxes, carved wooden musical boxes, Bavarian mechanical toys and, in no particular place of honour, an Oscar he'd won thirty-odd years before for writing an award-winning screenplay. 'Geez, Kowalski,' said Mabel in mock horror, 'don't you ever clean this place?'

Anna suppressed a smile. From what she'd seen of Mabel's apartment, she doubted whether the Mexican girl had more than a nodding acquaintance with a dustpan and brush either.

'It's clean dirt,' shrugged Kowalski. 'Come in, come in. I'll make you some coffee. It's not every day I get a couple of pretty girls come to visit.'

They followed him out into the tiny kitchen which by comparison was spotless and orderly and obviously well used. 'I like to cook,' he said as he pottered around, grinding fresh coffee beans for the filter jug and setting out the cups and saucers just so on a tray. 'Such a smell!' he breathed. 'Viennese. Takes me back to the Sacher days. You like a piece of strudel? I bake it myself.' He produced the strudel from the refrigerator triumphantly. It looked mouth-wateringly fruity and feathery. 'It's a gift,' he said smugly. 'Making strudel.'

He caught Anna's approving eye and nudged close to Mabel, whispering in her ear. 'Who's the lady? A new room-mate? She looks sort of frail, like Joan Fontaine. When she walked in the room, I thought for a moment: That's Joan. Then I thought: Joan is almost as old as me. Nice girl.' He chopped his hand in the air as if dismissing a stale memory. 'So, tell me. Who is she?'

Anna held out her hand. 'I'm Anna Sterling, Mr Kowalski. My father was Malcolm Sterling. You worked with him, Mabel says, when he was in Los Angeles. Twenty years ago.'

She felt his thin, dry, sensitive fingers exploring the palm of her hand. It was an eerie sensation, not unlike feeling a large spider crawling over her flesh. She tried to withdraw her hand as inoffensively as possible but he kept hold of it, edging closer to her, peering at her face as if trying to place it.

His intense gaze disconcerted her. 'You wouldn't remember me. I was just a girl then. I don't think I ever met you.'

He nodded his head. 'Malcolm Sterling! A bastard, that man. I'm telling you, though I shouldn't. A daughter should respect a father. You sure you don't want strudel? Suit yourself.' He shrugged, poured the coffee and, picking up the tray, gestured them towards the living area. He cleared a space on the table, scattering a pile of typewritten pages on to the floor. 'Sit!'

He indicated a faded, over-stuffed chaise-longue. As Anna sat down a cloud of dust rose from the upholstery and hung suspended in a ray of sunlight before distributing itself around the room.

'I'll leave you two,' said Mabel, clearly amused at Anna's discomfiture. 'I'll call back later.' She caught the look of mild alarm in Anna's eyes and grimaced behind the old man's back.

'I'm sure Mr Kowalski . . .' Anna protested.

'What are you sure about Mr Kowalski?' He patted her hand.

'I'm sure Mr Kowalski is very busy,' she insisted with a hint of desperation. She didn't know why this old man should make her feel so uneasy, but she did know that she didn't want to lose the prop of Mabel's presence.

'Steven Spielberg can wait,' he chuckled. 'I'm not so busy. You run off and play, Mabel. Me and Miss Sterling, we'll find plenty to talk about. That's why you came, isn't it? Talk about your father?' He rested his hand again on hers. 'I shouldn't have said that. Everyone's a bastard sometime in their lives.' He looked up at Mabel. 'You still here, girl? Mabel! A Mex who calls herself Mabel!' He fluttered his bony fingers from side to side expressively. 'Screw loose.'

'Screw you, too, Kowalski,' she said cheerfully as she closed the door behind her.

He insinuated his wiry frame into a chair covered in a particularly drab shade of plum-coloured plush opposite Anna, dislodging another cloud of dust. 'You don't like your coffee?'

Trapped, she thought, and took a sip. 'It's delicious,' she said. It was, too. She rather regretted not accepting the strudel.

'Don't be so nervous, Malcolm Sterling's daughter. Am I such an ogre?'

He pulled a face and she laughed.

'That's better,' he said. 'Laugh a little. We Jews. We know a thing or two about laughter. When you have nothing, there's always laughter. We laughed in the ghetto. You know there were even Jews who managed to laugh in the concentration camps. Giggling all the way to the gas chambers. That's a good one. I should tell Woody Allen. He'd thank me. Your father, that was a man who never understood about laughter! He didn't like me. Hilde—you know Hilde?—she was the one who got us together. Your father knew how to write a book but he didn't know about writing a screenplay. I did. So Hilde fixed it with the studio that was buying the property that we should collaborate.

93

Beauty's Summer Dead. I always thought that was a lousy title. Shakespeare! What's the difference? It was a lousy title. I hear he died. Malcolm Sterling.'

Anna began to feel more comfortable. There was pain behind Asher Kowalski's banter and pain she could relate to. Pain removed threat. Even Malcolm had no longer seemed threatening in those last months of suffering. 'A few weeks ago,' said Anna.

'And he sent you to Los Angeles before he died?'

How could he possibly know that? she thought. Unless . . .

'Am I right?' he prompted her.

'Yes.' And she found herself telling him about Julie and Malcolm and herself, spilling it out as if he were no longer a stranger but a family friend.

He kept nodding his head jerkily like one of those jokey stuffed animals people stuck in the rear windscreen of their cars. 'Such a legacy!' he clucked when she'd finished.

'Mr Kowolski, what do you know about Malcolm that I don't? Mabel said I might learn something from you.' She had a strange feeling that this was where her search for Julie might originate, in the dusty recesses of Asher Kowalski's memory.

He took his time, pouring more coffee, offering strudel again and then lighting up a small, foul-smelling cigar. 'I don't suppose it matters any more. It was a long time ago,' he said finally. 'Hilde Klein was a powerful agent in those days, lots of important connections. She'd married that free-loader Louis Lederman because she needed a good-looking guy to flaunt. Maybe she loved him, too. But when your father came on the scene it was like Fourth of July and Thanksgiving Day all rolled into one for her. She really fell hard for him and everybody knew it. Maybe that's why your mother looked for solace in Louis. Hilde could be a bulldozer when she wanted something—or someone. I don't imagine Malcolm gave a damn about her. He liked to be the centre of attention and she was useful to him.'

'I sensed there had been something between them,' said Anna. 'What about the film, though? What went wrong? I remember when it all fell apart it happened so quickly. It was as if he couldn't wait to get shot of Los Angeles.'

She watched the ash from the old man's cigar fall on to his lapel. He didn't bother to brush it away.

'What happened had nothing to do with the script. The studio was still hot to make the film and—Malcolm and I didn't get on, you understand—but we were making headway in licking the problem of structure. I knew we had the basis of a good, strong picture. He was bitching about changing the title but that was a little thing. There's nothing like a hundred grand for sweetening a compromise and a hundred thousand dollars was a lot of money in those days.'

'So why did he always say it was the fault of the studio? That they pulled out of the deal?'

'A face-saver, I guess. You won't like this. But, what the hell, it's the truth. Your father left California one jump ahead of the law.'

'What?' She looked at him incredulously.

'He had, it seemed, a penchant for little girls. Well, maybe not so little. But under age. And LA is a great place for any kind of vice you can name. The police department or the mayor's office was having one of its periodic fits of morality. There was a raid at one of those private parties where twelve-, thirteen-, fourteen-year-old girls meet up with guys whose tastes run to the very young of either sex. Malcolm was present. God knows how he got involved. There were discreeter ways of indulging your fancies. But I guess he liked to live dangerously. He was taken in but not charged. They called Hilde and she squared it with the cops somehow. The case was hushed up but at a price. The studio got nervous and dropped its option on the property. Malcolm was advised to leave the country before some eager beaver assistant DA started asking questions.'

He watched her with infinite compassion as she sat there numbly listening. 'I'm sorry. It's not a pretty story.' At first she felt nothing, no emotion. Then she felt the tears welling into her eyes and as they streamed down her cheeks, she hugged herself tightly, rocking from side to side and moaning softly. The agony was not that she hadn't known, but that, deep down in her subconscious, perhaps she always had.

CHAPTER 10

By the time Mabel returned, Anna had regained the outward composure with which she had armoured herself since girlhood against unpleasant realities. It came so naturally to her, this strict observance of her own code, that she was unaware of the effect it had on other people until she saw the look of wonder in the old man's eyes as if he'd witnessed an amazing transformation, which, indeed, he had. A few minutes before she had been stricken and defenceless: now she was rationally questioning what he'd told her as if it were some academic case history in which she had no personal involvement or interest.

'It's this place. It corrupts people,' she said briskly. She cursed herself for that lapse of control earlier. Keep your feelings to yourself. Don't let on how you're hurting inside from all those half-remembered clues about the secret self of Malcolm Sterling she'd always preferred to ignore. The occasional unsavoury visitor. The gossip between his acquaintances that stopped when she entered a room. An unexplained visit from the police. The heated discussions with his solicitor and agent and the time when she'd happened to find him weeping to himself, that great, roaring, uncontrollable lion weeping!

'Father!' She'd put her hand on his shoulder, timidly, for he didn't like to be touched unexpectedly. He'd looked up blindly and then pushed her aside so savagely that she'd missed her footing and fallen to the floor. 'Don't ever . . . don't ever . . . Leave me alone,' he'd raged and then roughly pulled her to her feet.

'It's nothing,' James Quill, his agent had said soothingly when she'd broached the subject. 'You know what he's like. Any little thing. It's just some drama with the publishers

96

over the new book. Don't give it another thought.' And oh, how gratefully she'd taken that advice! How willingly she'd agreed that it was just another of Malcolm's tantrums! How comfortingly she'd assured herself that really it was a matter of no consequence, nothing for her to worry or even think about!

'Such a sadness!' Asher Kowalski shook his head at her pityingly.

'Malcolm?'

'No—you, my dear. How sad to feel the need to wrap your emotions in a shroud. Is that what he did to you? Did he always make you feel *that* inferior or was it only when this sister of yours arrived?'

She pulled herself up rigidly, hating his perceptiveness. 'I don't know what you mean,' she said frostily.

He shrugged his shoulders, scattering more cigar ash down his front. 'Suit yourself,' he said amiably and she was relieved when he shifted the focus of attention from her, even though his next remark sent a chill down her spine. 'You know, Malcolm made enemies here. He was all flash and thunder. Some people don't like that and, even in this land of instant forgetfulness, there are those who have long memories. Could it be that someone might want to get back at him through your sister?'

'Or me?' The rider to his question suddenly seemed to her frighteningly logical. She was as much a part of Malcolm as Julie; indeed, as she'd found out, more. Julie wasn't even his flesh and blood.

The clever eyes noted the shiver of realization that had prompted her question and he made a conscious effort to calm her fears by casting himself as a silly old scaremonger. 'What am I saying? Inventing plots. It's the curse of a writer, seeing dramas where none exist. Forget I brought it up.'

She smiled. He was trying so hard. And perhaps he meant it. Perhaps he had just been exercising a fertile imagination. But, recalling the scrawled graffiti on her car, she doubted it.

'I hear your BBC made a TV series out of *Beauty's Summer*

Dead.' He changed the subject. 'I didn't see it, but it was probably better than the movie would have been. A pity, all the same. It was hard on everybody when the studio dropped the option. Bad news for me. I really needed the job. Bad news for Hilde. She tried to get it off the ground with other companies. But the moment had passed. All they were looking for were blockbusters. It was tough all over at that time,' he ruminated, not needing to add that his own career began to slide into oblivion, scuppered by Malcolm's depraved fancy for underage playmates.

'And what about Hilde Klein?' She was genuinely curious. The woman had seemed so cold, almost cruel. Yet apparently she'd taken a risk shielding Malcolm and been paid off by losing out on a picture deal that would surely have been lucrative, for it wasn't only Malcolm she represented in connection with the proposed film. More importantly, she'd risked losing her credibility as an infallible agent.

Asher Kowalski yawned. He suddenly looked drained, not the spry old man who had greeted her and seemed to defy his years. She realized that the interview had probably been a strain for him. Remembering.

'I told you she was obsessed with him.' He sounded bored, his voice fainter, as if the subject were receding further and further back into the distant recesses of his mind. 'Maybe he was the one unselfish love of her life, more than poor Max or Louis and that son of hers. She got him out of trouble and picked up the pieces afterwards. But I never heard her blame him.'

'But they never met again,' she persisted, despite his obvious withdrawal of interest. 'At least to my knowledge.'

He passed weary fingers across his forehead, rubbing eyes no longer bright and alert. 'Maybe she didn't want to see him again. Maybe she preferred her memory of a great unrequited love. If it was unrequited. Not seeing him she could convince herself that all he had been guilty of was a little indiscretion. What more do you want to know?' he said irritably. 'Who knows why anyone does anything?'

'But they must have kept in touch or why would Julie have come to her?' She knew she was pushing him as she'd pushed Hilde Klein and surprised herself by feeling no shame. The old were as accountable as everyone else, probably more so.

'She was still his agent on the coast. And business is business. Who knows what goes on in Hilde Klein's mind? I said that. Anyway—' he shrugged—'anyway, she dropped me years ago. No longer bankable. Me! Asher Kowalski! No longer bankable. Whadda *they* know?'

He flapped his hand feebly in front of his face. There was hurt and disgust in his eyes. Then his slight body seemed to fold up inside itself, his eyelids drooped, his chin sunk down on to his chest.

At first Anna feared he might just have packed up and died, berating the industry that had once lauded and had now abandoned him. Then a faint, whistling sound escaped from his slack lips and she realized he'd simply nodded off. She rescued the lighted cigar butt from his fingers before it could do any damage and stubbed it out on an ashtray. She collected the coffee tray, washed up the cups and saucers and stacked them on the shelves in the kitchen. A reflex action. She had always been neat and orderly.

Then she sat silently across from the sleeping man, digesting what he'd told her, wishing she could disbelieve him yet knowing that she couldn't.

'So, he flaked out on you?'

For a while Anna, wrapped up in her thoughts, had been unaware that Mabel was standing in the doorway. 'You don't have to babysit. The guys in the block keep an eye on him, look in now and then to see if he needs anything.'

'You surprise me.'

'We're not all scumbags in this town,' Mabel said quietly. 'Some people actually take trouble to care about other people. He's coming up to eighty, maybe older. Everyone lies about their age here. And none of the big wheels give a shit about him any more. And the young guys look at him and think: "That could be me when it's my turn for the scrap heap." So they try to make it easy for him.'

'I'm sorry, Mabel. It's just that Los Angeles doesn't seem all that friendly to me. I was thoughtless.'

'No, you're not thoughtless. You're too goddamned thought*ful*. Thinking will drive you crazy. You have to learn to coast along with the current.'

Anna smiled. 'You're positively poetic, Mabel.'

'Yeah, well, it's talking all that crappy dialogue that does it. Did the old guy give you any satisfaction?' She nodded at the sleeping Asher Kowalski, then grinned. 'Talk-wise. Otherwise, I guess he's passed it.'

'He told me that my father left Hollywood under a cloud, to put it politely.'

'Impolitely—it's more fun. Drugs? Murder? Meddling with minors?'

'I suppose that's one way of putting it,' said Anna. 'It just takes some getting used to the idea that your father was a deviant. And you know the silly thing?' She turned to Mabel. 'I never knew. I kept house for him, arranged his appointments, took all his damned flak and at the end nursed him. And I didn't know.' She pounded the wall with her fist, flushing out another cloud of dust.

Asher Kowalski stirred, grunted, but didn't wake. A small smile played around his lips as if in memory of the day they'd called out his name at the Academy Awards Ceremony and he'd thanked the world, including Hilde Klein, for this great honour the Academy had bestowed on him. His speech had rated a couple of lines in the *Hollywood Reporter* and the next film he'd scripted had flopped at the box office.

They left him to his slumber and quietly closed the door behind them.

Mabel, it transpired, hadn't been wasting her time. She'd checked with the company that had cast the extras on *Starlit on Sunset*. It seemed that she was taking her self-appointed role of minder to Anna seriously.

'I'm grateful,' said Anna, although even as she said it she suspected there was no cause for gratitude.

'No luck. They booked Bettylou and she introduced Julie. The address they had for her was one of those crummy hotels downtown where they do weekly rates. No questions asked. They hadn't heard of Julie Sterling, but she could have registered under an assumed name. So I guess we struck out on that one.'

Anna smiled wryly. It was getting to be a familiar story. If she could ever bring herself to write about this benighted trip to Los Angeles it would probably be entitled: *I Struck Out.*

'If I ever strike lucky you'll let me know, Mabel.'

'That's better, kid. Keep your sense of humour.'

'That's what Asher Kowalski said. Giggling all the way to the gas chambers!'

'Yuk! Sick! Still, he's a European Jew. He's entitled.'

The telephone was ringing as they reached Mabel's apartment. She rushed in, shedding her flip, laconic pose in her haste to pick up the receiver before it could ring twice. 'Could be my agent,' she threw at Anna over her shoulder, adding 'the bastard!' as a matter of routine.

'It's about time . . .' Her face, eager and hopeful, resumed its habitual expression of cynical resignation. 'Oh, it's you.'

She handed the instrument to Anna. 'Georgie!'

'How does he know I'm here?'

'How does the sun know when to shine?'

Anna lifted the receiver to her ear gingerly as if it were a lethal weapon. She didn't like surprises and she hadn't yet decided how to confront George with the fact that he not only knew but had worked with Julie before spotting her at the Double Take.

In the event she found she was too angry with him to mind what she said or how she said it. When she simmered down he explained that he'd located her through a careful process of deduction and chatting up the hotel receptionist who'd given her Mabel's message.

'You're pretty clever at finding *me*,' she retorted. 'It's a pity you aren't as clever at finding Julie. Or maybe you are.'

'What's that supposed to mean?'

'*Starlit on Sunset*?'

'So—it's a TV movie.' He sounded genuinely puzzled, but then, she reminded herself, he was an actor.

'Julie was in that film. She had a scene. With you. Dressed as Scarlett O'Hara with another girl.' She enunciated each syllable with insulting clarity.

He was silent for a moment. 'Oh, that movie. Honest to God, Anna, I didn't even know it was Julie. I still can't recall . . .'

'Oh, for Christ's sake, stop it, George. What are you calling me for? Concerned about my welfare or just keeping tabs on me?'

'Both. You wanted to go to the police. So I'm bringing the police to you. Or, rather, I've fixed up a meeting with Joe Hatchett, the cop I told you about. It's his off day tomorrow. You can pour out your troubles—'

'And he can tell me I've nothing to worry about and there's nothing anyone can do and a nineteen-year-old girl can just vanish into the ether with no one the wiser and anyway it's not a felony and therefore not a police matter,' she exploded.

'Jesus, you sound just like Mabel. Are you sure you're not Mabel?' he joked.

'No, I'm not. I'm Anna Sterling and I'm looking for my sister and no one—' She pulled herself up abruptly. She had been going to say, 'No one is lifting a finger to help', but then she remembered Mabel and old Asher Kowalski, maybe even George and perhaps that cop he set so much store by.

'No one seems to know anything,' she ended lamely. 'I'll be staying with Mabel. The hotel gives me the creeps. What time tomorrow?'

'I'll pick you up at ten.' He seemed about to put the phone down, then changed his mind. 'Anna, I know how you feel about all this. Strange city.'

'You *don't* know how I feel. But I'm willing to believe you're trying,' she conceded.

'Anna. Don't go bull in a china shop at this. It's not like England here.'

'You're darned right, it's not. Ten, then.'

She handed the phone back to Mabel, who wrinkled her perfect nose in amused recognition. 'He does it every time.

102

Smooth as a baby's rump. Just don't go falling in love with him.' She sounded as if she'd taken that risk herself and lived to rue it. 'You'd better go get your things from the hotel. I guess they'll charge you another night. But I promise my rates are reasonable—just don't let the bath water overflow and, above all, no small talk before midday or you're out on your butt.'

Apart from the rows of parked cars, the hotel garage was deserted when she arrived. Like most car parks it was a gloomy cavern, strictly functional. She felt an unaccountable prickle of fear. The driverless automobiles seemed curiously threatening in their state of suspended animation, like those mechanical demons with a life of their own in a Stephen King thriller. She tried to shrug off the feeling. It was pure imagination, fuelled by all that had happened to her that day.

All the same, she thought, as she briskly locked the door of her hired car, it was no place to linger.

She was half way to the exit which led into the hotel when she sensed that she wasn't alone. She heard her own footsteps quite clearly clacking on the concrete and then an undertone, a scuffing of quieter footsteps, zigzagging between the cars, but gaining on her. She quickened her pace. Better not to run. The scuffling became more positive and she felt her heart pounding furiously. She'd heard of this kind of thing happening to people she knew. Waylaid by muggers in deserted places.

Against her better judgement she started to run. It was only a few yards to the exit. If she screamed someone would surely hear her. But before she could open her mouth a large hand gripped her jaw from behind and she felt the pressure of something hard digging into the base of her spine.

As she struggled, a throaty voice whispered in her ear. She could feel the hot breath giving off a whiff of alcohol. 'Stick 'em up, lady. Your money or your life,' the voice said.

The laughably archaic gangster *argot* dissipated the alarm she'd felt. At least, the alarm of the unknown. She knew the

103

voice very well. She just hadn't realized that its owner could be so dangerously playful.

Positioning her elbow for impact, she dug it sharply into the body behind her and was rewarded with a satisfying howl of pain. The grip on her jaw relaxed and she was able to swing round to face her phoney assailant.

'Whaddya have to do that for?' whined Bernard Klein. 'It was only in fun.' The words slurred into each other.

He was swaying from side to side hugging his stomach. A thick ballpoint pen clattered to the ground.

'You're drunk!' she said primly. 'What damnfool trick was that? You scared me half to death.'

He straightened up carefully and gave her a lop-sided smile. 'I am not drunk,' he said, marshalling his errant vowels and consonants precisely to back up his assertion. 'You sound like my mother.'

'God forbid!' she replied with feeling.

He let out a high-pitched shriek of laughter which trailed on hysterically until it finally ran out of steam.

'You're mad!' she said, and realized that might seriously be true. No wonder Hilde Klein kept her son on such a tight rein. 'What are you doing here? Did Hilde send you?'

He leaned forward staring down at her, his eyes dark with anger, and the sight made her more fearful than she'd felt at the prospect of a stray mugger. 'Don't say things like that to me. I'm not *mad*! Just . . .' he giggled. 'Just a little crazy. So I've had a few drinks. That's no crime. I was waiting for you and I saw you drive into the garage. Besides, you should be nice to me. I've brought you some good news.'

'What kind of good news?' she asked warily. She had the feeling that the Kleins' good news could only be her bad news. 'About Julie?'

'Right!' He dug a forefinger into her ribs. 'Right. Why don't we go into the hotel and have a little drinkie and I can tell you all about it.'

'I don't want a little drinkie and neither do you. We'll talk in the lobby.'

'Lotsa people!' He clamped a finger to his nostril and winked. 'Smart. You don't like me, do you?'

104

'Not much.'

'Pity. I like you. You're—you're different. Not like Julie and all those others.'

She prodded him forward through the garage exit into the lobby. She cupped her arm around his and steered him unsteadily towards a settee, braving the dubious glance of the receptionist.

As he plopped himself down into the cushion he fumbled in his pocket and produced, after a couple of misguided efforts, a rumpled postcard.

'Wouldya believe it, this came just after you left.'

His hand was shaking as she took the postcard from him. On one side was a view of an Indian totem pole in Vancouver. On the other a scrawled message addressed to Hilde Klein: 'Miss LA, but having a great time. Guess it's time to head for home. Thanks for everything. Julie.'

She looked at it disbelievingly. It was too much of a coincidence. Yet the handwriting looked like Julie's.

'So y'see, you didn't have to worry about her. By the time you get back to li'l ole England she'll be there. Probably a card from her waiting for you.'

She turned the postcard over and back again. 'The stamp's American, not Canadian.'

He furrowed his brow, then giggled wildly again. 'Could have given it to a friend to mail. There was some guy. Maybe they split.'

'Why, suddenly, should she make contact with your mother after all this time?'

He shrugged. 'Maybe she felt like it. My mother . . .' He wagged his finger in her face. 'My mother was very good to her.'

She looked at the postcard, then at him, suspiciously. 'You think this will buy me off, send me back home, stop me looking for Julie? I'm surprised. I thought Hilde Klein was cleverer than this.'

Suddenly her wrist was encircled in a vice-like grip. Bernard Klein might have been drunk and he might have been stupid, but the menace in his voice was all too real.

'You'd better believe it. You'd better.'

105

CHAPTER 11

'Are you through?'

The woman standing over them had long blonde Jerry Hall hair that she kept flicking out of her eyes. Her face was hard and having an uphill struggle trying to appear younger than it was.

She was wearing a good deal of gold jewellery draped around an obviously expensive jade green dress that clung to her figure, accentuating the ample positive provocatively. She looked not like a model, but like a woman who would like to look like a model. She was tapping her perilously high-heeled strap shoes impatiently.

'Kelly! Loved one! This is Kelly.' Bernard flicked his fingers in Anna's direction as if trying to remember something important that he had unaccountably forgotten. 'Anna,' he said finally, triumphantly.

Kelly nodded indifferently at Anna and repeated a touch more tetchily: 'Are you through?' She looked around her moodily, apparently disapproving of Anna's choice of locale. 'Hollywood's a dump these days.' She cast a shrewd eye at the hung-over Bernard and sighed a sigh of long experience. 'More to the point: are you sober? We're supposed to be dining out tonight. But I guess I'll just have to haul you home. As usual.'

He hoisted himself to his feet and fluttered his hand at Anna. 'Bye-bye, birdie. Remember what I said.'

The woman looked coldly at Anna, then yanked her lover to the door. 'Creep!' she muttered, targeting Bernard but including Anna.

Charming, thought Anna, as she watched them leave, the unconvincing postcard still in her hand. Curiouser and curiouser. But she'd think about that later, meanwhile she made a mental note not to take Bernard Klein too lightly at face value.

When she'd finished her packing back in her room she

106

glanced at the telephone. It was the first time since she'd been in Los Angeles that she'd seriously thought about Hugh; but now the urge to hear his sane, reasonable, slightly plummy voice soothing her fears and reminding her of the ordered, familiar world to which she belonged became overpowering.

Although even as she thought of that world it no longer seemed so ordered or so familiar. It was just that it kept its secrets hidden so skilfully that it was possible to deny they existed, as Anna had done for all those years.

It seemed an eternity before Hugh answered the phone. Finally a gruff voice announced his name and telephone number. She realized too late that she'd probably woken him up from a deep sleep, but even so he'd observed one of his many little rituals: name and telephone number. That way you avoided convoluted conversations with wrong numbers.

'It's me, Anna!' she said, adding, 'I'm calling from Los Angeles,' to excuse the nocturnal intrusion.

'Anna! Do you know what time it is?'

'About seven here,' she said apologetically.

'Well—' he yawned loudly—'it's three in the morning here.' Having established that, he changed his tone. 'How goes it there? I was hoping you'd call. I was worried.' Apparently it hadn't occurred to him to ring her, but then he wouldn't. Their relationship at all times and in all circumstances was a tentative one. Neither presumed too much on or from the other. Even their love-making was based more on respect and affection for each other than on any wild passion. Wild passion would have been anathema to Hugh. It argued a lack of control which would have been against all the rules. How, she wondered, could two brothers be so unalike?

'Has George been helpful?' he prompted her gently. 'And Julie?' He sounded sympathetic. She knew the sentiment was genuine. Everything about Hugh was genuine. And that was why, for all his finicky ways, she loved him in her fashion. Or perhaps, she was now beginning to wonder, it was his fashion, not hers. And, as she knew it would, the sound of his voice triggered off all the pain that had been building up inside her. She found herself telling him everything about Malcolm, Hilde Klein, Mabel, Bernard, Asher Kowalski; about her fears and suspicions and frustrated efforts to find Julie; about her feeling of strangeness in a strange land.

'Hold on, Anna.' She could sense him reaching for the inevitable cigarette on his bedside table. It was his one admitted vice and he never made apologies for it, although he could be ruthless with schoolboy offenders he found smoking in dark corners of the Winchester courtyard.

'I don't like the sound of all this. I don't like the idea of you being alone out there.'

'I'm not alone. There's your lovely brother George. He keeps popping up. I don't know whether he's being helpful or what.'

'George isn't bad.' Sibling loyalty. 'It's just—he's just become thoroughly Americanized. You can't blame him for adapting to the territory.'

'I'm not.' She was beginning to wonder whether it had been wise or fair to involve Hugh. It was he, after all, who had urged her to ignore her father's last request. He'd never had any time for Julie and, she suspected, he probably felt whatever she got she deserved. And he hadn't been too surprised when she'd told him that Malcolm wasn't her father. Come to that, he hadn't been all that shocked by her revelations about Malcolm himself. 'Did you know about Malcolm?' she said accusingly.

'No, of course not,' he replied wearily. But his denial had a false ring to it which, in turn, cast Hugh in a different light. He'd always been so exruciatingly honest. If he'd been trying to protect her it had been a misguided good intention.

'I shouldn't have called,' she said.

'Anna, listen to me.' He sounded fully awake now and anxious to be persuasive. 'You know I'd have been concerned if you hadn't called. Particularly as you're going through this—this traumatic experience.' It was so like Hugh to give the barrage of emotion and confusion and, yes, alarm she'd been subjected to its proper definition. A

108

traumatic experience! That put it all neatly in its place.

'I shouldn't have called,' she repeated. 'I'm sorry, I know you like a good night's sleep.'

He was silent for a moment as if cogitating about the impossible or unthinkable.

Then, finally, he said: 'I could come over. If you'd like me to.'

She laughed out loud. Impossible and unthinkable. 'But it's term-time.'

'I could manage it somehow. For a couple of days. Just to see you through this. After all, if I were sick . . .' His voice trailed away and she knew what he was proposing went seriously against his conscientious grain. 'Anna, I mean it,' he insisted.

She felt a wave of gratitude to the man who, like herself, considered any sudden alteration to the ritual of his life at the very least a gross inconvenience. And a part of her yearned to accept his offer purely for the comfort of having him there, good old reliable Hugh. But she realized it would be pure selfishness. What would it gain? What could he do that she wasn't trying to do herself? How he'd loathe all these unreal people she was having to deal with in Los Angeles! How he'd hate their values and their life style! And all for, in his eyes, a silly girl who disappeared.

But even as she was about to refuse him, she knew there was more to it than that: her own reluctance to measure these two unlikely brothers, Hugh and George, one against the other; to see them in close proximity. And maybe there was a secret fear that it would be Hugh she would find wanting.

Very carefully, she tempered her tone, making it sound softer, lighter, nothing-to-worry-about. 'It's kind of you, Hugh. But I couldn't let you do that. It would be too much trouble for you. And, besides, I'm sure I'll get a lead on her soon. After all, maybe that postcard she sent to the Kleins was genuine and she'll be home before I am.'

She could sense if not hear his sigh of relief. 'If you say so, then. If you're sure. And, if the police aren't able to help, then pack your bags. There's nothing more you can do.

109

Hire a private investigator.' She doubted whether he knew what first-class private investigators cost in California, but let it pass.

'I'll do that, Hugh,' she lied. 'Meanwhile, how are things back home?'

'You've only been away two days, three.'

'Is that all? It seems like such a long time. It's all so harsh and bright and angular here. I'd give anything to walk through the water meadows on a spring Sunday morning, just to put my mind in order.' And momentarily she could conjure up the warmth of that gentle sun as it played on the streams by the footpaths, alive with wild English flowers and the muted sound of strollers taking their constitutionals at that idle pace that would be defined as loitering with intent in the streets of Los Angeles.

He caught the longing in her voice. 'We'll be doing that, very soon. Promise. Let me know what plane you'll be catching.'

She laughed. 'You mean, you'll meet it?'

'Well, no. But I'll phone the airport.' Of course. How much more sense that made. To Hugh.

As she gathered up her toiletries from the bathroom and meticulously examined drawers she hadn't even opened in case she'd left something behind, she felt even more glad that she hadn't allowed Hugh to disturb his routine to hold her hand in Los Angeles. It was a matter of obligation and she was realizing that she didn't want to be under too great an obligation to Hugh. It would unbalance their relationship, a form of commitment on her part which she wasn't yet ready to make. Probably, she thought ruefully, she was one of those people who were incapable of commitment and dubious about anything less.

She was taking one last glance round the impersonal room when the telephone rang. Her first instinct was to ignore it. She'd told reception that she'd be checking out—'we'll have to charge you for an extra night' they'd informed her, briskly indifferent—and it was probably just an inquiry as to whether she wanted a porter. Even if it weren't, she couldn't wait to get back to the lazy, dusty comfort of Mabel's. A

110

fact which surprised her. She'd always regarded excessive informality before as slightly immoral, an infringement of social mores. Now she welcomed it, welcomed the warmth of being treated as someone of more than passing interest. Eccentric, maybe, but interesting.

But the nagging ring of the telephone persisted. Like an unopened parcel, it preyed on the curiosity. And for a wild moment she wondered if perhaps, just perhaps, it could be Julie. Who else, after all, would want to call her here?

She dropped her case and lifted the phone expectantly. A second later she knew it had been just a mad hope.

'Gottcha!' The voice sounded odd, high and husky at the same time. It certainly wasn't Julie's.

'Who is this?' she said brusquely.

'You've gotta help me.' There was desperation in the voice, too.

'Who *is* this?'

'Bettylou. Listen—it was wrong, all wrong. Julie . . .' she was rambling incoherently.

'What about Julie? What's wrong?'

'I saw . . . you're nice . . . you're nice lady . . . not fair . . . but you gotta help me.' She was making no sense. And in her obviously unbalanced state it seemed doubtful whether she had any sense to make.

'How can I help you?' No good. 'Goddamn it, what are you talking about?'

''bout Julie. If you help me . . . tell you about Julie.'

'Where are you? Where can I reach you?'

'No, I'll get you.' It was hard to tell whether the impression of fear was genuine or the self-induced fear of the addict.

'But where . . . ?'

'Myrna.'

'What?'

Quite suddenly the voice changed, no longer hysterical, merely blank, anonymous. 'Forget it . . . just kidding . . . forget it . . . like I said. S'morning. Julie. Like I said.'

The phone went dead abruptly as if cut off in its prime.

*

111

Waking up in the unfamiliar bed she stretched her limbs luxuriously, aware that, despite all the odds, she had enjoyed a wonderfully relaxing good night's sleep. She delayed opening her eyes. The feeling was too good.

Even the memory of her encounter with Sonny and the strange telephone call from Bettylou didn't, after all, seem so disturbing.

'So, what do you expect? They're a couple of crazies. This town is full of them. They're getting their kicks frightening the life out of you.' Mabel's lowdown common sense, when she told her, was just what Anna needed. Later, it would probably be different. Later, she'd recall the menace in Bernard Klein's warning, in effect, to abandon her search for Julie; the veiled message in Bettylou's wild rambling. Later, the frustrating knowledge that she seemed to be getting nowhere in her quest, the nightmare she'd been living through during the past few days, would return to haunt her. But not now. Not yet.

Mabel had read her the house rules, rummaged through the linen to find a pair of crumpled but clean sheets, demonstrated the eccentricities of the fridge, the microwave, the cooker, the air-conditioning, and the TV, told her to holler for help from a friendly neighbour if she were in trouble and wished her good night. She was, she explained, going on a night shoot for a TV series Anna hadn't even heard of and wouldn't be back till morning.

It was morning now. Early. She could tell by the pounding of bright light on her closed eyelids from the slats in the blinds on the window. Mabel had told her she should wear eye-shades. She was debating the question of tea or coffee as she opened her eyes.

The room was a shambles. Clothes scattered across chairs, wardrobe doors and drawers half open, empty Coke cans on a side table and the top of the dressing-table was a distaster area of make-up pots, spilled powder and perfume. Her first thought, that they'd been burgled in the night, quickly evaporated as she remembered that this was Sissie's room and Sissie had warned her not to mess with her things. Obviously she preferred her own mess.

Then as her eyes became accustomed to the room, Anna was aware of something blocking the open doorway. Only it wasn't a something. It was a someone. A figure, tall and muscular. She couldn't make out the face as the sunlight from behind framed the outline. It didn't move. It just stood there.

She wondered if she had the nerve to call for help from that friendly neighbour. Or maybe, indeed, this was that friendly neighbour.

Instead, she clutched the sheet tightly around her like some threatened movie heroine of the 'twenties, despite the fact that her chain store nightie was more than ample armour against immodesty if not actually a deterrent to unbridled passion. 'What—' she uttered in a voice so small she barely recognized it as her own, 'what do you want?' Screaming would certainly have been beyond her.

The figure moved forward and she could see him clearly now. She recognized one of the boys who had been clowning around by the pool the day before. He didn't look as young or as benign as he had then. He was wearing frayed jeans and a leather waistcoat decorated with brass studs incongruously formed into flower shapes. His feet were bare and his tousled straw-coloured hair flopped over his eyes.

'What do you want?' she repeated. 'And how did you get in here?'

He dangled a key from his little finger and moved slowly towards her, studying her intently. But he still didn't speak. Under his curious gaze she felt embarrassed, although more angry than frightened. If he had rape on his mind it's doubtful if he'd have left the front door wide open and he didn't appear to have a weapon. Even so, her hand inched towards one of the Coke cans on the side table.

Gradually a smile spread across his face, not a particularly agreeable smile, but an improvement nevertheless.

Still keeping his eyes fixed on hers, he sat down on the end of the bed while shaking his head at her feeble attempt to reach the Coke can.

Finally he spoke. 'Malcolm Sterling was your old man. Mabel told me. Well, that old man was *shit*. You hear me— *shit!*'

113

'He wasn't so old,' she said stupidly. What did it matter how old he'd been?

'Andy! For Christ's sake! What the hell are you doing here? And where did you get that key?'

'I know where you hide it.' He spoke with a lazy, South Californian accent. Not an alien in a foreign land.

Mabel was standing, feet apart, in the living-room, her arms clutching paperbags full of groceries. She dumped them on the kitchen table and slung her shoulder-bag on the floor. She looked weary and irritable from the night's shooting.

'So! Lover boy!'

Andy still kept staring at Anna. 'I wanted to see what the daughter of a shit looks like.'

'No kidding!' sighed Mabel. 'Look around you. Los Angeles is lousy with shit.'

He leaned towards Anna and she felt only shame. Would she ever be free of the legacy of Malcolm? 'He messed with my sister when she was only twelve years old and you should see her now. *He* should see her now.'

'Yeah, yeah. "It took more than one man to change my name to Shanghai Lily".' Mabel's Dietrich impersonation was better than that of the hapless performer at the Double Take. 'It's tough all over, Andy. Now run along. Go knit yourself a sweater.'

'You think I'm not serious,' he persisted.

'He's dead,' said Anna flatly.

'That ain't good enough.'

He leapt up from the bed, brushed past Mabel and out of the open door which she firmly shut, chained and double-bolted. 'I should have warned you about bolting yourself in. I'd forgotten about that key. I'll get the lock changed. You all right?'

Anna nodded. 'I was. Now it's all building up again. Asher Kowalski said someone might want to get at my father through my sister or me.'

'Andy? He's just stupid.'

'He didn't sound so stupid to me. Do you suppose he meant what he said?'

Mabel shrugged. 'Could be. His sister's an ageing hooker, than which you can't get much lower in Los Angeles. An old bag. She had to get started somewhere, turning tricks.'

'An old bag!' Anna repeated listlessly. 'She'd be about my age.'

Mabel sat down on the warm spot on the bed vacated by Andy. 'Honey, why don't you stop crucifying yourself? You can't change anything in the past. But you can let it screw you up inside.'

She levered herself up, digging the palms of her hands into the small of her back. 'Gee, I'm pooped. What'll it be? Ham, eggs and pancakes?'

'Mabel, what . . . what if I can't find her? I've been kidding myself all along that it's impossible for a human being to vanish without trace in this day and age. But that's not true, is it?'

She looked at Mabel for comfort, for an assurance that her fears were groundless. But the Mexican girl lowered her eyes and said nothing.

CHAPTER 12

'I don't know why you have to drag me out here. Why couldn't I have gone to the police station like anybody else?'

George Allenby had picked Anna up that morning and they were now driving up beyond Hollywood Boulevard into the hills above the city. She realized that she was channelling the alarm and anger that had been accumulating inside her over the past few days into a disgruntled attack on George. Maybe he understood that, too, for he seemed determined not to take offence.

'You'll like Joe. But you wouldn't like him nearly so much in his official capacity.'

'I don't have to like him. I just want some answers and some action.'

'And I wanted you to see something of Los Angeles that won't confirm all your prejudices.'

His equable tone vexed her even more. 'I'm not a tourist!'

He stopped the car abruptly and nerve-rackingly on a steep incline. 'No. You're a pain in the ass,' he said agreeably, as if he were paying her a rather nice compliment. 'If you'd be happier, you can get out of the car and call a cop. Any cop.'

He reached across her and opened the door on the passenger side.

She looked at him a trifle sheepishly. 'How can I . . .?' she gestured helplessly.

'Then stop acting the prima donna.' He shut the door firmly and put the car into drive again. 'All right, so you've had a rough deal since you've been out here and it's scary! Maybe you feel threatened with good reason. Maybe I haven't been as forthcoming with you as I could have been. But, for Christ's sake, Anna, you should have known before you came what you were taking on. What did you expect? A couple of phone calls, a friendly word with the British Consul and Julie would miraculously materialize? You're into something deep and perhaps dangerous and the sooner you recognize that the better.'

'You think I don't? After Hilde and Bernard and Bettylou and that—that *boy* at Mabel's accusing Malcolm of God knows what?' She rubbed her forehead wearily. 'It all comes back to Malcolm, doesn't it? It's twenty years since he was in Hollywood and he's been dead and buried for weeks. Yet it's as if he were still all around us.'

'I know,' he said quietly.

'It isn't easy facing the fact that I really didn't know him at all.' She opened the window and sniffed appreciatively. The air was fresher as they climbed out of the densely polluted streets of Hollywood. 'Where are we?'

'Griffith Park. Just ahead. It's got everything. Picnic areas, playgrounds for kids, hiking trails. Zoo. Planetarium. Bird sanctuary. And people. Real people. People like you thought didn't exist outside your precious Hampshire. Families with the same problems and virtues and values

116

and failings as families anywhere. Couples who are planning on getting married when they can afford it. Students with a streak of rebellion in them. Yougsters who make a nuisance of themselves. And old people who are cantankerous. Also, muggers, druggies, dealers and other assorted villains. All human life is here, Anna, as they used to say in the *News of the World*.'

She smiled, her first of the day. 'Even vicars indulging in sex orgies?'

He smiled back. 'More than likely. Joe brings his boys here on his days off. It gives Mamie a break.'

'Who's Mamie?'

'His wife.'

'Why—?'

'—does she need a break? You'll see.' They picked up a map at the entrance to the Park and then parked the car.

They found Joe Hatchett sitting on a bench pensively eating peanuts in the children's section of the enormous zoo set in natural surroundings.

'Hi, Joe!'

The man turned round alertly, then, as he saw George, the tense expression on his lined, craggy face relaxed into a welcoming smile. 'Georgie! How goes it?'

They were much of an age but Joe Hatchett looked older and tougher. He was wearing a T-shirt and jeans which seemed too small to contain the strongly muscled chest and arms.

'Where's Rolly?' said George.

'Jeff's taking him to see the monkeys. He likes monkeys.' He closed his eyes for a moment, letting the sun play on his face and Anna could see the deep crevices that creased his forehead and traced dark patterns from his eyes to his jawbone. It was a face that had experienced more pain than she could imagine.

'This is Anna Sterling. I told you about her.'

He opened his eyes and looked at Anna, extending a calloused hand. 'Welcome to LA. If that's what I mean.' He patted the bench beside him.

George nodded towards her and she took a seat. 'I'll go

117

find the boys. I've got those Eddie Bauers I promised from Canada.' He fished two Eddie Bauer anoraks out of a paper bag. 'I had the wardrobe girl on my last movie embroider their names on the breast pocket.' There was a sweetness in his expression as he fingered the fabric that she'd never seen before.

Joe nodded. 'They'll like that.' He pointed a direction. 'They went thataway. You can't miss them,' he said gruffly.

'George!'

'That's OK, Anna. Joe knows about everything. You don't need me.'

As George strode off, Joe turned to Anna and she was uncomfortably conscious of the keenness of his gaze as he studied her intently. 'He never forgets, George. Every week, unless he's working on location, regular as clockwork. Always something for the boys. A toy. A study aid. Something special to wear.'

'You must have been—must be—good friends.'

'The very best. Didn't he tell you?'

She shook her head and for a moment she could have sworn she saw a moistening in his eyes, the suggestion, though she could hardly believe it, of a tear.

'We roomed together years ago after I left Nam. I was a wreck, like a lot of the vets, no hope, no nothing. Georgie had just come out here from England and we met, just by chance, right here. In Griffith Park. I didn't know where I was at or where I was going. And I guess he was still feeling pretty much of an outsider too. He had this tiny apartment downtown and invited me to share it. It did cross my mind that he might be gay, but in those days—heck, even now— I couldn't have cared less whether he was Godzilla. He looks sorta frail, easygoing. Sometimes not even bright in the head.' He grinned. 'But he really worked me over. He made me shape up and get my act together, to take a pride in myself again. I met Mamie. She was a nurse. And I joined the LAPD. The police department. It may not be the greatest, but it's better than where I was heading before I met Georgie. He's Rolly's godfather. Did you know?'

Again she shook her head. There was no limit, it seemed,

to what she didn't know about George. But at least she was being saved from the terminal blindness which had afflicted her relationship with Malcolm.

'You don't know a lot, do you, girlie?' And she knew he wasn't merely referring to her lack of information about George's background.

'I'm discovering that,' she conceded. There was something about this blunt, open man whose nature belied his surname that dispelled anger and encouraged confidence and she doubted whether it had anything to do with his police training.

'When you've been through the mill you either come out stronger or dead,' he mused as if reading her thoughts. 'Don't sell Georgie short.'

'Why . . . is there . . . ?' She didn't know quite how to frame the question, but Joe Hatchett caught the gist of it as she imagined he would.

'He was married once. But she was a tramp. A bit part actress. She left him for some big-time operator in Vegas. They got a quickie divorce and he's been a free agent ever since, playing the field. Mamie's always trying to fix him up with some nice woman. But he's not the settling down kind. Why? Are you interested?'

'No, of course not,' she said hurriedly. But was she? she wondered.

He twisted his pencil-line mouth into a grimace that could be taken for amusement, disbelief or derision. 'Beer?' He reached into the cold compartment of the picnic basket on the ground beside him.

'Thanks.'

He flipped up the metal tabs of the cans and handed one to her.

He looked around appreciatively at the children chasing each other from one excitement to the next, the grown-ups soaking up the sun and issuing directives about noise and littering, the lovers taking pensive strolls and the loners isolated in their solitary thoughts. It was a polyglot, multi-coloured society of all shapes and sizes, as various as the animal species in the zoo.

119

'Once in a while,' he mused, 'it's nice to reassure yourself that the world isn't exclusively populated with sleazebags and mother-fuckers.' He reddened. 'Begging your pardon, ma'am. You treat with dirt, you get in the habit of talking dirty. Mamie, she balls me out all the time. So, Georgie tells me you're looking for your sister.'

She felt his keen eyes observing her as she sipped the beer from the can. 'A friend told me I should ask to see your badge.'

'That's your privilege. If you don't trust me, that's your privilege.' He reached behind him to unbutton the back pocket of his jeans.

She felt suddenly silly. 'I'm sorry. That was stupid.'

He took a deep swig from his can, crumpled it in his hand and aimed it accurately into a litter bin stamped with the words TRASH IT a few feet away. 'It's just as well. I don't carry it when I'm off duty. I should. But it reminds me all the time that I'm a cop. So, sweetie, you could say I'm doing you a favour. Let's cut the gab. What's the story?'

She told him as succinctly as she could, omitting only the references to Malcolm's ignominious departure from Hollywood. She didn't know Joe Hatchett that well.

He raked his fingers viciously through his short-cropped grey hair. 'You people! Why didn't you come to the police in the first place? We're not so different from your guys back home.'

'You carry guns,' she countered, pointlessly trying to defend her reluctance to make Julie's disappearance official.

'It'll happen, lady, it'll happen. The way I hear things are going in England. Look, you can register her as a missing person and we can see what we can turn up. You've got a photograph?'

'Yes.' She produced a not too recent snap of Julie from her wallet. 'Also, she had a tiny part in a Television film, *Starlit on Sunset*. She was supposed to be impersonating Scarlett O'Hara.'

He grinned. 'Who doesn't, these days? They hold contests like that in Atlanta. The whole country's *Gone With The Wind* crazy. I guess it takes people's minds off the civil war that's raging right now,' he said bitterly. 'Drugs, violence, race—'

'—pollution, poverty, the greenhouse effect. Mr Hatchett, that's not helping me find Julie.'

'Joe.'

'Joe. How many registered missing persons do you actually find?'

He shrugged his shoulders. 'Not too many, I guess,' he admitted. 'We concentrate on the kids. Your sister's not a minor. Adults can have all kinds of reasons to vanish. It's a free country—or so they tell me. But we could strike lucky. I take it you've tried your own consulate?'

She nodded.

'Well, leave it with me. Maybe my partner'll have a couple of ideas. It's not strictly through channels. Like I said, I'm doing you a favour. They can dump all over you in my job if you don't go through channels.'

He satisfied himself that she was duly appreciative.

'There was something.' He smacked the side of his head as if trying to liberate the elusive 'something'.

'About what?'

'The Kleins. Something you said. The husband. Louis . . . Louis . . .'

'Lederman.'

'Yeah. That's the guy. Louis Lederman. You said the old lady told you he'd been killed in the earthquake. On the Bay Bridge. San Francisco.'

'She was very cut up about it. I remember.'

'And that son of hers, Bernard? He said the same thing?'

She tried to remember. 'I can't . . . well, he didn't deny it.'

'That's funny. It's coming back to me. Six, eight months, it's a long time. You forget.'

'Forget what?'

'Louis Lederman wasn't killed in any earthquake. He was shot dead during a burglary at a beach house between Venice and Santa Monica. He either owned it or rented it.'

She stared at him, hardly believing what she was hearing.

'But why on earth would Hilde Klein invent a fiction that he'd been killed in an earthquake?'

He shrugged that eloquent shrug of his. 'Who knows? Maybe she'd convinced herself that was a better way to die than being shot by some punk. Old people have a way of shutting things out they'd rather not believe. She suffered a stroke soon after, maybe she actually mixed up the two events. The earthquake, his death, same time. If it gives her some comfort, what's the difference?'

'How can you say that? It could make a lot of difference,' she rounded on him.

'Now hold on. What difference? The guy's in the house, he surprises an intruder and gets it—wham bang.'

'No one else was there?'

'I guess not. The Kleins, mother and son, turned up later when the body was discovered.'

'Did they ever catch the killer?'

'Not so far as I remember. But there were several break-ins along that stretch of the coast. It all fitted.'

She was tempted to offer the smug opinion that it didn't speak too highly of the efficiency of the LAPD, but refrained.

'Look, it wasn't my case, lady. I'm just dealing the cards as I remember them. In any case I guess the guy who got him might have been doing Louis Lederman a favour.'

'What makes you say that?'

'Again, it's just what I *recall*.' He had a habit of emphasizing the statements he wanted to hit home with a short, sharp, chopping gesture of the hand as if slicing bacon in a temper. 'There was some investigation going on into his business dealings. He part-owned this gallery in Westwood.'

'Fine art?'

'Hardly in that league. Antique—what do you call 'em?— artefacts. Stick a label "antique" on anything and the rich in this town buy it up like jelly beans. Only they're getting a lot smarter these days. It seemed some of our Louis's antiques were mint fresh off the boat from South America and South-East Asia. There's a big business in forgeries.'

'And that's what Louis Lederman was involved in?'

'Let's say the evidence pointed that way. It was probably

only a matter of time. But then time was running out for Louis quicker than he thought.'

Anna conjured up a picture of that arrogant, tough old lady Hilde Klein and imagined what a blow to her pride her husband's arrest for fraud would have been. 'Was—was *she*—his wife—interrogated after his death?' she said suddenly.

'I imagine so. Everyone associated with the victim is interrogated—as you so nicely put it—after a killing. Even in Los Angeles,' he added, sarcastically.

'And?'

'You've heard about cast-iron alibis?' he replied obliquely.

'Is the gallery still operating?'

'So far as I know. It had a good reputation, Lederman's. Until this thing. His partner seemed to be in the clear, probably relieved when Louis turned up dead before the investigation became a public scandal.'

'And the beach house? Where's that?'

Not thinking, he gave her rough directions, then stopped abruptly. 'Why do you want to know this? If you're thinking what I think you're thinking, you're not only stupid but crazy. Mixing with police business is a sure way of ending up dead yourself. And it won't help you find your sister. What do you care if Louis Lederman was making a little something extra on the side?' The hand chopped the bacon even more vigorously.

'Maybe his death had something to do with his fake art dealing.'

'Maybe. And you can bet the thought had occurred to Homicide, too. What are you? Lady Sherlock Holmes? Leave the fine tuning to the experts. I'll see what I can turn up on your sister. And that's all I'll do for you.' He turned round, fished another beer out of the basket and set his face squarely into an impenetrable mask. The subject, he indicated, was closed.

Then the face relaxed into an expression of infinite tenderness that made him seem strangely vulnerable. His eyes were focused on three approaching figures. George Allenby and a stringy lad, barely into his teens, were ranged protectively on either side of a wheelchair which they were wheeling towards Joe and Anna.

The boy in the wheelchair was frail to the point of emaciation. His spindly arms and legs twisted unnaturally, the skin almost translucent. His large head was crooked on his shoulder, digging down into a shrunken chest. But his eyes were brightly alive, burning with an intensity that seemed to fuel the rest of his frail, deformed frame.

'Pop!' He spoke haltingly but clearly. Whatever a cruel nature had inflicted on his body, it had left his brain intact. His fingers clutched the Eddie Bauer anorak George had brought for him. The other boy had draped his round his shoulders.

Anna glanced at Joe. 'Rolly, buddy boy,' he shouted out loud. 'How were the monkeys?'

'Great . . . great . . . monkeys.'

'Hungry?'

The boy nodded his head.

'Let me.' The stringy boy, the younger of the two, clicked the brakes on his brother's wheelchair capably and then foraged in the picnic basket for a package of sandwiches. 'Peanut butter and jelly. Your favourite,' he told Rolly as he gently tucked a paper napkin in the neck of the boy's shirt and prepared to unwrap the sandwiches.

'Can I help?' said Anna, moved by the sight of the two boys—one so dependent, the other so protective.

Joe put a restraining hand on her arm. 'No. Jeff likes to do things for Rolly. His mother, Mamie, brought him up that way. He's two years younger, but ever since he was a little kid he trotted around looking out for Rolly. It's a comfort. Sometimes you can't help wondering—if we go . . . But, what the hell, we're lucky.' He spoke quietly so that his boys shouldn't hear.

'Come say hello to the lady, Jeff.'

Jeff reluctantly left Rolly's side and held out his hand. 'Hi!'

'Hi, Jeff.' She smiled and was rewarded with a smile.

'I have to get going, Anna.' She'd forgotten George and

124

now she looked up into his face with renewed interest. ' 'Bye, boys. See you later.'

'Alligator,' groaned Jeff, then he grinned. 'Thanks a lot, Porgy. These—' he fingered the anorak—'they're real neat.'

'Porgy?' queried Anna.

'Georgie—as in "Kissed the girls and made them cry", Porgy,' George explained, grimacing as he did so.

Joe hoisted himself upright. She was surprised to see that he towered over both of them. 'I'll be in touch,' he assured Anna and then to George: 'You should watch this dame. She's liable to land herself in more trouble than she can handle.'

'I know,' said George thoughtfully. 'I know. That's what I'm afraid of.'

CHAPTER 13

Lederman's Gallery looked as if it thought it should be preening itself among the Cartiers and Armanis on exclusive Rodeo Drive rather than nestling among the bookshops, casual wear boutiques and student hang-outs of the West-wood area of Los Angeles, mindful of its town-and-gown proximity to UCLA. It had, Anna suspected, ideas above its station, rather like its dead co-owner, Louis Lederman.

After she'd parked the car, she'd had difficulty locating the gallery, set back from the sidewalk in cloistered seclusion, as if anxious to dissociate itself from its common neighbours, a lively restaurant decked out in 'thirties décor and a store specializing in movie memorabilia. It was discreet to the point of ostentation, proclaiming its superiority by austerely disguising any signs of it.

A minuscule brass plaque on the wall bore the name, underneath which 'Directress: Lois Galloway' had been quaintly added in newer lettering, presumably to reassure clients that the gallery's only association now with the doubtfully reputable Louis was his surname.

In one small window set in a scrolled, imitation marble

125

surround like a picture frame, an intricately moulded necklace in metal and semi-precious stones was draped around a moulded 'neck and shoulders' covered in purple velvet. A backdrop of artfully arranged velvet in a complementary shade added to the shimmering splendour of the exhibit which carried no price or explanatory note.

She looked at the necklace long and hard, but her thoughts were far from antique jewellery, which she assumed it to be, or cunning fakes of the real thing. She was remembering George's reaction when she'd told him she intended finding out more about Louis Lederman's past life and death.

After they'd left Joe Hatchett and his boys she'd felt a great swell of gratitude to him for introducing her to that other side of Los Angeles life, to people who were wrestling and coping with problems that were real and universal removed from the ephemeral, high profile world of movies and television and the grim underworld of drugs and vice and crime.

'It makes me feel . . .'

'I know, humble.'

She wasn't sure whether he was being serious and realized there was a touch of irony in his assessment of the emotion she genuinely felt after watching Joe's sensitive devotion to his handicapped son Rolly and the fierce, almost truculent, protectiveness of the younger Jeff.

'What's so comic about feeling humble?' she'd challenged him.

'Nothing. If you mean it. I'd just never figured you for humble. Oh, sure, you've got loads of pity. Isn't it sad that Rolly has muscular dystrophy! You probably spread it around like manure in all your charitable works. But humble's something else. Humble is empathy. Entering into another person's experience and sharing it. You can't just feel sad for Rolly and the sacrifices Joe and Mamie and Jeff have had to make, not that they regard them as sacrifices anyway. You can't even throw money at them. They wouldn't take it. Humble is giving of yourself. I don't think you've given much of yourself to anyone or anything in all your life.' Unexpectedly he'd thrown back his head and

126

laughed so loudly she'd feared he'd steer the car up the sidewalk or into a bollard. 'Get me! Sounding off like the wise guy in a daytime soap. Forget it. Forget I said it. It's nice you feel humble. Truly. I'm happy for you. So, what else is new? Was Joe helpful?'

She felt curiously rejected, not by his critical lecture but by his assumption that it would be falling on deaf ears, that she'd be incapable of facing his perception of the truth about herself or putting up an argument in her own defence.

'As helpful as he could be, with nothing much to go on. What he did tell me is that Louis Lederman hadn't died in the earthquake. He'd been killed during a break-in at his beach house and that he was being investigated for fraud, selling fake antiques.' Her tone was deliberately brittle and cold. She'd be damned if she'd let him see how deeply his words had hurt her, or was it merely her pride? She couldn't yet force herself to make that distinction.

'Poor old Louis! He didn't have much luck, did he? Couldn't even pull off an art scam successfully.'

'Is that all you have to say? Maybe you knew about Louis's death, too.'

'Maybe.' He shrugged. 'What difference does it make?'

'My God, you're thick. You're so clever at judging people, but you can't even see that perhaps his death has something to do with Julie. After all, she worked for a time at his gallery. Perhaps she knew something she shouldn't. Oh, I can't believe she was involved in anything underhand. But something happened in those last months to change her. And why would Hilde Klein feed me that lie about how he died? She had to have a reason. Surely she'd have realized I'd have found out the truth sooner or later.'

'Why?' George sounded irritatingly laconic. 'Why wouldn't you believe what she told you? After all, it was the day before yesterday's news. It happened months before. How could she know you'd take it upon yourself to forage out past history or that you'd even want to? Or maybe she has actually convinced herself that he didn't die at the hands of a chance thief.'

'That's what Joe thought, too. I don't buy it,' she said

127

firmly, amused, despite herself, that she was lapsing into the lingo of the territory.

'Oh, sure, you know better. The police probably spent weeks investigating his death, but *they* don't know anything,' he said with exaggerated sarcasm. 'Leave it to the little lady from England who's spent all of three days in Los Angeles to come up with the truth. How are you going to play it? Third degree the old lady and make a citizen's arrest? Find out that Julie has holed up somewhere in fear and trembling waiting for her gallant sister to come to the rescue? You know something?'

'Else?' she said bitterly. 'Like, not only fake humble but foolhardy, too?'

He looked at her, through Hugh's eyes, with a mixture of disbelief and discovery. 'No, not foolhardy. That's a paltry fault. Vengeful. You're behaving as if you're carrying through some kind of vendetta.'

'Vendetta!' she echoed, not affronted because she wasn't quite sure she'd heard him correctly. It was such an odd, unexpected accusation.

'That's right. Vendetta. Against Hilde Klein. That's why you're so intent on all those pointless investigations. Going to his gallery, visiting the beach house where Louis died. What can you possibly hope to achieve, except something to discredit or discomfort Hilde Klein?'

'But think about it. Everything stems back to Hilde Klein—Malcolm, Julie . . .' Her voice trailed away as the full import of his accusation dawned on her. Vendetta. Vengeance. Revenge. Ugly, alien words. Was that really her motive: to get back at Hilde Klein?

'Admit it,' he said, more gently. 'She made you feel silly, inferior. But she's old and ill and abandoned by the industry she helped to create.'

'She's dangerous.' She wouldn't give in so easily.

'Suit yourself.'

As he reached across to open the car door for her, his hand brushed her cheek. They were both aware of the contact. She felt his lips on hers and she found herself responding more eagerly than he, exploring his mouth, prolonging what was probably no more than a courtesy kiss on his part. Then she pulled away abruptly, embarrassed at having taken the initiative.

He touched her cheek again. But the gesture was more that of a brother than a potential lover.

She shrank back into the corner of her seat. 'You—you must think I'm very naïve. I mean, at my age. Old-fashioned, anyway. I don't usually make advances,' she said haltingly, sounding as dated as she felt. In this world of Jackie Collins she was behaving like a time-traveller out of Jane Austen. She shuddered to think how he must be secretly laughing at her.

But he didn't laugh. He continued to examine her face as if it were a map to hidden treasure if only he could locate the key. She tried to avoid his eyes, but there was no escaping his persistent gaze.

'There's nothing so tough to bear as unrequited love, is there?' he murmured finally.

To Anna the implication compounded her embarrassment. 'What makes you think . . .?' Now she was on firmer ground. His assumption gave her the right to be angry.

He smiled and shook his head. 'I wouldn't flatter myself. And neither should Hugh. Malcolm. You've been in love with Malcolm all your life. No other normal relationship stands a chance. Even hating him, warts and all, you loved him. And now you know what he was, you still love him.'

She stared back at him, appalled. 'You're out of your mind.'

'Face it, Anna, to him you were just a general factotum. He didn't deserve all that love you wanted to give him. It may not be Juliet's love for Romeo. But it sure as hell ain't just a daughter's fondness for a father.'

'That's obscene,' she whispered, unable to move, to think, even to articulate a cogent protest.

'No. What's obscene is persuading yourself that you're doing all this out of some righteous filial commitment, a promise to a dying man. Part of the reason you hate Hilde Klein is probably because of the influence she once had over Malcolm, the fact that she could offer protection when he needed it. You're not exorcizing his ghost you're perpetuating a hopeless love-affair. Perhaps you feel if you find his precious Julie he'll give you his spiritual blessing from wherever it is a man with his gross ego and appetites retires to when the final curtain comes down.'

He gripped both her wrists tightly and forced her to look at him. '*Think*, Anna! The man was a monster and he treated you like shit. How much more of your life are you going to sacrifice on the altar of Malcolm Sterling?'

She struggled to break free from his grip but he wouldn't let go.

'How can you believe all this?' She heard her voice echoing in her head and was surprised it sounded so level, so reasoned. 'He was a great writer.'

'You make it sound like an absolution.'

'It is.' Well, wasn't it? Isn't that how she'd always rationalized his rages, his excesses, his inconsistency, his neglect of her and her mother? Great talent was entitled, almost required, to break the rules: to make its own rules and break *them* too. 'It is,' she repeated defiantly. 'And you've no right to make assumptions about me or my father. You—you opted out, escaped, took off to this—' she spread out her hands, tensing the fingers as if trying to clutch at something that didn't exist—'this fantasy world.'

But as she looked around her she realized this was no fantasy world, just people and houses and traffic and vegetation that was unreal only in the sense that it didn't grow in Hampshire. She was hitting at George in the hope that hurting him would somehow cancel out the hurt he'd inflicted on her: those deadly home truths she'd never dared acknowledge, let alone examine.

'True,' he admitted amiably. He didn't rile easily. That was the insult he always added to injury. He didn't even bother to sulk when he was annoyed like Hugh.

'And you lie.'

'Incorrigibly.' He was positively enjoying her irritation.

'About Julie. How you met her. Where she might be. First, you're helpful. Then you can't wait to bundle me on a plane back to England.'

'For your own good. I don't like you messing with the likes of Hilde Klein. She's ruthless.' He didn't sound so amiable now.

'*You* don't like! What God-given right do you have to like or dislike anything I do?'

He nodded. 'Spot on, again. Now, if you'll excuse me I'm off to see a man about a job. I may seem to spend my life loafing around and giving you a bum steer, but, contrary to whatever you may think, I have to earn a living. So, go play your little detective game. I've heard that Lois Galloway who runs Lederman's now is a real dragon. You'll enjoy that.' Despite his scornful remarks, she could tell she'd underestimated him. His flippancy was just his way of reining in his temper.

'Why do we—I,' she corrected herself, 'always end up having a thundering row?' she said, feeling suddenly contrite.

He shrugged. 'Because . . .' Then, whatever homily he was about to utter, he changed his mind. 'Because I'm here, I suppose.' And then he'd seemed anxious to be rid of her.

She didn't know how long she'd been standing outside Lederman's Gallery, staring blindly at the gaudy necklace on its purple velvet mount in the window, remembering George's accusations and wondering how closely they mirrored the truth about herself. But she became aware of curious looks from passers-by. A salesgirl in a hip-hugging red mini skirt from the movie memorabilia store next door had asked if she'd needed any help. But she didn't sound helpful, just suspicious. Although Westwood was far less guarded than Beverly Hills, loiterers weren't encouraged unless they were patently students or tourists.

'No, thank you. I'm . . .' Anna gestured towards the gallery window.

'You'll have to ring the security bell to get in,' the girl volunteered. 'Usually people make an appointment.' She clearly didn't have much time for Lederman's Gallery.

'Of course. Silly of me.'

The girl turned on her heel and swivelled back into her

131

own store, her compact little buttocks undulating from side to side in a fair imitation of the Marilyn Monroe walk.

Inside Lederman's Lois Galloway tapped one immaculately manicured shocking pink fingernail on the marquetry surface of a Venetian occasional table. She was a singularly unprepossessing woman in her mid-forties, but early on she had discovered the happy knack of exaggeration rather than disguising her short-comings. In consequence she was regarded as attractively unusual, striking rather than ugly. A short black cap of hair framed her large, angular face with its protuberant eyes and thin, hooked nose. The Chanel suit, the same vivid colour as her fingernails and garlanded with heavy gold chains, was not the height of fashion, but it sat well on her skeletally thin figure. A pair of dove grey patent Ferragamo pumps displayed her most becoming features—her tiny feet and model slim legs—to perfection.

She was not in the best of tempers.

The voice on the telephone had been peremptory and she didn't take kindly to being dictated to. And she especially resented the assumption that she had no option.

'Watch what you say,' it had warned her. Just that. Well, if she couldn't handle some little busybody from a hick town in England, who could? For all her adopted airs, Lois Galloway had been born Ida Flick, of dubious parentage in the Bronx. Her vagrant father had deserted her waitress mother early on in her pregnancy and little Ida had pretty much raised herself, clawing her way out of the ghetto via the cut-throat garment trade and assorted lovers always shrewdly chosen for their potential usefulness. You didn't survive that upbringing without knowing the score. She'd met Louis Lederman when he was peddling third-rate contemporary paintings in a seedy gallery in Greenwich Village, long before he'd married his meal ticket, Hilde Klein. Under his tutelage she'd developed a taste for quality and an eye for antiques. She'd always been grateful to Louis for that, even though he'd been nothing but trouble before—and after—his death. How many times had she warned him in their last few years as partners at Lederman's that he was a fool to even contemplate trading in fakes when the pickings were so rich without resorting to fraud. But poor Louis, given the choice between making a straight or a crooked deal for the same reward, he'd pick the crooked one. It was his nature. At least she'd had the sense to distance herself totally, financially and legally, from his dealings when she suspected the law might be breathing down his neck. And she'd kept the gallery afloat, restored its reputation, the clients were recommending other clients. Now this woman was stirring up the Louis business again. And why? Because of some little tramp who should never have left home in the first place.

Her assistant, Barry Douglas, tapped on the door of her inner sanctum. The sight of him always gave her pleasure. He was in his mid-twenties, well set up, with crinkly Richard Gere eyes and prematurely greying hair that accentuated his youth while conferring on him an aura of distinction and incorruptibility, not wholly deserved.

He was also suave and silky and gave the impression of knowing where the bodies were buried, whether or not there were any bodies.

But his prime asset was his handling of wealthy matrons whose artistic judgement was as suggestible as their financial standing was solid. He'd been in her employ for two years and he suited very well.

That he was a confirmed, though discreet, homosexual made it easier all round. The matrons enjoyed his flattery without expecting anything more and Lois Galloway didn't feel obliged to put herself through the wearing process of seducing him. Except as a means to an end, sex had either bored or repelled her. It also, invariably, at last, interfered with business. But it would have been a matter of pride to have at least tried had he not made his preferences known to her from the start of their association, some time before she'd decided to break off diplomatic relations with Louis.

He hadn't waited for her to answer his tap on the door: a touch of insolence that reminded her of herself when young. That pleased her, too. He wasn't in awe of her: most people were, if only because of her appearance. And she hadn't the slightest idea whether he liked her or not. That wasn't so pleasing; sometimes positively disturbing.

'Someone is asking for you.'

'Do I know them?' she asked, sure that she didn't. His manner would have told her if the visitor were a regular client.

'She *says* she's interested in the Aztec,' he said pointedly, plainly indicating that he doubted whether she were. 'She even asked the price.'

She laughed or, rather, snorted: a low gargle that originated somewhere in the middle of her bony chest. 'Where does she come from? Outer space?'

He stroked his chin, as if actually considering the question. 'I'd say somewhere in England. Country, not big city. Clothes well cut, natural fibre, ten years behind the times. Hair a disaster. Features regular. Figure not bad. Attractive in a quiet way. A little over thirty, give or take. Voice dreamy—Joan Fontaine with a touch of Deborah Kerr. As interested in Aztec as I am in sheep-farming.'

She smiled. 'You don't miss much, do you, Barry?

He bowed. 'I try to be of service.'

'All right. I'll see her. Meanwhile . . .'

'I'll get right on to London about that Chippendale for Mrs Carrington. Pearls before swine, but money talks.'

She looked up sharply. Now and then he sounded too much like Louis for comfort. 'Be nice, Barry. It's *our* money.'

'Yours, dear, yours. I'm just the hired help.' The eyes crinkled endearingly, but the smile was steely. 'I suppose Joan Fontaine outside couldn't possibly be related to our lovely Julie, could she?'

Waiting in the main salon of the gallery, Anna perched gingerly on a chaise-longue that might have been Regency but probably wasn't. She felt vaguely foolish at having expressed an interest in the Aztec necklace in the window. From the young man's reaction that clearly wasn't the way you did business when buying antiques in this rarefied atmosphere. But at least it had got her in to see Lois Galloway, although she now realized she hadn't the slightest

134

idea what she hoped Louis Lederman's partner could tell her, even if she felt so inclined.

Her worst suspicions were confirmed as the shocking-pink-tipped elongated fingers touched hers in a disinterested excuse for a handshake. The bulging eyes beneath the jet black fringe of hair were both bored and wary. 'What can I do for you, Ms . . . ?'

'Sterling. Anna Sterling.' She drew a deep breath, deciding to plunge in without the niceties of small talk. 'I'm Julie Sterling's sister. I want to find her. She worked here, I gather. And I think you can help me.'

Lois Galloway took her time. 'Do you indeed, Ms Sterling. Then I'm afraid I must disillusion you. I don't know where she is and I don't want to. She ruined my partner and she almost ruined this gallery. Frankly, if I heard she was dead I wouldn't shed a tear,' she said, staring at Anna through eyes that hadn't been washed by a tear since she'd been raped by a neighbour in the hallway of a Bronx tenement at the age of eleven.

CHAPTER 14

The small, reptilian smile that played around the corners of Lois Galloway's lips appeared to Anna even more lethal than the indictment of Julie she'd just expressed with such damning authority. It baited her across the silence that lay between them, challenging her to respond somehow. I can wait, it said smugly, certain in its crushing superiority.

At first she felt nothing, merely appalled at the vehemence of the other woman's attack on her sister. Then a slow panic began to percolate through her body from the pit of her stomach. The room seemed airless and stifling, despite the air-conditioning purring almost soundlessly in the background. It was all happening too quickly.

She had a curious sense of unreality, as if she were standing outside herself, observing her own disintegration. Her hands, she noted, were shaking. If she could just clasp them together the shaking would stop, but she was incapable of making even so simple a move as putting one hand over the other. And all the time that smile taunted her. The rest of Lois Galloway's face faded into soft focus behind it. Like the Cheshire Cat, she only existed through the smile.

This must be what it is like when you start hallucinating, thought Anna, as she tried to avoid looking at it. But her eyes kept staring at that expression of mirthless malevolence.

Then, quite suddenly, under her scrutiny the smile started to tremble as if it could no longer hold the pose. The face swam back into sharp focus again, the lips just lips, part of a whole.

She realized that the challenge was as much hers as Lois Galloway's. The woman hadn't wanted to see her: the only artillery she could muster against her was abuse and arrogance. Why should Anna accept as fact what she was told? Julie might have been many things, but she couldn't surely have become the scheming bitch Lois Galloway had depicted. Her hands stopped shaking; she began to breathe more easily and her mind was clearer, now it was free of the spell cast by that damned smile.

She rose to her feet, unsure of what she was about to say, anxious only to exit with as much dignity as possible intact. It had all been a dismal mistake, just as Joe Hatchett and George had predicted. How could she have imagined that she could crack the surface, let alone the secrets, of any of these wretched people? To her surprise she realized she was expressing the thought out loud.

'I won't waste any more of your time. I should have left it to the police, after all. That's what Detective Hatchett told me. I should have listened to him.' She didn't know why she had said that or where the nerve to say it had come from. At best she was embroidering the truth and she doubted whether such a loose reference to the police would be likely to dent the armour of Lois Galloway.

But, oddly, it drew an unexpected response from her. Perhaps she was even regretting her attack on Julie.

'I'm sorry if I sounded hard on your sister. Maybe I overstated it. She was just—awkward, you understand?'

136

Anna understood very well. Any regrets the woman may have had were not from any charitable motives but from a sense of self-preservation.

She leant hard on the pretty Sheraton reproduction desk between them, so hard in fact that a line of anxiety creased Lois Galloway's forehead. Perhaps, after all, it wasn't a reproduction.

'I want to find Julie. You must know something.' Her voice sounded unfamiliarly crude and loud, but she didn't care. She was fed up with being played for a fool.

'I've already told you . . .' For the first time Lois appeared distracted, not quite in control of herself.

'You must know something,' Anna repeated, even more crudely and loudly.

'There was some young man she knew. That's all I can remember.' Lois flicked her pink-tipped fingers at Anna as if warding off an attack from some singularly irritating but not strictly dangerous insect. Then, very firmly, she pressed a button on the intercom on her desk.

'Who? Where?'

'I've no idea.' She thumped the button again, more agitatedly. 'That was Louis's affair. And Louis Lederman's dead and you've no business coming here under false pretences . . .'

'What false pretences?'

'The Aztec necklace. Couldn't you agree a price?' a voice drawled.

She hadn't noticed the door open behind her, presumably in answer to Lois Galloway's summons.

'Ah, Barry.' There was a note very like relief in the woman's voice. 'No, we couldn't agree a price.'

'Pity!'

'Will you show Ms Sterling out.' She smiled sweetly at Anna. A versatile smile. 'It's been a pleasure. Don't call again.'

'Don't bank on it,' said Anna. She swept past the young man who was standing there insolently, apparently enjoying the clashing exchange.

'I spoke to London about the Chippendale and called la

137

Carrington. She wants some reassurance. It's a lot of money. I promised to see her. You know how she likes the personal contact.'

'I can't spare you.' Her voice was all business again.

'Wayne's back.'

'Don't be long, then,' she said grudgingly.

'As long as it takes. You know that's what you always say, Lois.' The emphasis he placed on her adopted name was less than flattering.

In the anteroom Wayne, an identikit image of Barry Douglas, was languidly flicking through a catalogue. He looked up, judged Anna correctly as a woman of no importance, and went back to the catalogue.

As she reached the door, Barry caught up with her. 'How about lunch?' he said making sure they were out of his colleague's earshot.

She frowned. 'I thought . . .'

'Mrs Carrington? She can wait. She always does.' He smirked, but not unpleasantly. 'Now, don't say this is so unexpected.'

'It is. But I won't.' He was, she judged, a rogue. A likeable rogue. 'Isn't it a little late for lunch?'

'It's never too late for lunch. Do you like Italian? I know a nice little place round the corner. Tony's. Very *un*-chic. No risk of running into the dragon lady or any of her cohorts.'

'Why?' She carefully lifted her arm out of his grasp. She felt uncomfortably hot. It was mid-afternoon and the sun bounced off the sidewalk and plate glass windows, intensifying the glare. And her sinus was beginning to trouble her. God, I'm a mess, she thought.

'Why doesn't the dragon lady eat at Tony's?' he said, deliberately misunderstanding her.

'No, you fool.' She sneezed and blew her nose loudly into an inadequate handkerchief. 'Why me? Why lunch?'

'No reason. You really shouldn't frown like that. At your age. The skin begins to lose its elasticity. The lines solidify.' He was mocking her in an amused yet agreeable way. Agreeable was, after all, his stock in trade.

138

She sneezed again, relaxed and smiled. 'I *am* hungry.'

'There, you see, it's easy when you try. You wanna watch that sinus here. It's the Los Angeles curse. Among others, of course. I can get you something to fix it at the drug store.'

'I still want to know why,' she said, allowing herself to be led across the baking paving stones and tarmac.

'Let's just say when you've a score to settle you take the first opportunity that presents itself. You really put the breeze up darling Lois. As did Julie.' He noted her curious glance. 'Sure, I know all about that. If I can throw a little help your way it has to be bad news for Lois. You know, on the principle that my enemy's enemy must be my friend.'

'Why do you hate her so much?'

'I don't hate her. I hate her type. She's a leech and a snob and she hasn't an ounce of human compassion. She dumped poor old Louis the moment he stepped out of line, but if it hadn't been for him she wouldn't be running Lederman's. She wouldn't even *know* how to run Lederman's. He taught her everything. He had a real eye. He just got greedy. It's a common enough disease. Even in your country, I guess.'

She nodded, ruefully. 'They call it the Thatcherite revolution.' She mopped her dripping nose. 'Why do you work for her, then? You don't strike me as a typical antique dealer.'

'I'm not. I'm just a persuasive front man. Haven't you noticed? A glorified messenger-boy who's been taught the right jargon. There are a couple of hard-core dealers who work with Lois and really know their job. I'll get out when the time's right. The pay's good, the bonuses better and Lois is a pain in the ass I can live with. Thank God, not literally.'

'And what happens when the time's right—to leave, I mean?'

'Have you ever been up to the red woods and the Napa Valley?' She shook her head. Now that he was no longer courting a customer or his boss his voice had subtly changed, revealing a flat mid-Western accent which presumably came

139

naturally to him. With the change he seemed easier, more comfortable with himself. Were there *no* native Los Angelenos? she wondered.

'That's the best place in California. Near San Francisco. I met a guy—a rich guy—who owns a vineyard out there. He comes to the gallery now and then. He's into English porcelain. He said if ever I wanted a change of scene . . .' He shrugged. 'Maybe he means it . . . who knows?' He didn't sound too sure. But like everyone else in Los Angeles, it seemed, he had his dreams. She felt suddenly rather sad for him. Underneath the cultivated air of indolence and cynicism he was just another vulnerable human being sustained by the hope of a better life that would probably never materialize.

'I hope it works out for you,' she said, meaning it.

'Ah, who am I kidding? This town is like an octopus. Once it gets you in its tentacles it never lets go. What the hell!'

They stopped outside what appeared to be a small apartment block. 'We're here.'

'Where?' She'd almost forgotten his luncheon invitation.

'Tony's.'

He pointed to the basement. The restaurant was tucked away down a flight of stone steps leading to a cool courtyard where a few tables and chairs were arranged under a striped awning. The inevitable rampant shrubs with their garish blooms spilled out of tubs reaching up the walls of the courtyard towards the sun. Even so, it had a secretive air about it. If you didn't know where it was, you certainly wouldn't have stumbled on it by chance.

First he insisted on calling in at the pharmacy next door and dealing with her sinus. 'The pills may make you a little drowsy, so don't overdo the dosage. But they'll give you relief for up to twelve hours,' the druggist recited solicitously. 'There's a lot of it about,' he added, sounding just like the girl in Boots back home.

They obviously knew Barry Douglas well at Tony's. Despite the fact that only a handful of late lunch-time customers remained, the proprietor, who actually sounded

140

Italian, welcomed him effusively with more hugging and handling than seemed strictly necessary. He winked at Anna. 'Nice boy, but not for you.' He wagged his finger.

'Tony! This is business.'

Tony shrugged expressively, as only Italians can. 'What isn't?'

'If you're hungry, have the pollo Antonietta. In other words deep-fried chicken seasoned with garlic, rosemary, white wine . . .' Barry didn't sound excessively interested in food.

'Fine,' Anna agreed.

'Is Jimmy around?'

Tony nodded. 'Sure. He's finishing up in the kitchen. You want him to wait table? Or just to talk?'

'Talk.'

'I'll tell him. You don't forget the party?'

'I don't forget the party, Tony. Promise.' Barry crossed his heart perfunctorily.

Two young men waved at him as they left the restaurant.

Watching her closely as her mind, already feeling the effects of the pill which was also effectively drying up her nasal drip, sluggishly put two and two together, he gave her a crooked smile.

'That's right. Gays come here a lot. Do you have a problem with that?'

'Why should I?' she said, smarting at the implication that she might be that bigoted.

'I don't know many English ladies,' he said, as if that were explanation enough. 'You know, you're a good listener. I don't tell people much about myself. But I tell you. Why is that?'

She took a swig of mineral water, wishing the sinus pills weren't quite so drastic, and tried to focus her thoughts. 'I understood you had something to tell me about Julie. That awful woman said something about a boy she knew, then she clammed up.'

'Why do you think I brought you here?'

'And will you stop talking in riddles? Why is it that

141

everyone manages to imply something without saying it whenever I bring up the subject of Julie?'

'What about Julie?'

She looked up, startled. A very young man was standing beside their table. He was dressed pretty much like most of the students in the Westwood vicinity. Torn jeans, T-shirt, trainers, the arms of a sweater tied round his waist. He had a frank, open face dotted with freckles, and a mop of auburn hair. He was still perspiring from his stint in the kitchen and his colouring made him look even hotter.

'Sit, boy. Have a glass of wine.'

He swung a chair round, sat down heavily, curling his legs round the back of the chair, and accepted the wine. 'I'm not your boy,' he said truculently.

'Too true you're not,' Barry sighed. 'James, I want you to meet Julie's sister. Anna Sterling. Jimmy Bean. Jimmy works part-time here. He's studying cinema at UCLA. Going to be the next Spielberg. You have to be nice to him. Someday he may be able to get you into pictures.'

The boy, for that is how he appeared to Anna, brushed aside the banter, obviously used to it. He'd dropped his aggressive stance and there was an expression of pitiful expectancy in his eyes.

'You've seen her?' He turned his attention to Anna eagerly.

He's in love with her, she thought, and wished she were the bearer of good news. But there was only one way to say 'no' and that was to say it.

He rested his forehead on his hands which were gripping the back of the chair. Then he straightened up, cupping his palms over his eyes and she suspected he'd been close to shedding a tear. A tear for Julie. There hadn't been too many of those. Certainly she hadn't shed any. Yet this boy . . .

She reached out a hand, feeling awkward and a little ashamed. He looked at it as if it were some strange object he'd never seen before. 'She never could talk to you. That's what she said. You didn't approve of her. That's what she said. You didn't even like her. That's what she said,' he accused her suddenly, using the repetitions like sharp jabs to her conscience. 'So, what are you doing here?'

'I'm trying to find her,' she said haltingly. 'I promised her father. I mean, *my* father. I imagine you know about Louis Lederman. I think—I think everything you say is true. But there's my side, too, Jimmy Dean.'

'Bean. Bean.' He grinned just fleetingly, but it was enough to diffuse the anger he seemed to have pent up inside him. 'Everyone makes that mistake. They think I've taken James Dean's name, hoping a little of his fame would rub off on me. Like I tell them. There's another side. Forget the fame, who'd want a little of his early death rubbing off on them as well? I guess you're right. There's always two sides.'

Tony brought their chicken and salads with a flourish and urged them to enjoy. Jimmy Bean eyed the dishes hungrily. Barry reached for a fork from another table and handed it to him. Like the French, Anna had discovered, Americans were frugal with cutlery.

'Here, dig in. Don't they feed you here?'

Jimmy shrugged. 'Sometimes,' he mumbled through a mouthful of chicken.

Barry raised his eyebrows in mock horror at Anna. 'These students! Living on diet Coke, burgers and crack. Can't think what the world's coming to.'

Jimmy speared a leaf of Anna's iceberg lettuce, neatly skewering half a tomato on the end of his fork as well. 'You don't have to pay attention to this guy, you know.' He gestured at her with the full fork. 'He's OK, though. For a faggot.' The way he said it lacked any kind of offence. They were obviously good and probably staunch friends.

'When did you last see Julie?' she urged him.

'About six, seven months ago. I couldn't say exactly.'

'It was a couple of days before Louis Lederman was killed. I remember when you told me,' Barry filled in for him.

'Well, what did she say? Did she tell you where she was going?' Anna was trying to contain her impatience, but it wasn't easy. Not knowing the right questions to ask she could hardly blame them for not knowing what to reply.

He put down his fork and ran stubby fingers through his thick red hair. 'Look, I hate talking about her. I asked around after she'd left and when she didn't come back I made up my mind to forget her. She was special to me but I guess I wasn't special to her. Now you come around, bringing it all up again, making me remember things I don't want to remember.'

'I'm sorry,' she said quietly.

He leaned close to her, tipping the back legs of the chair forward. His face was within inches of hers. She bent her head trying to avoid his gaze, but knowing it wouldn't go away.

'No, you're not. Sorry. You just want to do what you gotta do and then split.' He jerked the chair back with a thump. 'Jeez, I don't know why I'm taking all this out on you. You seem like a real nice lady. I just don't understand how you could care so little about what she was going through.'

'What are you talking about?' she said quickly, while fearing what he was about to tell her.

'Julie—and that man.'

'Louis?'

'No, dammit.'

'Malcolm? He was devoted to her. Much more devoted than he was to me. But what's so strange about that?' Don't, she pleaded silently, don't say it. Let me be wrong.

'Is that what you call it? Devotion! Didn't you know he had sex with her? Forced himself on her. Is that polite enough for you?'

'You're lying,' she gasped, knowing it was true. Knowing she'd known it and hadn't wanted to face it.

'She told me. That's why she had this sex hang-up. We lived together but we never slept together.'

'How long? Malcolm and Julie?' she managed to utter.

'Well, not when she was a kid. If that's any consolation. But when she was in her teens. Not long before she left home for Los Angeles. I guess she was shattered. She loved him like a father. And her father was committing incest. It was then he told her about Louis. He thought that would make it all right. He was just an older man and she a pretty girl. Only somehow it made it even worse.'

'That's why she became so strange. She didn't . . . I didn't . . .' She looked at him helplessly, begging for reassurance that she hadn't been negligent, too cocooned in her own blinkered, self-contained prison to venture into those dark emotional regions where human frailty connived at human suffering.

'No, you didn't,' he said implacably.

CHAPTER 15

'So, folks! It's showtime. Da, da!'

They both looked at Barry Douglas and perhaps because neither could sustain the intensity of feeling they'd been experiencing, they laughed nervously at the sheer absurdity of his dizzy irrelevance.

The drop in emotional temperature seemed to reactivate the effects of the sinus pill. She felt sluggish, but she mustn't give in now. She drank another glass of ice-cold mineral water thirstily and felt better.

Jimmy Bean seemed suddenly sheepish. He was a small-town boy who had been brought up to be respectful of elders, polite to ladies and wary of anything that smacked of excess. He had, he reckoned, defaulted on all three scores. He impaled a leaf of lettuce on his fork and crammed it into his mouth.

Barry sat back with the self-satisfaction of a host who had succeeded in seating two controversial guests side by side at dinner and achieved a memorable exchange without bloodshed.

'You, my friend, are unbelievable.' He was addressing Jimmy. 'A student with scruples. A moral man in an amoral city. You'll never make it in the movie business.' He turned to Anna. 'Don't you think he's unbelievable, Fräulein Sterling?'

145

'I think,' she said quietly, 'I think he's probably rather admirable.'

'I'm sorry,' the boy mumbled. 'I shouldn't have talked to you like that.'

'Perhaps you should. A lot of people have opened my eyes to a lot of things—about my father, Julie—since I came to Los Angeles.'

'A changed woman!'

'Shut up, Barry!'

'How did you meet Julie?' she asked.

'Through this character here. He's quite a decent guy when he remembers to button his lip. When I came here to UCLA just over a year ago I was—like out on a limb. It was all so strange.'

'Join the club,' she said wryly.

'I come from Santa Rosa upstate. It's not a little place, but it's not a big city either. I hate big cities. It's just that I got hooked on movies and wanted to study cinema and this was the city to do it in. My dad's a horticulturalist. The gardens are famous in Santa Rosa. You should go there. My folks staked me and I've got a little apartment off campus. It's not much, but it's homey. Like I said, when I started working here to get some dough, Barry wised me up about Los Angeles. One day he brought Julie in to lunch and she was just—just magic.' He flushed, embarrassed at expressing so intimate a feeling in public.

Anna smiled. Julie had always had that effect on people.

'Had she always had this thing about Scarlett O'Hara?' he asked her.

'As long as I can remember.'

'It was as if she—how can I say it?—escaped into Scarlett. From herself. When she was Scarlett she was free and flirty and—liberated, I guess. But when she was Julie, she was all screwed up, tight inside. It was real weird. I think she liked me. I know she did. But she was always holding back. I respected that,' he said, rather primly.

'As you can see, I didn't do too good a job at wiseing him up,' Barry intervened.

146

Anna brushed the remark aside. 'How did she happen to move in with you?'

'It was after the blow-up. At the gallery. Barry knows more about that than I do. All I know is that she was dumped. No money. No place to stay. So I offered her a bed at my place.' He blushed again. 'I slept on the couch. I wanted to marry her, meet my folks. That's when she told me about herself, your father, Louis Lederman. I think in time, when she'd found out where she was at, it would have worked out for us.'

'Did she see Louis all this time?'

'Not at first. Then later, towards the end, she did. He came around. She left soon after that.'

'And did she see a girl named Bettylou?'

'*That* one!' Jimmy snorted. 'Yeah, she was around once or twice. She got her a job in some movie, extra stuff. I didn't like it. But who was I to tell her what to do? And she needed the money. She had a few jobs, waitressing, stuff like that.'

'She worked at a club in Hollywood. The Double Take.'

'That only lasted about a week. I used to pick her up every night. It's real scary down there and I didn't want her getting into drugs or turning tricks like girls do in this town when there's nothing else. Then one night she just wasn't there. It's the last I saw of her.'

'You don't sound surprised.'

'Frankly, I wasn't. For a couple of days she'd been talking wild. About meeting someone who had a beach house. She wouldn't say any more. I could tell she wanted to, but it was as if she'd been warned not to talk about it. It was a funny thing. I got the feeling that half of her wanted to go and the other half hated the idea. If I could just have been stronger, maybe I could have stopped her from going.' Now *he* was looking pleadingly at Anna, begging for absolution. 'I tried, I really tried to find her.' He shrugged, changing his mind. 'No, that's not true. I was hurt. I thought: What the hell, if she wants to go, let her go! Why should I care? It was only weeks later that I knew I was lying to myself.

147

But by then it was too late. I even went to see Louis Lederman and that woman, his wife . . .'

'Hilde Klein.'

He nodded. 'Only Louis was dead by then. And she'd had a stroke. And her son acted like he'd never heard of Julie. I even went to the police. But I wasn't a relative and she wasn't a minor and girls disappear all the time and they told me, not in so many words, to get lost.'

'They're not exactly your friendly bobby on the beat,' Barry murmured. 'Isn't that how you describe your cops?'

Jimmy glared at him.

'There aren't all that many friendly bobbies on the beat in England either,' she said. 'But I think they might have followed up a missing persons inquiry.' She looked over at Barry who was carefully toying with the remains of his now congealed chicken sauce. 'What was this rumpus at the gallery? Your boss, that awful Galloway woman, said Julie nearly ruined the gallery. I mean, it's pretty absurd. Julie. What could she do?'

'Nothing. She didn't have to do anything. She was just there. You have to understand that between them Hilde Klein and darling Lois had Louis totally under their thumbs. I guess when you get to their age it's satisfying to know you have a guy as personable as Louis completely sewn up—either as a husband in Hilde's case or as a business partner for Lois. I don't know what the attraction was but he certainly had a way with women. Well, you must know that.'

For a moment she didn't catch his meaning, then she realized he was referring to her own mother's affair with Louis all those years ago.

'I never met the man,' she said icily.

'Oops! Sorry.'

'Go on,' she relented.

'Hilde had helped set up the gallery. She was shrewd enough to realize that Louis knew antiques, Lois could handle the deals and the finance and, most important, she wasn't a threat. They may have had a little something going at first, but by the time they opened the gallery it was

148

strictly business between Louis and Lois. Then your sister, your Julie, comes on to the scene. A long-lost daughter for Louis and he just went ape. He was crackers about her. Nothing flaky. He was just genuinely knocked out at discovering he had such a stunning daughter who'd actually sought *him* out.'

'That's what I don't understand. Why did she suddenly decide to find her true father?' said Anna. 'There'd been no contact between them. She didn't even know he existed.'

'Can't you guess?' Jimmy's voice sounded strained as if he were tired of remembering. 'She told me she wanted to discover if there was life after death.'

'Death?' Anna echoed incredulously.

'Just a figure of speech. She talked crazy like that sometimes. What she meant, I think, was that after the trauma she'd been through she wanted, sort of, to settle accounts. With herself, so to speak. Find out what her real father was like, even if he rejected her. Then she could get on with her life.'

'Did she—did she ever say anything about me that wasn't . . . ?' she started haltingly.

'Critical? Sure. She looked up to you. She wished she could be like you—all calm and collected and sure of herself.'

'She never said.'

'You never asked. I guess.'

She shook her head vigorously, partly to lessen the drowsiness and partly to drag her mind out of the past and back into the present. 'When she went to work in the gallery I don't suppose Lois was best pleased.'

'You have to be joking,' said Barry. 'She was but *furious.* And so, I suspect, was Hilde Klein. But there was nothing either of them could do. Louis wanted her there and she was doing an OK job, making herself useful about the place. But that's when Louis started doing his little deals on the side. I got the impression he wanted to make a lot of money very quickly. We talked now and then when he realized I wouldn't tattle-tale to Lois. I also got the impression that when he had made enough money of his own he intended

149

leaving Hilde. Mind you, that's just my impression. It wouldn't stand up in a court of law.'

'And the little deals were selling fake antiques?'

'Mostly Chinese pottery, pre-Colombian artefacts—there's a big market for those here. And a thriving underground business in manufacturing and ageing them. In Taiwan, South and Central America.'

'Lois and Hilde didn't know anything about this?'

'That would have ruined the object of the exercise for Louis. But I've a shrewd suspicion someone cottoned on to what was happening.'

'Like you?' she goaded him.

'*Puh-lease*, lady! I may not be perfect but I'm no informer. Anyway, someone must have tipped off the law or else why was he being investigated?'

She thought about this, wondering where Julie might have fitted into this weird scenario. 'It could have been a client who wasn't as gullible as Louis thought they were. Or Lois—surely she was smart enough to catch on?' She wondered why she was bothering to conjecture about something that seemed so remote from the purpose of her visit to Los Angeles. What did it have to do with finding Julie? Yet even as she formed the question in her mind she knew the answer. Whatever had motivated Louis Lederman in those last months of his life was in some way related to his daughter. Unless Julie were the motivator which would throw a far more sinister light on her disappearance.

Barry was studying her carefully expressionless face with that knowing intuition which belied his flip response to just about everything. Each of us, she thought, observing him in return, erects some kind of defence against the too close examination of others. In Barry's instance it was amused cynicism. Only someone as young and bruised as Jimmy Bean had yet to learn the dangers of being transparently himself.

'Are you thinking what I'm thinking? Julie . . . ?' said Barry.

'No,' she lied, deflecting his line of questioning. 'You still haven't explained why Julie was forced to leave the gallery.'

'Well, I suppose that's one way of putting it. I'd have thought it was obvious, even to someone like you who doesn't care to face the obvious.'

'Can't you ever stop playing with words?' Jimmy's interruption was more like an explosion of pent-up feeling. It didn't have much to do with Barry's predilection for taking a roundabout route to a simple statement of fact.

'My, my! Aren't we being touchy today.'

'Drop dead!'

'I love you, too, baby.'

'Shut up, both of you.' Anna clamped her hands over her ears. 'Why does everyone talk in riddles over here?'

'You have to admit it's more fun.' His smile was teasing but sympathetic. You couldn't help liking him, she thought. 'Right,' he said firmly. 'When Lois and Hilde got wind of the investigation into Louis's sideline—always supposing, that is, that either or both hadn't set it in motion in the first place—they had the perfect excuse for making him toe the line. No more pandering to his paternal passion for Julie— or else! Oh, power's a beautiful thing, the most highly prized possession in this town. If you have power you don't need money. Although the two usually go together like Rocky and Rambo. That's a pretty good definition of Lois and Hilde—Rocky and Rambo. Anyway, there was a big bust-up to which I was not witness, I hasten to add. But when you find a more than middle-aged man blubbing in the bathroom you can't help deducing that there has to be a reason.'

'They told him that Julie had to go and they didn't give a damn what happened to her?'

'More than that. And this was the really elegant touch. They insisted that Louis do the dirty work, get rid of Julie. She'd know, of course, that he didn't want to. But she'd also know he was so weak that he had to do as he was told.' For the first time since she'd met him he sounded serious and genuinely concerned.

'And I don't suppose you did anything about it—like, maybe, make sure she was all right, had a little money, somewhere to stay?' she said softly.

'Anyone would have done the same,' he replied flippantly, as if, in his book, good deeds were something to be ashamed of.

'Louis didn't.'

'As it happened, Jimmy here was the knight in shining armour waiting in the wings. Poor old Louis was trapped like a pecan in a nutcracker. I guess Hilde took over. He was persuaded to lie low for a while. Maybe she still knew enough people to make sure that the investigation would—well, die away from lack of nourishment.'

'I've learned that Hilde Klein is very good at fixing things,' said Anna bitterly.

He looked at her again with that intuitive expression. 'More secrets?' he suggested.

'I think—if you don't mind—this is one I'd rather keep to myself.'

He shrugged. 'I'm all for secrets.'

Jimmy Bean snorted, his restless long legs winding and unwinding round the staves of the chair. 'So, what's the point of all this? You go round and round saying the same old things. It doesn't get us closer to Julie. She may not even be *alive*. Have you considered that?'

God, you're young, thought Anna. Couldn't he imagine that was all she'd been considering? Action, not words; that would be his creed. But what action?

To her surprise she felt pleasantly relaxed yet alert. The pills really were working and her nose had stopped dripping, too. She chided herself for not feeling as desperate as young Jimmy Bean. At least she could give him something to think about. 'Tell me, you said she was going to meet someone at a beach house—in those last few days before she disappeared. That's right, isn't it?'

He nodded sullenly.

'Louis was killed during a break-in at his beach house, even though the old lady insists he died in the earthquake,' Barry volunteered.

'I don't want to think about that,' Jimmy mumbled.

'Why?' said Anna. 'You can't think Julie . . . ?'

Jimmy was silent for a moment. He seemed to be wrestling

152

with a doubt that had been rattling around in his brain.

Then he braced himself to unload whatever it was that was bothering him, the long legs tightly coiled round the chair. 'During her wilder moments she'd talk about killing her father. I thought it was just the sort of thing people say, not meaning it. I assumed she meant the guy in England. But—I don't want to think about it.'

'Do you know where the beach house is?' Anna asked Barry.

'Sure. He used it for partying when he wanted to get out from under Hilde.' Then he realized where her question was leading. 'Whoah—there.' He tipped back his chair, holding up his hands. 'Not me. The game's in your ball park now.'

He was right. She'd involved him enough. She turned to Jimmy. 'You want to do something, don't you? Well, instead of mooning about the girl that got away, why don't you help me? We could at least go to the house, see if we can find something out—neighbours maybe.'

He looked dubious. 'The police did all that. What can we find out all these months after? Besides, you don't know this place, the people. They don't like speaking out, even if they had anything to speak about.'

'That's the whole point, Jimmy. I *don't* know this place or the people. You do. Surely you can spare that much time. I've got a car. We could drive out.'

He thought about it before answering. Then he clapped his hands on the table. 'OK. If you think it means that much.' He looked at her with a sort of wonder. 'She didn't tell me you were this determined.'

'I didn't know myself I was this determined.'

They became aware that the proprietor had silently sidled up to their table. 'I love you, you lovely people. For me, you can stay forever. But the help.' He gestured towards the kitchen and a waiter lounging by the door, picking his teeth in an elaborate show of boredom. When he caught their eye, he yawned ostentatiously.

Barry grinned. 'Sorry, Tony. How time flies when you're having fun.' He burrowed in his pocket for a wallet and a

153

credit card, forestalling Anna's attempt to pay the bill. 'Let's have it on Lederman's.'

'I'm not sure I want anything on Lederman's.' But she conceded grudgingly.

He took out a notepad, jotted down an address and handed the slip of paper to Jimmy Bean. 'Good luck, Mr Holmes and Dr Watson. Go solve the crime that's been baffling the entire Los Angeles Police Department.' He shook his head, amused. 'It's been a pleasure and privilege, Ms Sterling. And now I must go and pay obeisance to my lord and mistress for overstaying my lunch hour. No, I tell a lie. I'm supposed to be seeing Mrs Carrington.' He looked at his Swatch watch. 'Whoops! Mr Smack will pay a visit when she sees the time.'

As they left the restaurant, they noticed a lone guest sitting at one of the tables in an alcove under the awning. He lifted his glass of wine as they climbed the steps to the pavement.

'*Bon appetit!*' said Bernard Klein. The smile on his lips wasn't reflected in his eyes which were mean and menacing.

CHAPTER 16

'No press, no press! No cops! He's had enough of you scumbags!' The skinny little woman couldn't have been more than five feet and, despite the crude make-up and the dyed candy-floss hair, still pretty, with finely chiselled bones and a heart-shaped face that had defied the puffiness of age. She could have been anything between sixty and seventy, maybe more, maybe less. She was brandishing a shotgun, more as a warning than a weapon. And she was a fearsome sight to see.

Anna nervously retreated a step, just managing to save herself from toppling backwards down the wooden steps that led to the stoop. But Jimmy Bean held his ground. He put up his hand to stop the woman slamming the glazed front door.

154

'We're not press. Not cops.'

'I don't give a shit who you are. You're not wanted,' she grumbled, but she lowered the sights of the shotgun from the groin area to the shin. 'Curious, just curious. "Let's go take in the freaks on Venice boardwalk and maybe catch Ernie Lowe on the way. He lives around there some place,"' she affected a mocking, mincing accent, then, in her normal voice, 'Where were you when he needed you? Get lost. Just get lost.'

She made to slam the door again, but Jimmy wedged his foot in the space between the door and the frame. His persistence surprised Anna. He hadn't particularly wanted to join her in searching out the house where Louis Lederman was killed and where he might have met Julie. Yet here he was positively eager to question this weird neighbour who just might have seen something on the night of the death that she hadn't remembered before. She noticed his eyes were glowing as if he'd made a remarkable discovery.

The woman looked down at his foot and up, way up, into his face. He seemed twice as tall and three times as brawny as her. She wasn't deterred. 'You want I should call a cop?'

'You don't like cops,' he said reasonably. 'You said so. Besides, I'm a friend. No press, no cop, no freak-fancier.' He held out his hand. 'Jimmy Bean. I'm studying film at UCLA.'

The woman's slight body relaxed. She looked almost benign. 'You kids! What's the assignment for this week? Rediscovering Sweet and Lowe? Funnier than Laurel and Hardy? Smarter than Abbot and Costello? Up there among the greats—Chaplin, Lloyd, Keaton. Yeah—Keaton. For years they never gave a damn about Buster, then—bingo! He's a genius! Well, don't lay that apple sauce on Ernie Lowe. He's going to die in peace. I'll see to that.' She instinctively gripped the shotgun tighter.

'What gives, honey?' A great, lumbering man shuffled up behind her. He was older even than her and his bulk had disintegrated into flab. He was wearing a loose, none too clean overshirt and a pair of sloppy, long shorts. Socks and sandals covered his feet and ankles which supported incongruously spindly bare legs. His round face was puckered with a myriad of lines but there was a good deal of humour behind the eyes.

He towered over the little woman. He looked vaguely familiar to Anna.

'Some kid from UCLA,' she threw over her shoulder. 'Wants to *rediscover* you,' she repeated the word acidly as if she'd heard it too often and didn't believe it. 'I told him to get lost. Can't figure the girl.'

'C'mon now, April, honey. He don't mean no harm. Too young to know. You don't mean no harm, do you, feller?' He smiled at Jimmy and the smile illuminated his ravaged face. The memory clicked in Anna's mind and explained Jimmy's enthusiasm. She'd seen that face on the cinema screen with his partner, Bert Sweet. He was the slapstick stooge and Sweet the smart one who fed him the wisecracks. They'd been old films even then, made in the 'thirties and 'forties and revived occasionally by film clubs and at the National Film Theatre. The films had been low budget vehicles specifically designed for their talents, but she remembered laughing helplessly at the skill of timing and inventiveness they'd brought to the art of movie comedy. Then, suddenly, there'd been no more films, probably because there'd been no more Bert Sweet who had committed suicide in the early 1950s.

It never occurred to her to wonder what had happened to Ernie Lowe. It had all been long before her time. But now she knew.

'I—we—just wanted to talk,' said Jimmy. He spoke with a sense of awe as if in the presence of some revered deity. Perhaps the young students of cinema really were rediscovering Sweet and Lowe, thought Anna, while fearing that he might completely forget they hadn't come to chat up an old comic but to find out what had happened to his neighbour in the empty house next door adjacent to the ocean between Venice and Santa Monica. She'd been surprised at how shabby they had seemed, frame buildings that looked as if they could do with a lick of paint. Not at all the sort of hideaway she'd have associated with what she'd heard about Louis Lederman. The two small houses sat incongruously among the developing and increasingly gentrified area with its condominiums and shopping malls edging down the coast from Santa Monica. In time they, too, no doubt, would be taken over by progress. But heaven help the developer who tried to mess with April Lowe!

'We wanted to talk about . . .' Anna prompted, until Jimmy Bean gave her a warning glare. Better than she, perhaps, he realized that they were poised on a fragile tightrope between get-lost and welcome. Ernie seemed willing but April obviously still needed to be convinced.

'What do you want to talk about?' she asked suspiciously. 'We don't talk to people. No cops, no press . . .'

'You said,' Jimmy sighed.

'Now, now, April, honey. He's just a kid. You've seen the movies?' Ernie's old eyes watered with expectation.

'Every one, sir, six, maybe more, times. You know they're stealing your routines . . .'

'Yeah! That black comic on TV. I watch now and then. But like I say to April, he just misses. The pace is all wrong. Maybe it's the medium. Television!' He sounded as if he were spitting out a droplet of sour saliva. 'No time. You wouldn't believe how we'd rehearse for two minutes of film. Isn't that what I always say, April, honey?'

She looked up at the enormous man protectively. 'Yeah, baby, that's what you always say,' she agreed softly.

'Did you hear what he said? Seen the old movies six, maybe more, times.' There was no mistaking the hunger in his voice, hunger for the attention he'd been denied for so many years. 'I told you they'd come around.'

'Don't hold your breath,' she sighed, but he didn't hear her.

'Why don't we invite these folks in, honey, just for a few minutes? I could show the young feller the old scripts.' He cradled his arm around her thin frame. 'Ah, c'mon, April, it's been a long time.'

Grudgingly she opened the door and propped the shotgun up against the wall in the porch. 'Well, OK, just a few minutes. I don't want him upset,' she hissed.

157

Beckoning Jimmy and Anna, Ernie Lowe followed his wife obediently, his huge body obscuring her tiny one.

It was dark and cool inside, the windows supposedly shuttered to block out the glare of the sun. But it was evening now and the sun was already setting. When her eyes became accustomed to the dim light, Anna began to understand April Lowe's reluctance to invite them in. The living area was bare of anything but the most basic furniture and that was scuffed with age. The upholstery on the two sagging easy chairs angled towards a television set was greasy and torn. The walls were whitewashed in a slapdash fashion and the stark bare boards of the floor were relieved only by a strip of carpet in the centre. Stacks of manuscripts and albums were piled haphazardly in the corner. Either the Lowes were living on the poverty line or they just didn't care. Maybe they didn't even notice.

April faced them grimly, daring them to make a judgement. She spread her arms wide. 'As you can see, we weren't expecting to entertain royalty,' she said sarcastically, then defiantly: 'We like it.'

'Sure you do,' said Jimmy easily. 'It's home.' He plumped down on a wooden stool which promptly collapsed under his weight.

For a moment there was silence as the Lowes and Anna looked down at the sprawling figure. Then Jimmy puckered his face and started to whimper, screwing up a tuft of hair on the crown of his head like Stan Laurel.

A mighty bellow of laughter echoed round the room. 'That's great, boy,' Ernie Lowe spluttered. 'Ain't that great, honey?' The laughter was infectious. Anna and even April joined in. Jimmy's little stunt had relieved the tension.

'It's sorta gloomy in here, don't you think, honey?' Ernie looked around the room, but it was obvious that he wasn't really seeing it. Jimmy had been right. It was home. He'd grown so used to the grime and general seediness of the place that he didn't even register it any more. 'Why don't we sit out on the porch?' He made a grab for the little woman from the back, encasing her waist tightly in his arms and lifting her off her feet. 'How about a cup of coffee, honey?' he whispered in her ear.

She wriggled out of his arms. 'Now you just stop that, Ernie Lowe. You're not as young as you were. You could have a heart attack. Just like that.' She snapped her fingers as if to prove her point, then disappeared in the direction of what was probably the kitchen.

There was a hammock of sorts on the porch and a couple of canvas chairs, one had 'Ernie Lowe' in very faded letters stamped on the back, the kind provided for stars between takes on studio sets. The house and its neighbour were sad survivors of a past that was being swallowed up all around them. Like Asher Kowalski's apartment, they seemed to be existing in a time-warp. But their strangeness was barely remarked in an area that tolerated the eccentric in every shape and form, human or architectural.

Jimmy and Anna settled themselves awkwardly on the hammock and Ernie lowered his bulk into the sagging chair that bore his name.

'You mustn't pay any mind to April. She took it all to heart badly. Never got over it. Press, cops, cameras— they haven't been around for years. Me? I don't bear no grudges.'

Anna looked inquiringly at Jimmy. What was the man talking about?

Jimmy seemed to know. He leaned forward and the hammock swayed perilously. 'It must have been tough, though,' he prompted.

But Ernie Lowe didn't need any prompting. 'Sure, it was tough. We were really making it big, Bert and me. And April. She was the sweetest little leading lady we ever had. A great comedienne. Just a kid, she was. A real little trouper. She didn't know nothing from nothing about politics. When the UnAmerican Activities crowd homed in on Bert and me for supporting left-wing causes she should have just upped and left. I wouldn't have blamed her. They ruined us with the studios. No producer would touch us. We couldn't even get a spot on TV or radio. But she stuck by us. Then it all got too much for Bert. His wife left him. And

159

he just gave up. He walked into the ocean one day and never walked out. If it hadn't been for April, I might have gone the same way. It was the end of Sweet and Lowe. Luckily I'd had a bit put by and I'd bought these two beach houses when I was flush, so we were able to make out. She insisted we get married. I'd been divorced a couple of times and I wasn't even sure I wanted to get married again, not with the black list hanging over me. But she said if I didn't make an honest woman of her she'd cry "Rape!"' He let out another great bellow of laughter. 'No one's got more guts than April. It's been a lousy life for her, these past thirty-odd years.'

'Don't you go speaking for me, Ernie Lowe.' She was balancing four mugs of coffee on a tin tray. 'I knew you would set him off.' She darted a reproving glance at Jimmy and Anna, but she was no longer hostile. She perched on the other canvas chair. 'All those vultures! Those letters! Would you believe kids sent back their autographed photographs of Sweet and Lowe with "commie bastards" scrawled across their faces. And those wicked columns from Hedda and Louella saying they were a disgrace to the industry.'

'Didn't you work at all after that?' To her surprise, Anna found herself increasingly engrossed in this sad footnote of Hollywood history, almost forgetting why she was there in the first place. But she had confidence in Jimmy Bean. In time, she was sure, he'd get around to it.

'For years I couldn't even get arrested.' Ernie Lowe chuckled at the unintended irony of the remark. 'Well, I guess that's *all* I could have got. They'd have liked nothing better than to put me away on some charge or other. But work . . . !'

'So, what do you do? Did you do?'

'A little bit of this and a little bit of that. Odd jobs, electrical stuff, carpentry. I used to be good with my hands, always was. There's plenty to do around here if you don't care what you do. April got a job at the hospital, working with sick children. She's good with kids, April is. Pity is we never had any of our own.'

April shrugged. 'It was for the best.'

160

'Yeah, I guess you're right. Anyway, we didn't need much to live on. Now I'm too old for a regular job. We go down to Ocean front and watch the people doing crazy things. It's the best part of the city. Folks don't care who you are or what you are or how you dress, so long as you're— interesting, I guess. Young folks, old folks. We've made a lot of friends. Sometimes a few old-timers who've fallen on hard times call in. We sink a few jars, play pinochle, yarn. It's OK. April keeps on at me to write my memoirs. I've made a start. And once some guy from UCLA—like you— dropped by, wanted me to give some lectures. But I thought: What the hell! Who wants to hear me? After a while you get lazy. Maybe I could have made a comeback after the dust settled. But it all seemed too much trouble. And, without Bert, I didn't have the heart.' He sounded wistful, but resigned.

'You could have worked,' April rounded on him bitterly. 'If it hadn't been for that bitch, Hilde Klein.' The name, as it always did, started alarm bells ringing in Anna's head. So here they were again. Back to Hilde Klein.

'What about Hilde Klein?' she asked.

'You know her?' April didn't seem surprised. Knowing Hilde Klein appeared to be a condition of life in Los Angeles.

Anna nodded, sensing no explanation was needed. Yet, at least.

'After the heat died down, Paramount approached Ernie to collaborate on some scripts for a new comedy team they'd discovered working the clubs. But Hilde Klein was representing them and when she heard about it, she found some clause in the contract and threatened the studio that either Ernie was out or her clients would walk. There was no contest. How could a woman be that spiteful? Unless she just felt guilty about how she'd abandoned the friends who'd helped her in the early days when the Committee started investigating them.'

'That's history, April,' Ernie said wearily.

'Everything's history to you,' she grumbled. 'It isn't to me. When I caught sight of her that night I still felt I could have strangled her with my bare hands.'

161

'What night was that?' Jimmy slipped in the question adroitly, trying not to sound too interested. Although they seemed to have gained the Lowes' confidence, the couple—especially April—could as easily withdraw it and all they'd be left with was the sad story of a neglected comic who'd fallen foul of the Communist witch-hunt in post-war America.

But April didn't appear to find the query in any way suspect. 'About six, seven months ago. Our neighbour—' she pointed at the identical frame house next door—'he was shot dead in a break-in. At least, that's what the papers said. I don't know if they ever caught the guy. If there was a guy. When I saw Hilde Klein drive up with that woman of hers and the son, I figured it was no ordinary break-in.'

'Who lived there?' said Anna, knowing perfectly well.

'Hilde's husband. Louis Lederman. Nice guy. We liked Louis. You know Louis, too?' She didn't wait for an answer. 'Like Ernie said, we had these two places and we used to rent out the other one. Louis hired it a few years ago. Paid his rent regular. He liked to swing a little down in Venice and he used to come here for weekends, whenever he could get away from Hilde, I shouldn't wonder.'

'What happened on the night, then?' Anna wished she hadn't jumped in so eagerly when she saw a flicker of doubt in April's eyes.

'You're mighty interested in what doesn't concern you.' She peered closely at Anna. 'You're not from here.'

Anna drew a deep breath. The more she'd learned about Ernie Lowe and his wife, the more uncomfortable she'd felt about concealing the real reason for intruding on their privacy. Now she was relieved that it was time for the truth. 'No, I'm from England. I think my sister may have been at the house the night Louis Lederman was killed. After that, she disappeared and I'm trying to find her. You may be my last hope,' she said, giving her bald statement of fact a flourish of flattery that, in other circumstances, would have offended her sense of restraint.

April kept peering intently at her, apparently unimpressed by Anna's confession of a special interest in the

162

circumstances of Louis's death. 'Sure there was a girl,' she said frankly. 'But which girl?'

'What do you mean? Which girl?'

April let out an exasperated sigh as if she considered Anna seriously deficient in the brain department. 'There were two. They bundled one in a car and drove off before the cops arrived. And the other was lurking around at the back as if she didn't want to be seen. Didn't I say that?'

'No.'

April shook her head. 'I must be getting old,' she conceded.

'What actually happened?' Jimmy volunteered helpfully.

'It was dusk. There was a lot of activity. Louis was there with the girl. Pretty, young, dark hair. She'd been there a couple of times before in the previous week. Then the cars drove up with Hilde and that woman of hers and the son. We can see everything from the window out back. There was a shot. And a few minutes later the cars drove off with the girl. I thought I'd better phone the cops after the shot, but I didn't say who I was. Before the police arrived I noticed the other girl in the shrubs. Come to think of it, they looked alike, could have been twins.'

'By the time the police car drove up, the other girl had vanished. That's all.' Ernie Lowe had been watching his wife becoming increasingly distraught as she spilled out the details of the fatal night. 'Leave it alone,' he continued quietly. 'Just leave it alone.'

'Have you told any of this to the police?' Anna pushed her, ignoring Ernie's plea. Immediately she regretted it.

'Police!' The anger in April's voice was touched with hysteria. 'I wouldn't give the cops the time of day after how they treated Ernie.'

'History, honey,' Ernie repeated, soothingly.

'They questioned us, because we were next-door neighbours. But we didn't say a thing. See nothing, hear nothing.' April's eyes narrowed. 'Now I get it. You don't give a hoot in hell about Ernie Lowe. You're probably lying about a sister. You're from them!'

'Them? Who?' said Anna, weakly.

'What's the difference!' April's voice sounded high and wild, like the wailing of the wind as it whipped off the ocean. 'All of them. Cops, press, Hilde Klein. What's the difference? Get out, both of you, get out!'

CHAPTER 17

For a moment the small woman seemed to expand, the ferocity of her outburst pumping up the slight body so that it bulged like an over-pressured bicycle tyre. Then, as suddenly, she collapsed, sobbing.

They watched with a sense of shame and embarrassment as Ernie gently cradled her to him, enveloping her in those huge, ungainly arms.

'C'mon, honey. There, there! No sweat. You're just tired.' He turned to Anna and Jimmy. 'She's just tired,' he repeated. 'I'll take her inside. She just needs a little rest.'

They stood there on the porch, awkwardly, as dusk settled and Ernie took his wife into the ugly little frame house. Neither spoke. They had no need, for they shared the same unspoken guilt that they had been the cause of April's breakdown.

In a few minutes Ernie returned. He didn't seem surprised to find them still there. He sat down heavily in his canvas chair.

'I told you to leave it be. I could see the signs.' He spoke without rancour or reproach. He merely sounded resigned as if all the anger had been used up years ago. 'Everything hit her harder than it did me. I was used to the knocks, you have to in my business. What *used* to be my business.' He puckered his lips in a sort of smile, correcting himself. 'When folks start asking questions, any questions, it reminds her of the bad times. The guys in suits from the FBI who kept on asking: Who did you know, what did you do? Pressing me to name names. And when I didn't, the threats . . . ! All that. She took it hard. Not for herself, but for me.' He sliced his hand in front of his face in a gesture of disgust as

164

if swatting a noisome insect. 'History! I never made any secret of my left-wing politics. Neither did Bert. Why should we? We thought it was a free country.'

Anna noticed that the little finger of his hand curled into the palm and the knuckles were thick and malformed. She wondered how painfully he suffered from arthritis and how much effort it took to disguise that pain. She thought of Malcolm who had had it all and squandered everything but his talent and in the end there'd been nothing but a ghostly shadow, not raging at death, but irritated in a petulant way that it should seek him out.

Ernie Lowe was worth a dozen of Malcolm Sterling, but it wasn't Ernie who won the accolades or would rate tributes like those glowingly written about Malcolm. It wasn't Ernie who had adoring acolytes rallying around to protect him when he needed them.

Yet here I am, she thought, doing Malcolm's bidding and because of that I have to harass this old man with questions and, if the answers aren't good enough, maybe threaten him with the law. Just like 'them'.

He was looking closely at her and she realized that he knew, even if he didn't understand, the burden she'd accepted and she searched for forgiveness in those gentle, weary eyes.

'Go on,' he prompted her as if she'd faltered in the middle of a conversation.

'I wondered if you could remember anything about the girl who visited Louis in those last days, the one who might be—is, I'm sure—my sister,' she said, at first hesitantly, then gaining authority as he seemed to positively invite her confidence.

He shook his head. 'Not a thing. Like I said, she was dark, pretty, young. Nervous, I guess. But maybe not. It was none of my business what Louis got up to. So, I can't help you there. But could be, this can.'

He was holding a roll of paper, secured by a rubber band. They hadn't noticed that he'd brought it out with him from the house, perhaps anticipating that Anna would be waiting with more questions.

165

'The police went over the place after the shooting and then the Kleins moved out what was left of Louis's things. The usual stuff had been taken, money, bits of jewellery. Nothing much. They figured Louis had happened on the guy who broke in before he could really do the place over and it was a panic shooting. There'd been a lot of break-ins in the area.'

'But you don't believe that. April didn't.'

'I've given up believing much of anything.'

'The Kleins could have faked the break-in?'

He shrugged. 'I guess I should have spoken up about what we saw that night. But I couldn't do that to April. You saw how she was when you even mentioned the police. Don't you want to see this?'

He poked the roll of paper towards Anna, who grasped it gingerly. It was pockmarked with stains as if it had been rescued from the waste disposal.

Ernie grinned, reading her thoughts. 'It won't bite you. I've cleaned it off. When we went into the house after they'd all gone to see if it needed tidying up, I found this in the trash outside. There was a whole lot of papers, kitchen waste—and this, screwed up. I was going to leave it there and then I opened it up and it looked cute. Corny but cute. It seemed a pity to destroy it. They do a lot of that sort of thing with old movie posters these days. Can't think why I hung on to it.'

As Jimmy peered over her shoulder, she unravelled the paper. It was a facsimile of a poster for *Gone With The Wind* but in place of Vivien Leigh as Scarlett O'Hara another face was substituted. Julie's. It was only a sketch, not a photograph, but the identity of the sitter was unmistakable. On the back of the poster there was a scrawled inscription. 'For the girl who is Scarlett.'

'Is that her? Your sister?'

Anna nodded. She felt numb. The face, that provocative face, stared not at her but at Clark Gable as Rhett Butler. But there was something there she hadn't perceived or perhaps hadn't noticed when last she'd seen Julie. It was a kind of desperation bordering on frenzy. This wasn't an aggressive, challenging, liberated Scarlett, but a young girl on the verge of madness.

'Can I have it?' she asked.

'Sure. I suppose you're going to ask me why I didn't wonder what it was all about, with that inscription and everything. Well, I did wonder. But then I figured I'd never find out so I might as well mind my own business. April didn't even know about it. If I'd shown it to her she'd have worried that I'd take it to the police. Can't think how they missed it anyway. I guess they'd made up their minds about what happened.'

'Louis was Julie, my sister's, father.'

He shrugged carelessly, not especially surprised. 'It happens,' he said.

He sounded suddenly awfully tired, as if there were nothing left in the world *to* surprise him.

'It's Julie all right,' said Jimmy. 'That look!' He shivered slightly.

She glanced at the house next door outlined in the gathering darkness. It looked haunted, empty and haunted.

'Has anyone lived there since . . . ?'

Ernie sighed. 'No. We never bothered to put it up for rent again. Too much trouble. I guess it'll become derelict and the city will want to take it over, along with this place. They can always think up a reason. But we'll be dead by then.'

He sounded as if he almost welcomed that blessed release from a life that had ceased to have much meaning over thirty years ago.

'Now if you young people will excuse me,' he said, 'I ought to see how April is. And I guess you've got all you came for.'

Anna started to speak, to utter the usual platitudes of courtesy, thankful for his help and sorry to bother him, but Jimmy forestalled her.

'I want to apologize, sir,' he said respectfully. 'Maybe your wife was right. We did come here under false pretences, I suppose. But it's not true that I don't admire you. As an artist. I'd really like to come sometime and read your scripts.' He paused, then went on a trifle bashfully. 'You

167

see, I've made a little comedy film. A sort of exercise. But I'd sure like to show it to you. I'd value your opinion. And maybe you'd meet some of my friends at UCLA. Talk to us about how it's done. How it's really done. I mean—like in the old days.'

Tears welled up in Ernie's eyes, the rumpled face was striving hard not to show too much emotion but he was visibly touched by Jimmy's gauche enthusiasm. 'That would be a right pleasure, young man. I'm in the book. Under Lowenstein. Ernst Lowenstein. That's my name.'

He wiped away a tear, smiling. 'They made a lot about that, too. Like Edward G. Robinson changing his name from Emmanuel Goldenberg. I don't know how they figured that was subversive when half the immigrants at Ellis Island got stuck with a new label because the old one was too hard to pronounce. But they did.'

The smile broadened, with something of the old twinkle that had charmed filmgoers all those years ago. 'History! It don't do to dwell on history.'

He bade them farewell with grave formality as if concluding a royal audience. Then, fixing his eyes on Anna, he said a strange thing. 'I hope you find your peace, little lady. Just remember, you're your own person, not somebody else's idea of you. Don't ever let them take that away from you.'

Flustered, she withdrew her hand from his too hastily. How dare he presume to know so much about her? And then a small, knowing voice punctured the instant anger: How dare he be so right? What, after all, had her whole life been but a front she'd designed to conceal whoever the real Anna Sterling might be from the bewilderment of her mother, the tyranny of her father and, now she realized, the torment of her sister.

She regretted her brusque gesture. But already he had mooched back into the dark little house, the porch door squeaking on its rusted hinges behind him.

'Ernie! Is that you?' She heard April's voice through the shuttered window and the gruff rumble of Ernie's reassurance.

168

'What was that all about?' said Jimmy.

She looked at him: so young, so surprisingly unworldly in this ruthlessly worldly city, so uncontaminated by the cynicism and lack of wonder affected by many of his peers. How could he possibly understand what Ernie Lowe had seen in her?

'Nothing,' she said.

It was a long drive back to Mabel's through the preening suburbs of Santa Monica and up through Beverly Hills to West Hollywood. She was glad to hand over the wheel to Jimmy Bean, who drove with that comfortable ease and unconcern with which Americans seem to be born. She doubted whether anyone had ever so drummed into him that he had a lethal weapon in his hands (as her own driving instructor had done) that he never touched the accelerator without anticipating the worst.

As he stared straight ahead undazzled by the headlights of oncoming cars she studied his frank, open face and wondered about his relationship with Julie. Perhaps if he'd tried just a little harder, if he hadn't been quite so diffident . . .

'Did you *really* love her?'

'You said "did". Don't you believe she's alive?' He continued to stare ahead, not taking his eyes off the road. 'Yes, I did. I do.'

'If you felt that strongly . . .'

'Why didn't I work harder at finding her?' he finished her sentence. He was silent for a moment and she felt, not for the first time since she'd arrived in Los Angeles, that she was asking too much of strangers whose need to protect their emotions was quite as strong as her own.

'I'm sorry,' she said.

'No, you're right to ask. I just—I just didn't want to take the risk. If I found her and she'd . . .' He brushed his cheekbone with the palm of his free hand, but she couldn't tell if he were flicking away a tear or a memory. 'I just didn't want to take the risk.'

'Of being rejected?'

'No, dammit, why should I be?' he replied heatedly. She'd

169

hurt his pride. She was getting awfully good at inflicting damage, she reflected.

She tapped the poster, changing the subject. 'What an odd mixture Louis Lederman must have been. I suppose he must have mocked this up to please Julie, yet it's such a daft, sentimental gesture. And this is the same man who put up with Hilde Klein and Lois Galloway all those years, who wasn't above tricking his clients with fake antiques and cheating on his partner. Doesn't he sound strange to you?'

'He sounds like someone who loved Julie,' he said flatly, then, with a hint of humour: 'I know. I've been there.'

'I'm not giving up,' she said.

'I didn't think you would, your type never does.'

'Why do you say "my type"?'

'All knotted up inside. Point of honour to get the job done whatever it is, provided you don't have to get your hands dirty in doing it.'

'Another riddle!' she dismissed his remark. 'A tiresome riddle.'

'For "hands" read "emotions",' he elaborated. 'Ernie Lowe had you angled right, didn't he?'

So Jimmy Bean wasn't as young and unperceptive as she'd thought.

'Look, let's leave me out of it,' she said irritably. 'There's Julie. You can think what you like about me, but you have to help.'

'OK, I'll help. What do you suggest, first? There's only the whole of the U-nit-ed *States* to explore. That shouldn't take too long. If I cut a couple of lectures we could wrap it up in no time.' He shook his head. 'Don't you think I've gone over and over this in my mind, long before you came into the picture?'

'Yes, well, you didn't get far, did you!' She sounded and felt snappy, tired of being analysed and found wanting. 'Who do you suppose she, April Lowe, mean by "that woman of hers"?'

'Search me.' She shrugged. 'Lois Galloway?'

'Hilde Klein came that night before the shot, with her

170

son and "that woman of hers".' She snapped her fingers. 'Myrna!'

'Myrna?'

'Hilde Klein's housekeeper, watches over her like a hawk. When Bettylou phoned me she mentioned Myrna, too. For no particular reason. I've just remembered. Not that she made any sense anyway. Yet . . . do you suppose Bettylou had been blackmailing the Kleins? After all, if she was there that night, watching, maybe she saw something. Why was she there, anyway?'

He didn't speak for a minute or two and she thought he hadn't heard the question or simply couldn't figure an answer. 'I guess maybe I told her,' he said finally. 'Not meaning to. The day Julie left for good, Bettylou came around. She'd heard of some sort of job for the two of them. I was angry and I told her she'd left me, she was seeing someone at a beach house in Venice. I wasn't very helpful. I didn't like her.'

'And she put two and two together. It wouldn't have taken much for her to realize who Julie was meeting and where. She obviously knew the Kleins. I'm damned sure she was there yesterday when I called on Hilde Klein. Maybe she went there to the beach just when it was all happening. That's it! I'm sure she's been blackmailing Hilde.'

'You're way ahead of me.'

She doubted whether he was that dense. Maybe he had other reasons for not wanting to get involved. But her mind was made up. 'I'm going to the police,' she said firmly. 'With this—' she tapped the poster again—'and what the Lowes saw . . .'

'You can't,' he blurted out suddenly. 'What do you think would happen? They'd have to question those people, the Lowes, bully them because they didn't come forward before.' He sounded desperate, as if meeting Ernie Lowe had imposed a trust that he couldn't betray.

'You're exaggerating,' she said, but less forcefully.

'Maybe. But for the past thirty-five years they've been trying to put the nightmare of being interrogated and inves-

171

tigated and judged behind them. Now you want to open up that whole can of beans all over again when they're old and vulnerable. I know it's not the same thing, but to them it would be.'

'But this could be a criminal offence. Murder maybe. Blackmail. At the very least it's a clue to what happened to Julie. Don't you *want* to find her?'

He clapped his hands on the steering-wheel, shaking his head from side to side, and the car veered perilously towards the oncoming traffic. He righted it just in time to avoid an affronted Jaguar, horn blaring. She felt sorry for him, sorry to be facing him with the dilemma of choosing between two loyalties. 'Of course I do, but I don't want to destroy the Lowes either. I don't know, maybe like April said, you *are* "one of them". But I know sure as hell I'm not.'

She started to say something, anything, but then decided not to.

They continued the rest of the journey in silence. As she sat there, watching the lights of Hollywood flashing their signals into the neon night, she felt curiously disembodied, not the woman she'd been but someone quite else. She knew she should be distraught with worry about Julie, crushed by the revelations about her mother and especially Malcolm, appalled at the recognition of her own sins of omission. But she felt none of these things, just a sense of exhilaration. For the first time that she could remember she was experiencing the fearful pleasure of being truly alive, a participant with all that entailed, instead of merely an observer. The cleansing pain would come later and she would welcome it.

When they reached Mabel's apartment he refused to come in.

'How will you get back to Westwood?'

'I'll manage.' He sounded truculent, yet unsure of himself and her.

'You can take the car. Bring it back tomorrow morning.' She knew she was making the offer only to ensure that he didn't disappear, like Julie. And in a positive way she needed him.

'Fine.' He half-smiled, understanding her motives but

determined to exact his own price. 'If you promise not to contact the police yet.'

She returned his smile, giving nothing away. 'Until tomorrow.' It was only a half-promise but it seemed to satisfy him.

In the event there was no need for her to decide whether or not to call the police. They had called her.

Mabel was looking uncharacteristically agitated. The apartment seemed to have undergone a slaphappy spring clean as if she'd needed to do something to keep her busy.

'Where have you *been*?' she thundered when she'd closed and locked the door behind Anna. That was uncharacteristic, too. Bolting herself in from the outside world.

'I told you. George . . .' Anna began, puzzled.

Mabel waved the explanation aside with one of her exaggerated, flouncing gestures.

'I know. I know. I'm sounding like a den mother. Or, worse, *my* mother. God forbid!' She crossed herself with mock piety. 'You've had a message. It's important and I didn't know where to reach you.'

'What message?' Anna said anxiously.

'A cop named Joe Hatchett called. You saw him this morning—right?'

Anna nodded. Was it really only this morning?

'He thinks they may have found your sister. Julie. Only brace yourself, amigo.' She took Anna gently by the arm and led her to one of the floppy cushions scattered on the floor, urging her to sit down. 'The girl they think is Julie is dead, Anna.'

CHAPTER 18

It wasn't within Joe Hatchett's division, but he came anyway with the plain clothes detective from the LAPD who accompanied her to the morgue.

True to his word, he had made inquiries and what he'd

173

come up with was an unknown dead girl who seemed to match the photograph of Julie Anna had given him.

The detective was over-solicitous and polite, calling her 'ma'am' a lot, clearly anticipating he'd have a screamer or a fainter on his hands. But if she could identify the body it would lighten his workload.

The girl had been seen wandering crazily along Santa Monica Boulevard in nothing but a flimsy shift the night before. Several passing motorists had notified the police, although the one that had mown her down hadn't stopped.

Technically it was the car that killed her, but sooner or later, it seemed, she would have died of a massive heroin overdose. Just another young, unaccounted-for OD among many, unless Anna could put a name to her.

It was cold in the morgue but the chill didn't penetrate the numbness in her bones as the dead face that might be Julie's was unveiled. Please God, don't let it be her, she thought. There's too much left undone, unsaid.

'I'm sorry to have to put you through this, ma'am,' someone said.

She shut her eyes tightly, preparing herself, then opened them. The face in death was not peaceful. The mouth was drawn back in a garish smile, the skin sallow and blotched. The worst of the injuries she'd sustained were mercifully concealed. But the stench of death was overpowering.

She felt Joe Hatchett's hand gripping her elbow, ready to support her if she needed it.

She looked long and hard at that ghastly excuse for a face, mesmerized by the horror of it. And by the added horror that it was a face she recognized.

'It's not Julie,' she whispered. 'It's not my sister. It's Bettylou.' Then she heard a weird, irreverent sound and realized she was laughing. In this place of death she was laughing with relief. It wasn't Julie.

They drove her away to a near-by coffee shop, figuring, no doubt, that a police station might be too much for her to take in one night. She told them all she knew about Bettylou, which wasn't a great deal. About her relationship with Julie; about the strange meeting at the Holiday Inn and the phone call the night she was killed; about her possible association with the Kleins. Mindful of her half-promise to Jimmy Bean, she omitted any reference to her conversation with the Lowes about the night Louis Lederman died.

'What about parents, relatives, where she came from?'

Anna shook her head. Then she found she was burbling recklessly, not making any sense, all her suspicions and frustrations of the past few days poured into a garbled, pointless narrative.

The detective listened to her patiently until she ran out of steam and she realized he was looking at her with kindly disbelief. After all, she'd had a shock. Identifying dead bodies, even if they aren't your nearest and dearest, isn't pleasant. People react differently. She could see all that in his eyes.

'I'm not making much sense, am I?' she said, consciously pulling herself together.

'You'll feel better in the morning,' he assured her soothingly. 'We'll want a statement, but it's just a formality. We'll be in touch. You won't be leaving town.' It wasn't a question or a request, but a statement.

She shook her head again. 'Not till I've found Julie.'

'We'll see what we can turn up,' he told her without conviction. Girls went missing all the time. Sometimes they turned up. Sometimes they didn't. Sometimes the police found them and sometimes the relatives wished they hadn't. Missing persons was a growth industry in southern California.

But he couldn't tell Anna that.

'You'll talk to Mrs Klein. You *have* to . . .' she said urgently.

'Sure thing. We'll explore all channels.'

She laughed again. A short, silly laugh. Amazing, that policemen all over the world should use the same ponderous, give-nothing-away language. She could be reporting the theft of a budgerigar to the local constabulary in Winchester. Or maybe, because she was English, that's the way he thought he should speak to her.

175

'I'll drive you home,' said Joe Hatchett, nodding at the other officer.

'Home,' she echoed sourly. 'I've forgotten where it is.' And then, to her embarrassment, she started to weep, not loudly but uncontrollably. The pain was beginning.

The detective who had seen it all before discreetly disappeared. At least he had a name for his corpse.

Joe Hatchett let her weep until the tears began to dry up and then he handed her a fistful of Kleenex.

'I'm a mess,' she apologized as she scrubbed her nose, feeling the sinuses throbbing again. 'I bought some pills at the pharmacy, but they make me drowsy.'

'Wait till you get home. You're upset.'

He led her to his car.

She looked at his battered face, lined with weary wisdom, and remembered the disabled son to whom he was dedicating his life. 'I'm sorry, dragging you away from the family. On your off-duty day.'

'They're used to it. It goes with the job. And as a favour to George.'

'Tell me—' she began, but he interrupted her, his tone stern and exasperated.

'Look, lady. You don't want to waste any sympathy on me. You'd be better off looking to yourself. You shouldn't go around making accusations you can't prove. The Kleins still carry some clout in this town.'

'You mean, like getting away with murder,' she said.

He snorted. It was just a phrase, the sort people use for any minor infringement of the law or business ethics. Then he realized she was serious.

'*What?*' He sighed. 'There you go again.'

'Bettylou could have been murdered,' she persisted.

'Look. She was a junkie. You said she must have been on the stuff yourself.'

'Why don't you question Hilde Klein?'

'Lady, it's not my department. If you say the girl knew Hilde Klein, she'll be questioned. But it's not my department. I can't go flashing my badge for no good reason.'

176

'You'd flash your badge pretty damn quick if Hilde Klein were sixteen, hard-up and black.'

'Whoa, now, slow down! I'm a straight cop, but this isn't my case. It's for the Beverly Hills Police Department. I'm doing you a favour talking to you now.'

'At least they've got an identification on Bettylou,' she said heatedly.

'True! But they'd have figured her out sooner or later.'

'It's a pity they can't figure out where my sister is.'

He let out a slow whistle of air. 'That's it. I'm taking you back to where you came from and I suggest you get a good night's sleep. You'll think a whole lot more clearly in the morning.'

He looked at her, curled up like a rebuked child in the corner of the car, small and vulnerable, her face still blotchy from crying, her hair tangled. She was, she knew, a sorry sight, though not as sorry as he imagined.

He took her hand gently in his. 'You've had a bad shock. On top of being worried about your sister. Don't take on more than you can handle. Just let it ride. I promise if there's anything that can be done, it will be. Just . . . don't do anything crazy. You don't know this town.'

He ran out of words, for which she was grateful, allowing her the peace to contemplate the small idea that was germinating in her mind. If she couldn't get official help, maybe there were other ways of getting at the truth.

George was waiting for her at Mabel's apartment. He'd rushed over when he'd heard from Joe Hatchett about the dead girl on Santa Monica Boulevard. He looked distracted and had obviously polished off the better part of a bottle of bourbon.

'Is she OK?' he asked Joe over her head as if she weren't capable of speaking for herself. Without thinking, she ran fingers through her straggly hair trying to arrange it in some sort of order. There was nothing much she could do about the rest of her dishevelled appearance. She didn't want him to see her like this and she tried to suppress the tingle of excitement his presence generated in her.

'She just needs some shut-eye. I'll be going.' Joe lifted his hand as if to give her a paternal pat, a there-there-don't-cry pat, but she shrugged it aside.

'Like the man says, I'm fine,' she said firmly. 'But I could do with some of whatever that is.' She nodded at the bottle.

'I wouldn't, honey.' Mabel was draped in the doorway to her bedroom in a negligée and nothing else. 'It'll knock you out cold in your state.'

'My state is fine. I told you.'

'On your head be it,' said George, pouring her a minute dram. The liquor went down like a bolt of lightning. She swayed unsteadily and felt herself being helped to the one upright, conventional chair in Mabel's living-room. She saw Joe Hatchett looming over her, his face blurred, warning her to take it easy.

After he'd left, her head cleared and she felt suddenly ravenous. Mabel produced a pastrami sandwich and she wolfed it down as if she hadn't eaten for days. 'I needed that,' she said, licking the last crumb from her finger.

George had been watching her intently, but his voice was casual. 'What did you tell them?' he asked. 'The police.'

Her eyes met his, but she couldn't read anything there. They were blank, an actor's eyes.

She was trying to think of a suitable answer when Mabel intervened. 'She's had enough for one night. She'll either have indigestion or a hangover in the morning. But I guess she'll survive.'

'I just wanted to . . .'

Mabel looked steadily at George. 'You can just *want* until some other time. If there's anything worse than a nervous doll it's a nervous guy. And, remember, you owe me a bottle of bourbon.'

She pushed him towards the door.

'I'll look in tomorrow morning, Anna. Don't let this dragon lady bully you.'

'No!' They both turned towards Anna, surprised at the vehemence of her protest. 'No. Don't come tomorrow morning,' she said more easily. 'I'd rather just . . . you know, calm down.'

'OK, later then. I worry about you, you know,' he said

softly, blowing her a kiss in the manner of some swaggering, silent screen dandy.

'What a ham!' laughed Mabel, closing the door behind him. 'That's what's known as the Rudolph Valentino school of acting. It comes out when he's had too much to drink. When he's really drunk he's Dirty Harry. But I guess he's right about one thing, he was worried about you.'

She caught Anna's curious look and wrapped the negligée tightly around her. 'No. He didn't. We didn't. Just in case you're wondering. Now get to bed and you can tell me what you want to tell me in the morning.'

'Mabel, you know something odd? He didn't ask me whether the dead girl was Julie or not. The first thing he asked me was what I'd told them. Doesn't that strike you as odd?'

Mabel wrinkled her perfectly formed nose. 'Nothing Georgie does or doesn't do strikes me as odd. Anyway, I guess he assumed it wasn't Julie or you'd have said straight away. That's what I thought. It wasn't, was it?'

'No.' Now that she was standing, Anna realized that the bourbon and the pastrami might be about to declare a state of war with each other. 'It was Bettylou.' Then she made a dash for the bathroom and just made it in time.

'You know what, you're *loco*! What makes you think this boy will go along with a crazy plan like that? What makes you think *I* will? Don't you know you could get yourself killed?'

Intent on lecturing some sense into Anna who was nursing a mug of thick black coffee and a splitting headache, Mabel ignored Jimmy Bean, perched comfortably on a cushion, his long legs shot awkwardly out in front of him. He'd returned Anna's hired car early and was now supposedly unconcernedly munching a whopper hamburger with all the trimmings slopping down the sides of the bun which he'd brought in with him for breakfast.

'Are you listening to me?'

Anna nodded, although the effort was roughly akin to a road drill boring a hole in her skull. She winced.

179

'Here, stupid!' Mabel handed her a couple of aspirin tablets. 'You shouldn't be allowed out without a leash.'

Anna swallowed the aspirin gratefully. It had been a tough night. She had hardly slept. The dead, grinning face of Bettylou kept swimming into her restless dreams, waking her up with a start. And then the whole process would start again. The thinking. The remembering. The relief that the face hadn't been Julie's. The fear that she might have to look at a similar face, similarly dead, and it would be Julie's. And somewhere slotted in between the nightmares and the memories she'd evolved the plan. She couldn't wait any longer for the slow, convoluted procedures of the law and she couldn't afford the services of a private detective she wouldn't trust anyway. All she needed was a little help from her friends. She didn't allow herself to dwell on the suspicion that she didn't know who were her friends. Having made her decision in the early morning, she slept peacefully for a couple of hours and woke up with a new, exhilarating resolve and a thumping head.

The aspirin was beginning to work and it helped that Mabel had turned her irate attention to Jimmy Bean.

'And *you*! Either you're two nickles short of a quarter or you're as cracked as her.'

'Same thing.' Jimmy looked up from his hamburger and blinked at Mabel.

'Don't double-talk me, you little shit. The pair of you! You're getting me so I don't know what I'm saying.'

'Oh, you're making yourself pretty clear.'

She took a swipe at his provoking smile, but he caught her hand before it landed on his cheek. 'She's neat. When I make my first movie you can play the lead.'

'When you make your first movie Mexico will be the fifty-first state of the union,' she said, smiling despite her rancour. 'What am I saying? It already is, except it doesn't know it.'

'Smart, too!' He let her hand go.

'You know your problem? You're not a serious person.'

'I'm serious. I'm very serious. That's why I'm here.' He

turned to Anna, who'd been listening to their exchange with a kind of puzzled admiration. The people she knew didn't talk like that, so quick, so easy, where she came from. All those buttoned-up feelings and skirting around the truth with elaborate and sometimes cutting courtesies. Here, they sounded direct even when they were devious. And, she realized with surprise, she was becoming like that, too. She wasn't the Anna Sterling who had left England less than a week ago. She was somebody else and she was beginning to enjoy her company.

'When I left you yesterday, I could have parked the car somewhere convenient and called you to collect it,' said Jimmy. 'I could have said include me out. You find your sister and welcome to her. But then I got to thinking.' He ducked his head like a small boy caught in a conflict of conscience. 'About a lot of things. Julie. You. The Lowes. And the way other people get away with things. So . . . !' He screwed the remains of the hamburger into the paper sack, took aim and shied it neatly into a kitchen waste bin across the room. 'At least, we'd be doing something.'

'Like getting yourselves arrested or knocked off,' Mabel sighed.

'It's not so dangerous, Mabel. Just a matter of keeping watch. Maybe nothing will happen at all. But I've a hunch it will.' Anna was amazed at how calm she felt. Normally, the slightest deviation from routine would have bothered her. Only now wasn't normal.

'I'm sure when I overheard Hilde Klein talking about "insurance" she was referring to Julie,' she went on. 'Julie was insurance, perhaps in case of a police investigation into Louis's death. And then, another thing, "use the user". If Bettylou was blackmailing them she was the user, but they used her in trying to persuade me that Julie was fit and well so that I'd leave and go home. Then maybe she pushed her luck and they arranged her death to look like an accident. But if they thought I really knew what they were up to, where Julie is and that I was calling in the police, they'd have to do something about it. Pronto! All I'm asking you to do is to make a simple call to the Kleins in my name. Do you think you can sound sufficiently like me to fool whoever answers the phone?'

'Sure.' Despite her assurance there was no mistaking the reluctance in her tone. 'I saw *My Fair Lady*.'

'It takes an hour, say an hour and a half, to get to the Kleins' house, allowing for traffic. You make the call to them from here at approximately that time. By then Jimmy and I will be parked nearby and if they make a move we'll be waiting.'

'You don't even have the slightest idea what you'll be waiting *for*. Are they coming out guns blazing or begging for mercy? It's real *kids'* stuff!' Mabel exploded. 'Cops and robbers! I can't believe I'm hearing this from a mature, grown woman who, two days ago, wouldn't have walked down Hollywood Boulevard after six without a police escort. You're a fucking idiot. *Him*, I can understand. He's not much more than a kid himself. But *you* . . . !'

She clapped her hands to her head in a gesture of disgust. 'This is a rough city, woman. Maybe these are rough people you're playing with. It's not one of those cute little English mysteries. A puzzle to be solved and, if you do, you get a year's supply of Hershey bars. Let the cops mess with those people. That's what they're paid for.'

She thrust her face close to Anna's. Her own was contorted with anguish and a hint of fear. Fear for Anna, who stared back at her implacably.

Then her lips curled and she shook her head. 'You're listening. But you're not hearing me.'

'Will you do it?' said Anna imperturbably.

CHAPTER 19

As she sat in the red Toyota beside Jimmy Bean who had elected to drive, Anna realized that the heady determination of a couple of hours before was being slowly deflated, like air oozing out of a punctured balloon.

Of course, Mabel was right. It *was* kids' stuff. She

couldn't imagine what she'd been thinking of, trying to play amateur detective with the same mindless bravado of a child engaged in a game of bang-bang-you're-dead! in the safe knowledge that all the 'corpses' would revive in time for tea. It was, she worried, this place. It exists on manufactured fantasies and, after a while, you begin to think you can act out fantasy as if it were reality.

They were parked round a bend in the road from the Klein home off Benedict Canyon up towards Mulholland Drive, but within sight of its electronically secure gates. They could, in theory, spot anyone going in or coming out of the drive without being spotted themselves. But it was, as Jimmy pointed out, a dubious supposition in this well patrolled, exclusive area. Already they'd had a suspicious look from a large man with what seemed an even larger dog.

'It better work soon or we'll be pulled in on suspicion of planning a break-in. That guy didn't look too friendly. Suppose they catch on that Mabel isn't you on the phone? Suppose no one's home anyway? Suppose they just don't bite?'

Anna didn't answer. All that had gone through her mind. All that had reinforced her growing realization of the absurdity of what had earlier seemed such a clever ploy to lead her to Julie.

'What do you hope to get out of this? Honestly,' he prodded her. He sounded gentle and concerned, older than his years. She could understand what a rock he'd been for Julie in that terrible time when she must have felt abandoned by everyone in whom she'd put faith.

'Gum?' He offered her some spearmint and she unwrapped the strip with total absorption, depositing the wrapping neatly in the glove compartment.

'I don't know,' she said finally. 'Maybe just the satisfaction of knowing I'd made the effort. I came out here to Los Angeles not really, *really* committed to finding my sister. I was fulfilling a promise to a man who, I've been discovering, wasn't worthy of promises. But I had to do it. In a perverse sort of way I was proud that he'd asked me. "Make it right,"

183

he'd said as he was dying. I didn't know what he meant. Now I do. But you can't just make anything right through last-minute remorse. I spent practically my whole life refusing to see Malcolm, my father, as he really was. As I got older I was blinded by the fact that he was a great writer and I was just a scribbler with a small gift for words. He told me that so often I had to believe him. But worst of all I was jealous. Not of him. That would have been like envying Jesus Christ the knack of performing miracles. I was jealous of Julie. Jealous of his affection, his obsession with her. Why couldn't that be me? I did his chores, looked after his comfort, his house. I never answered back like Julie did. I was never indulged as Julie was.'

'That's an awful lot of self-pity,' he said quietly.

'You're right,' she admitted. 'But that's not how it felt, because I wouldn't allow myself that luxury. It became a nasty little canker inside that I couldn't put a name to. Well, now I have put a name to it. I was deeply jealous of Julie, so much so that I couldn't begin to understand her; and I doubt whether the thought even crossed my mind. But somehow I have to make amends, not for Malcolm's sake, but for mine. I know the police will probably find Julie eventually now that I've registered her as a missing person. But eventually isn't soon enough. I keep seeing Bettylou at the morgue. I'd seen my father dead and my mother. But I'd never seen anything like that. It could have been Julie. They did look awfully alike. And it could *still* be Julie.'

'You don't know that. It'll be OK. You'll see,' he said, although his assurance was just a formality, uttered in the falsely soothing tones of someone who was out of his depth and, perhaps, his understanding. 'Geez, I feel sorry for you. I guess I'm lucky to have had such a normal family life. I've known kids whose lives were messed up by their parents, but this is gross.'

She felt him shiver beside her and she knew she was imposing a terrible burden of shared confidence on him. But, selfishly, now the floodgates were open she couldn't close them, didn't want to. Exploring out loud the traumas of her life had the liberating effect of exorcizing them.

184

'Once when I was very little long before Julie was born I ran away from home. I'm not sure why. I think with hindsight it was something I'd heard between my mother and father that scared me. But at the time I know I had this overwhelming feeling that I had to run away from *me*. I thought if you removed yourself from where you lived and the people you lived with you'd be different. And for a whole day I was. I really was. Different. I wandered into a part of town I didn't know. Almost a slum. There were kids playing in the street, rough kids, and they let me play with them. When one of their mothers came home from work she gave me bread and jam and let me watch their telly. Then a policeman came along and took me back home. I suppose she'd called the station to report a stray child. But I wasn't different any more, ever again.'

'All kids run away some time. What did your parents say?'

'My mother was out of her mind with worry. She kept hugging and walloping me as mothers do when they're relieved and angry at the same time. But my father just thought it funny. I think it was the first and only time I ever amused or interested him, because I'd shown some initiative and run away. I'd always been such a model little girl. He said I'd suffered a kind of madness, as if it were a virtue he hadn't expected to discover in me. It was a strange thing to say about a child, except he wasn't regarding me as a child but as fodder for a new book. He used that phrase about a character in his next novel, although I didn't recognize it. At the time I didn't know what he meant; how could I? But I do now. I think during the past few days here in Los Angeles I've been suffering a kind of madness.'

She turned to Jimmy but he looked bemused. In his simple, caring way he was uncomfortable with the complexities of lives that weren't lived up-front and upright.

'I guess Mabel should have made the call by now,' he said, checking his watch with elaborate care, wanting to change the subject. 'Unless she's decided not to.'

'She won't. She promised and she'll do it,' said Anna. 'Sorry about all that.' She felt she owed Jimmy some sort

185

of apology. He'd been fond of Julie. He'd said he loved her. But that didn't mean he should be expected to assume or even especially care about the problems of her family.

He shrugged, chomping hard on his gum. 'It's OK.' But it wasn't. They were startled by a determined tapping on the car window on the passengers' side. The large man was peering in. The dog, firmly held on a leash, waited patiently but threateningly to heel beside him.

Anna wound down the window. The man's steely eyes took them in, sized them up and then raked over the rest of the car including the back seat, missing nothing.

It's all over, she thought with a sinking feeling, suddenly convinced he'd been sent to scare them off. She'd hoped Mabel's call would have panicked Hilde Klein into making a false move. She should have realized it might have the reverse effect. Hilde Klein was too cool a customer to be fooled by such an amateur ploy. And worse even than the sense of threat generated by the man facing her through the open window was the nagging fear that maybe all her assumptions about the Kleins were predicated on nothing more substantial than the fact that she disliked the woman.

'Are you folks in trouble?' His voice was soft, polite although prepared to brook no argument or excuse.

Anna sighed with relief. He might be a private guard or even a private citizen keeping a vigilant eye on dubious strangers, but he didn't sound especially menacing.

She leaned over hastily and grabbed a street map from the back seat. 'No. Really. We're just—just checking where we're going on the map.' She dug Jimmy in the ribs. 'It's pretty tricky finding your way around here, isn't it?'

'Sure thing.' Jimmy smiled weakly.

'Maybe I can help.' The man sounded as if he meant something quite different. His face had hardened. He obviously hadn't been taken in by her helpless tourist act.

'No need. We've sorted it out,' she said. She nudged Jimmy who switched on the engine.

'Where are we going?' he muttered.

'There.' She nodded ahead, then fluttered a hand out of the window at the man and the dog who growled none too peaceably at the departing car. 'Whew! that was nasty. I thought he'd been sent by Hilde Klein to beat us up or something.'

'What makes you think he wasn't?'

'Look ahead.'

A fairly elderly dark grey station wagon had glided sedately out of the gates of the Klein house. It was clearly a work-horse automobile, not for status or show, not the kind either Hilde Klein or her son would own.

Jimmy peered at the driver. 'It's just some fat old woman. Probably the help going on an errand.'

'You're darned right she's on an errand. It's Myrna. "That woman of hers"! You remember what April said about the night of Louis's death?'

'So what? She's probably just doing the marketing.'

'Maybe. Maybe not. Just drive, Jimmy. But try not to be too obvious. I don't want her suspecting she's being followed.'

'It won't be easy. What if we lose her in traffic? There are a lot of beat-up grey station wagons around.'

'I'm counting on you not to lose her, Jimmy.'

He chuckled. 'You really like to play long shots, don't you?'

'It seems to me they're the only kind on offer. Where's she going? You know this area a lot better than I do.'

He drove steadily for a few moments, keeping his eyes on the winding canyon roads and the rear of the station wagon. 'It looks like she's heading west, maybe on to Ventura.'

'And then?'

'I'm not a mind-reader,' he said irritably. 'Out to the Pacific Coast Highway maybe. Anyway she sure as hell ain't going to the Farmer's Market.'

When they hit the freeway west the traffic as always was fierce and Jimmy needed all his concentration to keep the station wagon in view, trailing a discreet three or four cars behind it. Fortunately both the station wagon and its driver weren't inclined to break speed records or, much more importantly, the state speed limit.

After several miles it took a left spur road and coasting

187

at a steady forty miles an hour eventually joined the Pacific Coast route north of Santa Monica and Malibu. They'd left the bustling, crowded and malodorous city behind them. On one side the crashing breakers of the Pacific Ocean battered the shoreline, throwing up an invigorating barrage of spray. The air was so fresh and clear it made Anna feel light-headed. For the first time since arriving in Los Angeles she felt she could breathe freely.

The traffic was fairly sparse now and if Myrna had cared to look closely in her rear-view mirror she might have wondered about the red Toyota behind her. The thought had obviously crossed Jimmy's mind. He slowed down to let a truck overtake, putting its bulk between him and the station wagon. The road sign pointed to Santa Barbara.

'Damn!' he cursed.

'What's the matter?'

'Gas. If I don't pull in to a gas station, we'll be stranded.'

'But we'll lose her.'

'Maybe not.'

The station wagon was indicating a right turn.

'Those canyon roads don't lead far. Mostly to private spreads. It shouldn't be too difficult to spot her.'

'Unless she's spotted us first and is trying to lose us,' Anna said gloomily.

He sighed. 'Don't blame me, lady. It's your hired car. You could have checked the gas.'

'I know,' she conceded. 'That's why I'm furious. We were so close.'

He pulled into a gas station and asked them to fill up the tank.

'Close to what?' he demanded, waving aside the attendant's offer to check the oil and water and clean the windscreen.

'It's a miracle!' Anna marvelled. 'In England you have to beg a garage to do those things and then tip handsomely and thank them profusely.'

'Are you listening to me?' Jimmy insisted, obviously unimpressed by a feature of American gas stations he'd known all his life. 'Close to what? We've driven—what, nearly eighty miles? Just on the off-chance that this woman, Myrna, is doing some sinister errand for Hilde Klein. She could be visiting a relative. Maybe it's her day off. She sure isn't driving as if the devil's on her tail. I'm telling you, we'd have done better to cruise around near the Kleins' house and see if anything happened. Or, better yet, walk straight up to the front door and confront them.'

'And get arrested for loitering? You saw that man and his dog. He could easily have called the local police and what would we have told them? Just what I told that detective last night and *he* thought I was crazy. Not that he said it in so many words. Jimmy, why are you such a negative-type person?'

She wondered why he was chuckling and then realized how Los Angeles she must have sounded. 'It's catching, isn't it? "Negative-type person"! I'd never have said anything like that at home. I wouldn't have known what it meant. All the same, you are—negative!'

'I guess I am. Cautious, anyway. In the regular way. This morning, you were kind of infectious. All that get up and go and do something. I actually felt we might buck the system, be heroes, fight off the villains, find the princess, all on our own.'

'And then live happily ever after?' She shook her head. 'I never believed that. But I still think it's worth an eighty-mile trip to follow a lead. Myrna *never* leaves Hilde Klein. There has to be a good reason.'

She paid the gas station attendant and they backtracked along the road to the turn-off Myrna's station wagon had taken.

They'd lost fifteen, maybe twenty, minutes. What, indeed, if Myrna had just been trying to throw them off the scent or, perhaps, trap them? What if she'd been alert enough to notice the red car shoot off after her the moment she'd pulled out of the Kleins' drive? What if this were a wild goose chase? What if . . . ? She shuddered. I won't dwell on that, she thought.

As they drove they passed a discreet sign reading 'Paradise Health and Beauty Resort' indicating that health and

189

beauty were there for the taking along the coast in the opposite direction.

'Wait! They said Bernard Klein co-owned a health farm on the coast near Santa Barbara. Perhaps that's where we should be making for.'

He stopped the car. 'Anna, there are *thousands* of fat farms in California. What would be the point of going to this one? Let's follow the route the station wagon took.'

'You're right, of course. But if it were Bernard Klein's it would be an added connection. Maybe the grounds of the resort meet the path Myrna took.'

'Maybe we should just stop maybe-ing and find out. Unless I'm much mistaken we've found the turn.'

The private road was little more than a dirt track and it took all Jimmy's skills as a driver to steer the Toyota past the pot-holes and up the steep inclines. They arrived finally at a pair of gates, fenced on either side. The drive beyond the gates led to a functional stucco building with a red-tiled roof. Parked outside the front door was a grey station wagon.

'Now what?' said Anna helplessly. She really hadn't considered their next move. 'We can hardly go up and knock at the door.'

'I'll go see if I can find another entrance round the bend.' Jimmy sounded suddenly very much in control. 'You stay put until I get back. Don't, repeat don't, attempt anything!' he added firmly.

She watched him disappear on foot round the bend in the fence wishing she could join him. She felt isolated and vulnerable.

She got out of the car and, out of sight of the house, tested the gates. They were old, unguarded. The whole place looked run-down as if in a state of suspended animation. She felt cold in her flimsy slacks and cotton shirt which had seemed so insufferably warm in the Los Angeles sunshine. Way below her she could see the ocean lashing the shore.

As she waited impatiently for Jimmy's return she became aware of the crunch of wheels behind her and the whine of brakes hastily applied. Then she froze as she heard footsteps, measured and sturdy, getting louder and felt a tap on her shoulder.

She stifled the scream that had started in the pit of her stomach and was clogging her throat. 'Jimmy!' she whispered instead. But she knew it wasn't Jimmy. It was more a call for help.

'Sorry if I made you jump.'

She turned to face a large, bearded man who looked beefy enough to take on the US Marines. He was wearing khaki shorts and a huge woollen sweater. His longish greying hair was damp from the ocean mist. His jeep was parked a few inches behind the Toyota.

'You looked sort of lost. Can I help?' Everyone in California seemed anxious to help at the most inconvenient moments. 'I live aways up in the hills and it's not easy to find places in these private roads.'

'I was looking for the health and beauty resort,' she improvised hastily, hoping she sounded confident and determined. But the words came out in a strangled, frightened whisper.

'Paradise?' He grinned, showing a great many white tombstone teeth. 'They closed that down months ago. This—' he jerked his thumb at the stucco house behind the gates—'this is where the staff lived. I guess that's closed too, although there always seems to be some activity there. Maybe you should have phoned first.'

'Maybe I should,' she said, glad that her voice was beginning to sound recognizably her own.

'You can make a turn over there.' He pointed towards a widening curve in the narrow road. 'You want me to see you down?'

'No, no, that's very kind. I can manage,' she assured him.

He was looking at her curiously. 'I wouldn't hang around. Woman on her own.'

'No I won't.' Go, for God's sake, go!

'Well, if you're sure. Drive safely. These tracks can be treacherous.'

He walked back to the jeep, climbed in and for what seemed like an eternity continued to look at her as if reluctant to leave. Then he switched on the engine, backed down a few feet, changed gear and slowly slid past the Toyota and on up the hill. 'I wouldn't hang around,' his voice floated back to her. She watched the jeep until it was out of sight.

Only then could she feel her heartbeat settle down to a relatively normal rhythm. The minutes continued to tick away. She could see that there was some movement in the house, figures appeared in the window and then disappeared. Luckily the Toyota was parked so that it was unlikely it could be seen from the house.

'Jimmy, where are you?' she pleaded out loud. Then she heard the scuffle of feet round the bend in the fence.

'Right here. Do you want to wake the dead?'

She hadn't realized she'd spoken so loudly. 'Jimmy,' she sighed with relief. 'There was a man in a jeep . . . I didn't . . .'

'I know. I saw him. I managed to avoid him. Listen . . .' He gripped her shoulders. 'Anna, I've seen her.'

'What?' For a moment she didn't comprehend what he was saying. 'Who?' Then she realized what he was saying. 'Julie! You've seen Julie?'

'That's right. I got through the fence further up and peeked through the window. She's in a conservatory attached to the house. She looks fine,' he anticipated her question. 'But, Anna, it's weird. If she's being held in there I don't think it's against her will.'

CHAPTER 20

He led her through the gap in the fence he'd found and, keeping close to the protective shrubs, they edged their way to the back of the house and crouched beneath the window of the conservatory.

It looked peaceful enough inside. Exotic creeping climbers in pots, obviously tended with care, crawling up the walls. The remains of a mid-morning snack on a wicker table. An

192

embroidery frame, anchoring a half-finished tapestry of some colourful seascape was lined up against the wall, along with a canvas bagful of tapestry wools, a pile of paperbacks, compact discs and hi-fi equipment. It all seemed pleasantly lived-in.

A girl was sitting contentedly on an upholstered rattan chair, her hands clasped decorously in her lap, watching television with the sound turned down. There was a feline smile on her lips. Her eyes were glazed with contentment. She was mouthing dialogue to match the lips on the screen. The film she was watching was *Gone With The Wind*.

'Julie!' breathed Anna.

In the corner of the conservatory, Myrna was talking to an enormous, muscular, middle-aged woman who had the appearance and manner of an old-style hospital matron. She must have been over six feet tall, but it was Myrna who looked the more intimidating. A wiry, older man with the face of a wary ferret was supposedly ministering to an ailing pot-plant but his eyes never left the two women.

'I'm going in,' whispered Anna.

'Wait!' hissed Jimmy. 'Look!'

Through the fanlight they could catch the conversation being conducted between Myrna and the other woman, although the girl in the rattan chair seemed totally unconscious of it. Occasionally she put her fingers to her mouth, miming a coquettish pout like Scarlett provoking Rhett. Lost in her fantasy, she was clearly enjoying herself.

The women ignored her. Myrna's eyes seemed to be mentally frisking the hospital matron, then settled on a bulge in the pocket of her loose, linen, overall-shaped frock. She reached into the pocket and pulled out a gun.

'What's this?'

'What does it look like?' matron said truculently, but there was an underlying nervousness in her tone. 'I keep it handy in case of prowlers. I thought I heard one just now. It gets pretty lonely up here—just me and Kurt and the girl.'

'Mrs Klein won't like that. The gun. It might scare the girl into doing something stupid. If she croaks on us, she'd be no use.' All the same, Myrna didn't attempt to relieve her of the gun.

'Use for what?' The man, presumably Kurt, stopped fingering the spotted leaves of the plant. 'You don't tell us nuthin'.' His voice rose to a fretful whine, but he looked scared as if it had taken some courage to speak out of turn.

Big matron rounded on him. 'Get lost, Kurt. This is between me and Myrna.'

Kurt looked from one woman to the other, shrugged his shoulders and shuffled off through the door that led into the main house.

The girl, Julie, took her eyes off the television screen momentarily. ''Bye, Kurt,' she simpered, then focused again on the flickering images. It was as if she were aware of the other people in the room only as extras on the periphery of the main attraction. 'She doesn't even hear what they're saying,' Jimmy murmured in Anna's ear. 'Either she's brainwashed or drugged.'

'She's not real!' said matron, shaking her head at Julie. 'But Kurt's right. You don't tell us anything.'

'You get paid to look after a sick girl, Arlene. That's all you need to know.'

'Just because you're my sister doesn't give you the right . . .'

'Arlene! You wouldn't want the cops to know about the little sideline you and Kurt had out here, now would you?' The satisfied smirk on Myrna's face seemed to flatten Arlene even more than the threat.

'You bitch! You always were a bitch!' she said limply.

Having made her point, Myrna was all business. 'This isn't a social call.'

'I figured not. How much longer?' Arlene said with a touch more spirit. 'You said a little while. It's been months. How long can you expect us to go on like this?'

'That's what I came to tell you. Mr Bernard's coming to take her away. Later. He's got some arrangements to make.'

'What kind of arrangements?' Arlene looked worried. 'Kurt and me, we're not getting mixed up in . . .'

'Arlene!'

'. . . something serious,' she ended lamely. 'You could have phoned.'

Myrna nodded. 'She knows I hate driving. But ever since Mr Louis she's been paranoid about the phone. She thinks it's tapped.'

'That old lady's nutty as a fruitcake. Why should she worry about it being tapped?' She nudged Myrna. 'You can tell me. We're sisters,' she said insinuatingly.

Myrna snorted. 'Your *bitch* sister! And don't you ever *dare* talk about Mrs Klein like that again.'

Arlene made a fist as if to sock Myrna, then thought better of it. But her fingers kept working, kneading into her palm, as if itching to do some damage.

The girl with the Scarlett face kept watching the television, unperturbed.

'I can't stand this,' Anna whispered, half-rising. 'That's Julie in there. I'm going in. What can they do to me?'

Jimmy pulled her back down. 'That's crazy,' he muttered urgently. 'Do you want to take your chances with that woman and her gun? She looks as if she wouldn't mind using it. Prowlers. Like she said.'

Arlene and Myrna looked up abruptly.

'What was that?' said Arlene. 'Kurt!' she called. The old man shuffled back in obediently. 'Go take a look-see round the place.'

'I'd best get going. Here!' Myrna opened her bag and took out a thick envelope.

Myrna grabbed it. 'The same?'

'Better. It's over, Arlene.' She looked across at Julie. 'Over for everyone.'

'I don't . . .'

'I don't want to hear another peep out of you or Kurt— ever. Do I make myself clear? Understood?' For all the fact that she was a foot shorter than Arlene, Myrna looked the more threatening.

Arlene nodded. 'Understood. I don't want trouble. You wouldn't, would you, Myrna?'

'Not if you behave yourselves,' Myrna assured her complacently.

'I'll go see how Kurt's making out.'

'What about her?' Myrna nodded at Julie.

Gone With The Wind had reached the point where Scarlett and Melanie were disposing of the dead body of the Yankee deserter who had sneaked into the war-sacked Tara.

'She'll be OK. There's another two hours of it,' sniffed Arlene. 'Christ, will I be glad never to see that movie again!'

They moved into the main house, shutting the door behind them.

'Now!' said Jimmy.

'What if they come back?' said Anna.

'We can't hang around here. That old guy might find us. We'll get her out somehow.'

They tested the glazed outer door to the conservatory, relieved that it was unlocked. Arlene and Kurt must have felt very sure that no one would penetrate the hiding-place where they were holding Julie.

Silently, they slipped into the conservatory. But Julie's eyes remained fixed on the screen.

'Turn off that damned thing,' said Jimmy, his voice low, indicating the television.

As Anna switched off the set, Jimmy moved swiftly towards Julie. She looked up, startled, as the screen went blank. She started to speak, but Jimmy clasped his hand over her mouth before she could utter. Only then did her frightened eyes take in the two intruders who had so rudely shut off *Gone With The Wind* in its prime.

'Julie!' Jimmy whispered. 'It's me! Jimmy! Remember? Jimmy! And Anna. Your sister. Look—Anna!'

Anna knelt down beside the girl and took her hand. It felt soft and pliant, like a small child's, in hers. She was so pitifully vulnerable and dependent. Anna was conscious of an overwhelming feeling of compassion such as she'd never experienced before, as if she were seeing her sister truly and clearly for the first time. Compassion and a sense of achievement, too. She'd been right, after all. The Kleins had reacted to Mabel's phone call. And she'd found Julie at last. Alive and well. And, whatever her mental state, there seemed nothing physically wrong with her.

'Julie, we've come to take you away. Home. You're safe now.' Then she heard muffled voices in another part of the house and the danger inherent in their situation stifled all other thoughts and emotions. 'You mustn't make a noise. If you do—those people will make you stay.'

The girl's eyes fluttered from one to the other, the fright receding to be replaced by recognition; the perplexed recognition of seeing familiar faces out of context.

Jimmy lifted his hand cautiously from her mouth.

'You turned off the TV,' she said listlessly.

'You don't want to watch TV,' Anna urged. 'You're coming with us. Jimmy and me.'

The girl started to shiver, then the shivers convulsed her whole body, her arms and legs jerking like those of an out of control marionette.

'I can't. I have to stay.' She spoke quietly in fits and starts, but there was an underlying hysteria that threatened to erupt into what?—screams, calls for help! Jimmy and Anna exchanged anxious glances. 'They told me. I killed him. They told me. I killed my father. They told me. The police—years and years in prison. I had the gun. They told me.' A yearning, puzzled tone came into her voice. 'But I liked Louis. Why would I kill Louis?'

Then she went suddenly rigid as if reacting to a programmed response to a question she'd asked often. 'I like it here. It's quiet. They let me watch . . .' She turned to Anna, eyes blazing with indignation. 'You turned off the TV.'

Anna looked at her with increasing despair. Time and treatment would heal Julie but not in the few precious moments they had before Arlene and Kurt returned. 'Julie, you didn't kill anybody,' she said, desperately trying to penetrate the web of lies her unstable sister had been forced to believe.

But the girl wasn't listening. 'They told me. I killed Louis. I had the gun. They're protecting me. They told me. I had the gun. The gun.'

She wrapped her arms tightly around her waist, rocking backward and forward gently, no longer seeing them, just the false guilt that had been foisted on her.

Anna tried to take her hand again but the gesture was brushed aside. 'Jimmy. It's no good. She'll never leave quietly. But we can't leave her here. You heard what they said. "Over for everyone." Bernard's coming to get her, then God knows what.'

Jimmy nodded. He was breathing heavily and he looked scared, but not so much at what might happen to him or Anna or Julie as at what he was about to do himself. 'If she makes a fuss they'll come running. There's only one way out of it. Get ready to make a break for it.'

He lifted his eyes skyward. 'Please God, I don't mean it!' Then he raised his fist and smashed the girl squarely on the jaw.

For a second her eyes cleared as if the fog she'd been living in for the past months had receded and she was rational again. Then she keeled over, sagging forward. He caught her in his arms and bundled her inert body over his shoulder like a sack of potatoes.

'Make for the car and get the engine started,' he said to Anna. 'I'll follow. Don't worry, she's no weight. I didn't play football in high school for nothing.'

Anna stared at him, frozen by the suddenness of his action. '*Move!*' he hissed.

The authority behind the command galvanized her into action. Without bothering to try to keep out of sight of the house, she ran across the lawn and dived into the shrubbery surrounding the estate, only to come up against the fence. Where had Jimmy found the gap? She circled round for what seemed like minutes and then saw the earth rise up to meet her as she tripped over a fallen twig.

Hoisting herself up, bruised and grubby, she saw what she had been looking for. The gap in the fence. Elbowing her way through it, she made for the spot where the Toyota was parked, slid into the driver's seat and turned on the engine. Perversely it refused to spark on the first few tries, then it began to hum reassuringly. All she had to do was wait. She tried to remain calm, but a flood of fear kept sweeping over her. What if Julie's captors had been too quick for Jimmy? What if, even now, they had him cornered in that house? How long should she wait? Should she wait at all? No, that wasn't even an option. She had to wait. And if he didn't come? What then? The police! She'd call the police. But by then it might be too late.

The moments ticked away, agitating new fears, unconsidered fears. She was conscious of a jab of pain shooting up from the base of her spine and cursed herself for falling awkwardly, for falling at all. But the pain in her back was nothing compared to the pulsing worry of that long, agonizing wait.

Then, with grateful relief, she heard a scramble of feet on the pitted road bordering the fence and saw Jimmy heaving the still unconscious Julie towards the car. There were beads of perspiration on his face and he was breathing deeply, taking in air through his mouth like an athlete on a marathon run.

'Get in the back with her. I'll drive,' he panted. 'We haven't got much time. I heard them. They could be right behind.'

Without ceremony he bundled Julie into the back seat, pushed Anna aside and was already putting the car into drive before she'd closed the rear passenger door. She winced.

'Trouble?'

'I put my back out running for the gap.'

He made a sympathetic face at her in the rear-view mirror, then lapsed into concentrated silence as he gunned the car down the narrow canyon road to the highway, taking the pot-holes as they came. The Toyota, grumbling but game, responded to the unaccustomed rough treatment.

When they hit the highway, he relaxed, keeping to just within the speed limit.

'Where to?' he threw back at her.

She hadn't thought about that, too concerned about just getting Julie out. 'Mabel's,' she decided. 'They don't know I'm staying there. Then we can sort things out. Let's just get out of here.'

He grinned. 'Did you know something like ninety per

cent of all American movies have that line of dialogue somewhere in the script?'

She stared at the back of his head, unbelieving. 'Is that *all* you can think about? Now?'

'Sure. I've got a lot to think about,' he countered angrily. 'Like maybe getting myself knocked off or fouling up some other way. Like getting us back to LA without being driven off the road by someone sent to stop us by those people. Like that girl back there, her mind all shot to pieces. Sure, I've got a lot to think about. But in the meantime we've got a long drive and there's nothing much we can do about anything unless someone does it to us first. So—just loosen up. You'll feel better.'

Immediately, she felt contrite. If it hadn't been for Jimmy Bean she wouldn't now he holding Julie in her arms and, whatever might happen afterwards, this one moment would be worth it. 'I'm sorry. Jimmy?'

He grunted.

'Thank you.'

'You're welcome.'

The girl in her arms stirred, moaned and slowly her eyelids fluttered open. There was an enormous swelling on her jaw where Jimmy's punch had landed. It must be hurting badly, but it didn't seem to bother her. Maybe she was beyond physical pain.

When her eyes were fully open, she tried to wrestle out of Anna's grip, then, seeing who was holding her, she slumped back, cooing softly and incomprehensibly to herself.

'It's all right now, Julie. It'll always be all right now,' Anna murmured, stroking the girl's hair. And she went on talking softly, soothingly, trying to communicate the confidence she didn't entirely feel herself to her sister.

'Grey station wagon up ahead,' warned Jimmy as they neared the outskirts of Santa Monica.

'Could it be Myrna's?'

'I'm not sure yet.' He paused. 'Yep. It's her.'

The station wagon was coasting at a sedate thirty miles

an hour. Myrna's preferred speed. Which accounted for the time lapse between her leaving the house and Jimmy catching up with her.

'She's probably not looking out for us. Unless she's got a car phone, which I doubt. But duck down in the back seat so that she can't see you. I'm going to overtake and she doesn't know me.'

Pulling Julie to the floor of the car below the window eyeline, Anna listened as the engine revved up ready to overtake and felt it swerve towards the centre of the road. It was stiflingly hot and uncomfortable and the jagged nerve in her spine was making itself felt.

'You can come up for air,' said Jimmy finally. 'We've passed her.'

'How did she look?' Anna eased herself and Julie into the back seat again.

'Like she hates driving. Isn't that what she said? But I can't say I paid too much attention. It should be plain sailing now. There's too much traffic around.'

It was late-afternoon by the time they reached Mabel's apartment and the door was opened before they'd rung the bell. Mabel had obviously been waiting for them or, at the very least, news of them.

As she stepped aside to let them in she showed no emotion. Perhaps, thought Anna, this is one imposition too many and she realized how much she'd depended on Mabel's goodwill.

'I'm sorry, Mabel, I couldn't think . . .'

'You crazy broad!' Tears welled up in Mabel's eyes. 'I was worried sick. That woman. On the phone. She scared me half to death.'

'But you did it, Mabel. You did it.'

She looked down at the girl clasped in her arms and registered the frightened expression she'd seen before in her eyes.

'It's all right, Julie,' she murmured as she'd repeated so many times on the drive.

Mabel was staring at the girl, seemingly unsure how to react. 'So—you found her, after all.'

'She needs help, Mabel,' pleaded Anna. 'Until I can work out what to do.'

Mabel continued to study the cringing girl. Then she nodded and smiled. 'Sure. First, let's get her to bed. She looks beat. And who gave her that belt on the chin. Them?'

Jimmy shuffled his feet. 'Me! It's a long story.'

CHAPTER 21

'Georgie's here.' Mabel poked her head round the bedroom door. She sounded sober and serious, unlike her usual flamboyant self. 'I've told him what happened. He's pretty shattered. And I've called Patty, that studio nurse I know. She's promised to look in and check up on Julie. How is she?'

'Sleeping,' said Anna. Mabel slid into the room and stared down at the girl curled up in a ball on the bed. It was an uneasy sleep. Her fingers kept twitching and every so often a spasm tensed the muscles in her body. After the spasm, a low moan escaped from her lips. The dark hair coiled into damp ringlets round the nape of her neck. Yet the expression on her face seemed oddly serene, as if, like the Scarlett about whom she fantasized, she was putting the past behind her and facing the future.

'She looked so—so untroubled.' Jimmy was squatting on a stool by the bedside. He'd refused to leave. Perhaps having helped save her life he now felt responsible for it.

'It's an illusion,' said Anna. 'She's troubled all right. God knows how long it will take. Mabel, I've got to have help.'

'Why would they want to persuade her that she'd killed that man? And why would they go to all that trouble to keep her in ignorance?'

'I don't know. But I'm damn well going to find out.'

Anna gently slid her hand out of the clutches of those twitching fingers. Julie had fallen asleep clinging to her as if to a lifeline. After the drive to Mabel's apartment, she hadn't demurred, had barely spoken, allowing herself to be led by the hand like a child, a particularly compliant child.

Only once had she registered any emotion, when Anna had told her they were going home.

The girl's body went rigid. 'Not him.'

'Who?'

'Him,' she repeated as if incapable of uttering the name.

'Malcolm?'

'Not him.' The sound was wild and shrill like that of a small animal suddenly alarmed.

'No, Julie. Not Malcolm. Not Malcolm ever again.'

She looked at the stricken face and cursed the father who'd caused such anguish. Later, much later, she'd have to tell her that Malcolm was dead, but she wouldn't know how to say it now or whether she should. There was too much repair work to be done on Julie's damaged mind before anyone, even a psychotherapist, could assess that.

She started as she felt the pressure of Mabel's hand on her shoulder.

'I've really buggered things up for you these past few days, Mabel.'

'What are friends for?'

'That's right. We are friends, aren't we?' The thought brought her a certain comfort. Friends! Mabel, Jimmy, George, Joe Hatchett. And all the time she'd imagined she was surrounded by enemies.

'I have to get her into proper care.'

'Sure you do. But right now no harm can come to her. I'm here. Jimmy's here.'

George was standing on the veranda outside the apartment, seemingly concentrating on a couple of young girls who were purposefully swimming in the pool below.

When he heard Anna behind him, he swung round urgently, sighed deeply and spontaneously took her in his arms. She sank gratefully into his embrace, luxuriating in the closeness, the safeness, of him.

He kept murmuring her name as if assuring himself that she was actually there. 'Why didn't you let me know what you were planning? Mabel shouldn't have let you do it on your own. I could have come with you. When I think what might have happened . . .'

Reluctantly, she released herself from his arms and looked up into his worried eyes. 'Mabel couldn't have stopped me. And I wasn't alone. I had Jimmy.'

'A boy.'

'If it weren't for that boy Julie wouldn't be safely sleeping in the next room now. Besides, what could have happened to me?'

He shook his head and she thought she detected a trace of fear in his eyes. 'You don't know these people,' he said lamely.

'What don't I know, George?'

He shrugged. 'Anyway, it's over.'

'No it isn't, George. First I have to go to the police. Then I'll see that Julie gets the right help.'

He considered that for a moment, his hand still fondling the back of her neck as if he couldn't bear to lose physical contact with her. 'Is she rational?'

'How do you mean? Rational?'

'Rational enough to give a statement to the police?' He stared at her intently, giving added weight and meaning to his question.

'I see what you mean.'

'If she's not capable of giving evidence you get a couple of cops in uniform around here and they'd probably scare her worse than she's scared now. They're not noted for their delicacy.'

She let his argument sink in. The sense of it was inescapable. The thought of those insensitive questions plundering Julie's fragile grasp on reality made her shudder. Worse, the girl might imagine they'd come to arrest her for the crime she'd been brainwashed into thinking she'd committed.

'What do you suggest?'

'I'll drive you to the local police. You can talk to a detective in private, explain what happened, how it's affected Julie and let them follow it up. After all, the only thing they'll have to go on is your suspicion. Think about it.'

She had been thinking about it and she knew he was

right. 'But they'll surely reopen the investigation into Louis Lederman's death, Bettylou's and there's Julie's kidnapping.'

'But she wasn't held against her will.'

She frowned. It all sounded so logical, yet why did she feel something in his reasoning wasn't quite right?

'Come on. The car's outside. It'll all turn out OK. You'll see.' He'd noticed the doubt in her eyes. 'I know what you're thinking. Maybe he's right, maybe he's not, but he makes a lot of sense. You've been through a hell of a lot, Anna. You've shown more guts than I ever imagined you had, maybe than *you* ever imagined you had. Now you need someone to lean on.' He lifted her chin and a trace of a smile crossed his lips. 'Am I right?'

She returned the smile and immediately felt it an act of betrayal in some strange way.

He'd anticipated that, too. 'There's nothing wrong in believing that the worst is over. Because it is.' The smile broadened. 'You did it, babe!' he said with an exaggerated John Wayne drawl.

She shook her head to disguise her sense of relief as the burden of responsibility for her actions shifted from her to George. 'You can never be serious for more than one minute at a stretch, can you?'

He thought for a moment. 'Sometimes actually two.'

She took one last look at the restlessly sleeping Julie before she left. 'Don't worry. Patty'll be along soon,' Mabel assured her. Jimmy looked up, blinked, but didn't say anything, returning to his tender observation of the girl on the bed. 'Dr Kildare is otherwise engaged,' joked Mabel. 'Ain't love grand?'

George's car smelt of perfume. Anna sniffed appreciatively. *Anais Anais.* Her own favourite. Maybe it *was* hers. Left over from the day before or was it the day before that? Time seemed to have been expanding and contracting since she'd arrived in Los Angeles, like one of those instruments of torture for exercising the pectoral muscles. She leaned her head against the upholstery and suddenly realized how weary she was. The ache in her back from her fall was starting to make itself felt after being briefly numbed by a painkiller. She willed it into submission and felt her eyelids close. She mustn't fall asleep. She'd have to be alert and practical and marshal her facts sensibly for the police.

But, as she came to, she realized she must have nodded off, because they'd left West Hollywood way behind and were heading up into the hills.

'This far?' she murmured, still drowsy.

'It won't be long.' His voice was strained, but soothing.

'I'm not thinking straight,' she worried. 'I should have called an ambulance for Julie. But I suppose Mabel's friend, the nurse, will do that. All I—we—could think about was getting her away from there. Then there was a sort of shocked relief when it was over. But I should have been more responsible . . .' Her voice trailed away as she saw he wasn't responding, intent on his driving.

She looked around her as they climbed beyond the smog of Hollywood. It was mostly residential, rich residential. Then she realized with growing alarm that it was also frighteningly familiar.

But he continued to remain silent, his face set and tense.

'Say something, damn you!' Louder now, but still pleading for reassurance. Not George! Not George who'd been so helpful, so reliable, so concerned! Not George who had acted as if he really cared for her! Especially not that George! Tell me I'm wrong!

For a few moments she allowed herself the self-deception of disbelief; not wanting to believe what her eyes were telling her, she tried to ignore the message. Until the message refused to be ignored.

The gun he'd joked about carrying in the glove compartment was placed on the dashboard within reach of his right hand. He'd probably taken it out while she'd dozed off briefly. The dark, lethal thing sat there, a brooding presence, biding its time, silent but not sleeping.

She was conscious of a sense of grief, even stronger than that of fear. Tears welled up in her eyes.

'You're taking me to Hilde Klein. What an idiot you must have thought me.'

There was no anger in her tone, only a flat, dull acceptance of the inevitable.

'Yes.' The acknowledgement seemed to release the tension in him, as if the declaration of betrayal was more worrying than the betrayal itself.

'Why?' she said listlessly. 'I should have realized when you said Julie wasn't held against her wishes. You couldn't have known that unless you'd known she'd been held there in the first place. How could I have been so gullible?'

Now all the pieces in the jigsaw fitted into place. George's strange behaviour on their first night at the Double Take club; his insistence that he'd only briefly known Julie when in fact he'd appeared in a TV movie with her; his sudden appearance on the morning after she'd been to see Hilde Klein. Only she hadn't wanted to see anything suspicious in his attitude towards her. She'd wanted to believe his lies.

'Why?' she repeated.

'Why does anyone do anything? Money. Loyalty.'

'Loyalty?'

'Hilde Klein got me started in Hollywood. If it hadn't been for her I'd have been just another bum with no future. I don't kid myself I'm any great shakes as an actor. But it isn't how good you are but who you know. Hilde knew the right people. And she liked me. For some goddamned reason she wanted to help me. When she called in her favours, when you arrived to find Julie, it didn't seem too much to ask. And there was the money. There's always the money.' He seemed relieved to be getting it off his chest at last. 'Why couldn't you leave well alone, Anna? You've got Julie back. She'll never get her head together . . .'

'Never get her head together sufficiently to inform against Hilde Klein and Bernard. That *they* killed Louis Lederman and probably Bettylou too?' She was angry now. It was his callous disregard for Julie that made her angry. 'What kind of man are you?'

'Weak,' he said with an expression of self-disgust. 'Hadn't you noticed? Isn't that what Hugh told you? Didn't he explain why I left Winchester? Because I couldn't hold down a job, because I gambled away money that didn't belong to me, because I was the misfit who in the old days would have been packed off to the colonies or joined the Foreign Legion.'

'Hugh didn't tell me any of that. He loves you. You're his brother. Whatever you'd done he trusted you,' she said bitterly.

'Trusted me to take care of you!' He let out a scornful snort of derision. 'That's a laugh!' For a second he took his eyes off the road to look at her and she saw in those eyes an expression that, against her will, re-activated the thrill she'd always experienced when he was near her: compassion and affection. 'I really did want to take care of you. That's why I urged you to go home and forget it, forget whatever it was that bastard of a father of yours wanted you to do. You have to believe me, all I did was to try to steer you away from Julie.'

'With your friend Mick's connivance.'

'Mick just took his cue from me. He didn't know anything about anything. Any more than I know whether Louis or Bettylou were murdered.'

'Didn't it cross your mind?'

'Why should it? So far as I was concerned Louis was killed by a break-in artist and Bettylou was killed on the freeway, smashed out of her mind. Hilde had her reasons for keeping Julie safe.'

'Safe? From what? You know *exactly* what happened, George. You just didn't have the nerve to ask them to spell it out. And what about Joe Hatchett? Or were he and his boys just extras in your little game?' She regretted the accusation as soon as it was uttered.

He rounded on her furiously. 'Don't say that about Joe or his boys! Do you hear me? Don't say that!' For the first time she was convinced that he was being completely genuine. 'My life may not be much. But they're the most— perhaps the only—decent part of it. I thought it would satisfy you if you met a real cop. And I knew there was not a lot he could do,' he admitted lamely.

She nodded towards the gun. 'They wanted you to kill

208

me, didn't they?' She felt light-headed, dispassionate, as if she were discussing someone other than herself.

He didn't answer the question. 'They just want to talk to you,' he said. 'Make you see there's no point in taking this thing further. Hilde will pay for any treatment Julie might need and you can go home. She just wants to talk.'

'That's what she told you?' she said cynically and wondered at how detached she felt, how cool her judgement, yet, by her own admission, she knew her life was in danger. 'You're not only weak, George, you're a fool!' She spoke with withering contempt, some of it for herself at being taken in so easily.

They'd reached the gates of the Klein house, a few yards from the spot where she and Jimmy had waited so patiently that morning before she'd even known that Julie was still alive.

He stopped the car and turned towards her, a wounded expression in his eyes, but she couldn't tell whether her words had touched a raw nerve or merely bruised his vanity. He was, after all, an actor. Of sorts.

Why am I sitting here, musing about this man who could be planning to kill me even now? Why aren't I scared out of my wits, making a grab for the gun—although she doubted whether she'd know what to do with it if she had it? Because George is weak and a fool and wouldn't have the guts to pull a trigger except on a fake weapon in front of the cameras.

He leaned across her and opened the door on her side. 'Get out! Get out and go! Do what you have to. But get out and go. *Now!* I'll tell them you'd already gone to the police and I couldn't find you,' he said urgently.

She looked at him bemused. 'Where?'

'You'll probably run into a patrol car around here. For Christ's sake, Anna, use your initiative. But go!' He sounded both desperate and absurd, as if fearful that his meagre supply of nerve might suddenly dry up.

'Anna Sterling! What a delightful surprise!'

They hadn't noticed that the gates of the Klein residence had swung silently open. Bernard Klein loped forward, put

209

his hand on Anna's elbow and made to help her out of the car. He didn't seem to have heard George's exhortation to her to make a run for it. She tried to resist but his grip tightened and, abandoning courtesy, he yanked her roughly to her feet.

She looked back to George. But he was sitting slumped in the driver's seat, avoiding her eyes. It seemed as if all his courage had been used up.

Then it happened, all in a rush. The terror that had somehow eluded her or been diffused by her feelings for George came flooding through her body. Why can't I scream? she thought. But her mouth was too dry and Bernard Klein had clamped his free hand, lightly but firmly, round her throat as he marched her up the drive. She heard George's hesitant footsteps behind them. They sounded to Anna like the final surrender of a spent man.

CHAPTER 22

'Anna, my dear!' Hilde Klein was seated in her upright chair, her good hand clasped around a silver-topped cane. She was dressed for a social occasion in lilac silk with a choker of pearls at her neck. Her twisted mouth made a gruesome attempt at a smile. She acted as if Anna were the honoured guest at one of those exclusive A-list dinner parties she used to give in the old days when, as she later bemoaned, there were enough people in Hollywood to warrant inclusion on an A-list.

She graciously extended the cane towards a chair in that haunted room with its photographs of dead celebrities and memories of Malcolm relishing being idolized by people he despised, not realizing how suddenly that idolatry could turn to—no, not contempt—indifference. For someone like Malcolm there was nothing crueller than indifference.

'Georgie's delivered the package you wanted, mother mine.' Bernard pushed Anna gently forward. He cast a mocking glance at George who had made straight for the drinks table and mixed himself a bourbon on the rocks. This gesture of familiarity seemed to Anna even more offensive than his betrayal, his lack of resolution. All the lies converged on that simple act of pouring a drink without invitation or permission, as he must have done so many times before. 'Frankly, I didn't think he would,' said Bernard.

'You've no faith in people, Sonny.' She smiled again, at least that caricature of a smile with no warmth behind it. To those who didn't know her well it might appear that, as nearly as her disabilities would allow, she was exuding sweetness, chiding a recalcitrant son, welcoming a longed-for visitor.

What new little game is she playing? thought Anna. The fear she'd experienced when Bernard had forced her out of the car and up the drive to the house was being replaced by a puzzled curiosity. She didn't minimize the threat but she couldn't help being mesmerized by the chameleon mentality of this weird, grasping woman who, even ailing and housebound, still wielded an awesome power over people.

Quite suddenly Anna was overwhelmed by a sense of the ridiculous. It was as if she'd been transported into a world that had no relation to the real world: a world lived out on a cinema screen and filtered through the labours and imaginations of writers, cameramen, directors and actors. And she'd been assigned a leading role. Hilde Klein was as much in thrall to fantasy as poor Julie in her obsession with Scarlett O'Hara, Mick and Mabel and all the others who came to Hollywood in pursuit of a dream.

Well, I'm not dreaming, she decided.

'Why don't you stop the benevolent old lady act? It's not working for me. Why did you have me brought here?' she demanded, amazed at her own bravado. Please God, it would last!

Hilde Klein looked at her with a hard, cool respect. There was no longer the flicker of an attempted smile. 'That phone call—you had me fooled for a while.'

Bernard had stretched out on a settee with a show of lazy indolence which Anna knew to be deceptive. She could still

211

feel the pressure of his fingers on her throat. He was watching a video of a baseball game, the frenzied commentary was turned down, but it could still be heard purring softly in the background.

'Sonny, can't you do that somewhere else? You're making Miss Sterling nervous.' As she spoke, Hilde kept her eyes on Anna, emphasizing the 'Miss Sterling' as if to establish a different, tougher relationship.

The suggestion that she was nervous was meant, obviously, to have that effect. But whatever she felt inside, she carefully fostered an outward show of composure. All her life, she'd been good at that. And she wouldn't give Hilde Klein that edge of advantage in knowing that she'd unsettled her involuntary guest.

Bernard uncoiled himself from the settee and switched off the video. As he passed Anna he bent down and whispered in her ear, his hot breath smelling strongly of sour whisky, 'Don't believe the bullshit my mother feeds you. She's crazy, you know. Old, ill and crazy. She only believes what she wants to believe.'

She looked up at him with revulsion. 'Then why do you always play her games?'

'Because she always makes it worth my while,' he murmured, as if surprised that she should even ask.

Hilde's cold eyes watched him leave the room. If she'd heard the exchange she gave no sign of it. Perhaps she was used to her son's contempt for her, secure in the knowledge that he was too much in her debt to do anything about it.

'Now, my dear,' said Hilde complacently. 'You've been a naughty girl, going behind my back,' she continued with a waggish attempt at humour. 'But I'm willing to forgive and forget.'

'Forgive and forget?' Anna was appalled at the banality of the remark.

'I can't imagine what dreadful fantasies you've been harbouring.'

'I don't think they're fantasies.' All the suspicions she'd accumulated during the past few days came pouring out recklessly. It was too late to debate her own dangerous situation. She no longer cared. 'I think you killed Louis Lederman because he wanted to leave you and take Julie with him. That's why he sold off fake works of art so that he could build up a nest-egg to finance his future away from you. I think Bettylou saw what happened and was blackmailing you. So you had her killed too and made it look like an accident. Most of all, I think you hated Julie because he lavished the love on her he never felt for you and somehow you managed to persuade her that she'd killed Louis. And you only kept her alive in case for some reason the investigation into Louis's death was re-opened.'

She stopped abruptly, suddenly realizing she'd demolished whatever hope she had of getting out of there unharmed, even alive.

Hilde had been listening with that infuriating twisted smile on her lips. She seemed completely unperturbed. 'My dear, my poor dear, such delusions! Louis was killed in the earthquake. I told you. I barely knew this Bettylou. And as for Julie, I loved her like a daughter. I felt sorry for her. She was quite unhinged after that experience with Malcolm. After Louis died she was inconsolable. I feared for her sanity. She needed peace and rest and quiet. That's why I sent her to stay with Myrna's sister. The last thing she needed was to be reminded of her family. And you were her family. So I lied to you about where she was. I admit that. But can't you see it was for her own good?'

She actually believes this is all true, thought Anna. She sounded so reasonable. If she hadn't been so sure it was lies, Anna might have been taken in, just as Bernard had warned her.

'You're not convincing me,' she said. 'So what are you going to do about it?'

Hilde tapped the silver-topped cane. On her face was an expression of satisfied recognition. This was something she could deal with. She'd been dealing with questions like this all her life and there was only one answer. 'I'm sure we can come to some little—accommodation.' She chose the word carefully.

'Accommodation!' Anna uttered the word with distaste.

'You think you can buy anybody, don't you? With money or deals or favours. You bought George, my father, your own son and Louis, too, until he decided he'd had enough of being your prize poodle. What do you suggest for me? And Julie? A comfortable recompense to forgive and forget?'

'What a loud woman you are, Anna Sterling!' Hilde Klein made it sound like the ultimate criticism of someone who simply didn't understand the rules of the game.

Anna had felt so confident, so sure of her own inviolability, but now she was conscious of a core of fear growing in the pit of her stomach, sending out tentacles all over her body. George! She whipped round swiftly, hoping he was right behind her, supporting her against all his instincts for self-preservation.

He *was* behind her, leaning against the white piano with its gallery of photographs on the top. But he looked neither supportive nor concerned. For a second their eyes met and she felt she detected a sign—of what? Perhaps it was only recognition that she'd talked herself into a hole and there was no way she could dig herself out of it.

At least she could go down—wherever 'down' was— fighting.

Hilde Klein was watching her with a predator's keen interest, waiting, waiting!

She was only an ailing, old woman, Anna tried to rationalize. But this was her territory. Outside, Bernard was waiting and God knows who else to carry out whatever whim might take her fancy. Maybe George, too! Perhaps she was even crazy enough to believe she could get away with another murder.

'You don't think I got Julie away from that place all on my own, do you?' she improvised wildly. 'My friends know where I am right now. They're contacting the police. And Julie! Whatever you've done to her she's lucid enough to give evidence against you and that Arlene and Kurt. She's probably doing that right now. Ask George!'

It was a risk, but she had to take it. She looked hard at George, willing him not to contradict her. He took his time and whatever thoughts were going through his mind they didn't show on his face. Then he lowered his eyes, seemingly more interested in the photograph of Hilde being toasted by an ageing Clark Gable at some studio function back in the 'fifties.

'She's right, Hilde,' he said.

Anna breathed a sigh of relief. Hilde would believe George. She'd probably paid him well enough. There was nothing now to stop her just walking out of this place if Hilde realized there was nothing to be gained by keeping her.

'Crap!'

She thought at first it was Hilde who had spoken, but then she saw that Myrna was standing at the open door. She must have entered while Anna was silently begging George to back up her story. She looked square and homely as she always did, except for one thing. She was holding a gun and it was pointed at Anna. In her sturdy shoes she circled the room forcing Anna to turn round and confront her. She moved closer, until she was barely two feet from Anna, her currant bun face screwed up into an expression of malevolence. Anna tried to retreat, but the look on the woman's face froze her into a kind of hypnotic impotence.

'Crap!' Myrna repeated. 'What have you been doing to my lady, my Mrs Klein?' She said it with such an air of possessiveness that it would seem that the roles were reversed and that she was the mistress and Hilde Klein her charge.

'You come here meddling. You're no different to that other one. That silly girl who took Louis Lederman from my lady! Well, I fixed her good. She didn't know nothing when I killed Louis that night. She fainted dead away. It was no trouble persuading her she'd killed him. She had the gun in her hand, didn't she? I put it there. Reliable old Myrna put it there!' She chuckled cruelly. 'They deserved it, both of them. How dared he leave Mrs Klein! But he was weak, like all of them. Men! Him!' She jerked her head back at George who was edging up silently behind her. 'Sonny, Louis! All weak. Only we're strong. Mrs Klein and me. I haven't cared for her all these years to see her destroyed by *men*!' She spat out the word with venom. 'And that little darling! Miss Scarlett! I liked to think of her stuck in that place with just Arlene and Kurt for company. I wanted her to rot there. Slowly. Mrs Klein would have liked that. Like she liked me killing Louis. I fixed that other bitch, too. That Bettylou.'

She was talking as if Hilde Klein didn't exist, was just a glorified figment of her imagination. This was no devious killer but an executioner who was beyond any thought but performing the act itself.

I'm going to die, thought Anna. Nothing can prevent it. Not reason or argument or compromise. I'm going to die.

In horror she watched the woman raise the gun and prepare to squeeze the trigger. It was pointing straight at her.

'Sorry, dearie, it's your turn,' said Myrna, a broad grin on her face.

'Myrna!'

For a second Myrna was distracted by Hilde Klein's call. Then there was the sound of a shot and a distorted scream. And the lifeless body of Hilde Klein slumped forward in her chair.

Only when she realized with numbed relief that the shot had missed her did she see that it hadn't even been aimed at her. George had one arm tightly wrapped round Myrna's tubby waist from the rear. His other hand was wrestling the gun away from her: the gun whose aim he had deflected from Anna, causing the shot to enter the raddled old heart of Hilde Klein.

But there was no fight left in Myrna. When she saw the inert body of the woman she'd served for so long, she let out a horrifying, keening howl, the like of which Anna had never heard before. And the howl continued as she cradled the head of Hilde Klein in her arms, oblivious of everything and everyone else.

The gun clattered against the piano and spun across the floor towards the door.

A moment or two after the sound of the shot, Bernard rushed into the room. He looked at his dead mother and

216

the wailing Myrna dispassionately as if they were tragic figures in a melodrama he had never much enjoyed.

He eyed the gun, tantalizingly close to his feet. Then he looked at Anna and George with a slight smirk on his face. Either he knew or had guessed what had happened.

'You're a man after all, Georgie,' he said, almost admiringly.

His eyes reverted back to the gun. He stared at it for several seconds as if he were considering a variety of options. He even bent down slightly, his hand outstretched towards it.

'Don't even think it,' said George quietly.

Bernard shrugged.

'Maybe you're right. I never was good with firearms. I guess maybe this way I might come to some little accommodation with the police.' He sounded as if he might actually relish talking his way out of the mess of murder and deception in which he'd been, however peripherally, involved. 'I never meant anyone to die, you know. It's too—yucky—if you know what I mean. What are you doing?'

George had picked up the telephone and was punching in a number. He and Anna had been listening to Bernard with disbelief. His mother was lying there dead and he was talking about accommodation, just as she had, with no hint of grief or even surprise.

She heard George speaking into the receiver but the words came to her like an echo filtering through a thick, swirling fog.

'Police! I want to report a shooting. Yes, dead.' He looked across at Anna and smiled wryly, adding, like a cheeky afterthought, not to be taken seriously, 'Two shootings— and an abduction.' Then he gave the address and details in a dull, matter-of-fact voice, proving he was very serious.

Bernard had poured himself a drink and was balancing it on his chest as he lay flat on the settee. In the corner Myrna was still nursing the emaciated dead body of Hilde Klein, rocking it to and fro and moaning, quietly now, softly, melodically. She might have been a mother caressing a sick baby.

217

George picked up the gun from the floor.

'Worried I'll make a run for it?' quipped Bernard. 'No need. Where would I go? Besides, that old woman still owes me. I didn't kill her, so they can't stop me from inheriting.'

'You really are a bastard.'

'Of course!' He raised his glass. 'Cheers!'

With the gun safely in his pocket, George rang Joe Hatchett. 'I'd like you to look after Anna. As a favour to me.'

It seemed hours before the squad cars arrived, but it was probably only a few minutes.

'Are you OK?'

She nodded. 'Why, George?'

'You asked me that before.' He shrugged. 'I change my mind a lot. Or maybe there's still a little bit of the Beau Geste—the old Wykehamist spirit—left in me. Honour and all that!' He was deliberately mocking himself, almost ashamed of having done the decent thing.

It wasn't the answer she'd hoped for. Was she fool enough to expect that he'd suddenly discovered he loved her enough to risk his life, certainly his liberty, for her?

He touched her cheek and looked at her with Hugh's eyes. Except, she now realized, they weren't Hugh's eyes at all. She couldn't imagine why she'd ever thought they were.

'I'm a disappointment to you, aren't I, Anna? You see, I'm part of this dream world. I play roles like everyone else. Maybe I'll have to play the role of a gaolbird for a while on a conspiracy charge—along with Sonny and, maybe, Arlene and Kurt. There's a thought to conjure with! God knows where Myrna will end up. But then I guess she's always been auditioning for *The Snake Pit*. What I'm trying to say is that you belong to the real world, Anna. Go back to the real world. But live life to the full. Out of the shadow of your father. You've learned how. LA has done that much for you. But here—here, you're a displaced person.'

They heard a slow hand-clap from the settee. Bernard raised his glass again. 'I have to hand it to you, George. You've got style.'

Then the house seemed to be filled with law officers.

218

Detectives from Homicide. Paramedics. Forensic experts. Uniformed cops, one of whom, a woman, managed to pry Myrna loose from the dead Hilde and then concentrated on being nice to Anna. It didn't come naturally to her.

Joe Hatchett helped Anna through the initial questions as they both watched George being taken out to a waiting police car. He didn't look back.

Suddenly everyone was paying her attention. The police. A representative from the District Attorney's office. An official from the British Consulate.

Hugh insisted on flying over immediately. But he made it clear that it would seriously inconvenience him and she had the feeling that he was less concerned about her than about the weak, wayward brother who had been guilty of the unseemly crime of letting down the school side. At first she thought how much Hugh had changed. Then she realized it was she who had changed.

They were all excessively considerate, apologizing for the fact that she would be required to testify when the case came to trial, and they arranged for Julie to get psychiatric care and a nurse to accompany her and Anna on the journey home.

Where were you when I needed you? Anna thought bitterly.

The bizarre tale made a splash in the media; newspapers dusted off ancient features about Hilde Klein and updated them; and several London tabloids offered Anna small fortunes for exclusive rights to her story.

Mabel, Jimmy and Mick rallied round to protect her from the unwelcome attentions of the press and the photographers and old Asher Kowalski kept her supplied in apple strudel and useless advice.

'So, what'll you do?' said Mabel. 'You know, I'll miss you.'

'First I have to get Julie well and then try to make amends for all the years. Maybe you—Jimmy—could visit.'

'You'd still make a great Joan Fontaine.' Mick pulled his James Cagney face. 'You'll be back, kiddo!'

She smiled. 'According to George, I don't belong here.'

219

'But that's the beauty of this place. No one starts out belonging here.'

It was painful saying goodbye to Mabel so they both agreed they wouldn't. But she stuffed the video of *Starlit on Sunset* into Anna's suitcase.

'To remind you. Me, George. In a funny kind of way I loved him.'

Anna hugged her tightly. 'In a funny kind of way I did, too.'

On the day she left LA with Julie they were dedicating another star on the Walk of Fame to some fleeting luminary of the silver screen. The black cabbie who drove them to the airport couldn't be sure who it was they were honouring, but he figured it was no one important.

'Just some movie star!'

He didn't sound much impressed. He was, he said, from out of town.